MATCHING

FEATHERS

TARA LYTLE

Editorial work by Eschler Editing

Author bio photo by Jana McGettigan

Published by Scribbled Reads

978-1-7363067-1-0

CONTENTS

ACKNOWLEDGMENTS

I would sincerely like to thank my wonderful husband, Seth Lytle, for believing in me enough to let me pursue my writing dreams. His help has been instrumental in every part of this journey, from letting me ramble my thoughts out, taking our kids so I could write, and pushing me to get my book published. I would also like to acknowledge my father, David Shelburne, for reading through every draft and pointing out what worked and what didn't. I would also like to thank Carolyn Lytle and Jeff VanDrimmelen for being beta readers. Last, I would like to express my gratitude to the Eschler Editing team for taking my rough manuscript and polishing it into something worth reading. Their help from editing to ebook publishing has been amazing, and I could not have done this without them.

CHAPTER ONE

AZURE

My cobalt, silver-tipped wings flutter. Energy accumulates, radiating down to the feather tips. My heart pulses. Eyes closed, I roll onto my stomach and snuggle my lavender-scented pillow. The blood pounding in my ears nearly drowns out the classical music playing softly from my nightstand. Sleep eludes despite my earnest desire to catch it.

An irritated flush heats my body. I kick off my blanket and sit up, my wings twitching. The digital clock on my dresser flashes 1:00 a.m. I slip out of bed and go to the window, wincing at the creaking sound as I open it. A cool pine breeze flows in. My feathers stretch taut, reaching for the air as if deprived of oxygen. My fingernails elongate, shifting into sharply curved talons. *What's spurred them to come out?*

My routine evening flight around my four-hundred-acre forested property usually takes care of the extra energy buildup my body produces. Did I not exercise my wings enough? My brow furrows. No, I remember being tired when

I turned in. Maybe I'm sensing some sort of danger? Why else would my talons come out?

I stick my face out the window, allowing my senses to sharpen. Dark shapes morph into Douglas firs, ferns, huckleberry and blackberry bushes. They surround the meadow serving as our front lawn. A couple of bats swoop around catching bugs. A mockingbird sings a mating song from his perch. A raccoon jumps from our garbage can and scurries off into the trees. Debris litters the ground. Crap. I forgot to secure the lid when I took the trash out.

I draw back, having not seen, smelled, or heard anything out of the ordinary. I shut the window and rest my head against it. I close my eyes in frustration, wishing I knew another Wingai to ask about this restlessness. I certainly can't talk to Josephina, my sweet, aging guardian. Besides the late hour, she's human. She wouldn't have any more of an idea than I would.

This is Mom's fault, I think, feeling a touch of anger and regret. She fled from the Wingai community when she was pregnant with me. For fear of a slap across my cheek or worse, I wasn't allowed to ask why.

My hands curl, talons pressing into my palms. A chill sweeps through my insides. It's been three years since her death in a head-on collision with a deer. Sometimes it still stuns me that I can feel acute relief and bitterness simultaneously.

My eyes land on the slash-like scars my mother bestowed on my forearms. I'm glad she can't hurt me during one of her mental breakdowns, but I despise how unprepared she left me. How am I supposed to know what's normal and be myself surrounded by humans?

I step away from the window. Gritting my teeth, I force my nails to retract until they appear human. A stinging ache remains as I flip on the light and grab my school bag hanging on the doorknob. The rest I need before my last day of finals isn't going to come. Might as well study instead.

I wake with a jolt, my phone alarm blaring in my ears. My English book slides off my chest as I sit up. I turn off the alarm and rub my eyes, surprised and grateful I managed to catch a bit of sleep.

Josephina stands at the stove stirring a pot of oatmeal when I enter the kitchen. "Good morning, Azure." She gives me a weathered smile.

I wrap one arm around her shoulders and give her a light squeeze. "Morning, Josephina." Because she's eighty-four years old and has increasing stroke issues, I worry my time with her is limited. I try to show affection whenever I can, though it doesn't come easy for me. The amount of love my mother showed me could be equated to a pea.

Josephina changed my perspective on love. Years ago on one of her flights, Mom got distracted and drifted onto the edge of our property, revealing herself to Josephina, whose land bordered ours. A somewhat stilted—on my mom's part—friendship formed. About once a month Josephina would come to our door with a plate of brownies or cookies and chat for a few minutes. I lived for those days. Mom would put on a show of normalcy, and I would get a treat.

When the car crash happened, Josephina wasted no time asserting herself as my new guardian. Her sweet presence has been my saving grace. Through her, I learned what a healthy family relationship actually is.

I pour a cup of orange juice. Josephina brings two steaming bowls to the table. "You're sitting awfully straight today. Something wrong with your wings?"

I nearly cried this morning when I hid them, leaving two tiny ridges near my shoulder blades. "Restless is all. I'm sure it'll pass." I don't want to worry her.

Her brown eyes twinkle. "Last day of school excitement, I'd wager."

I grin. "Probably," I say, even though I don't think it's that at all. My wings now pulse inside my back in exact rhythm with my heart. They've never done that before. I inwardly sigh. Something is up—I just don't know what.

I park at McMinnville High School a little past eight. Last day of high school. I take a deep breath and flex my fingers, keeping my talons under lockdown. I can do this, trouble with my body or not.

Bree, Ben, and Jack wait for me by the front of the school. Bree and Ben have been dating since homecoming. They're physically mismatched with Bree short and curvy, and Ben, a whole foot taller and lanky thin. I laugh at Bree when she has to jump to kiss him.

Jack and I became good friends over watching our besties fall head over heels in love. He's athletic and driven to become a major league baseball player. While I have no doubt he could get a girl if he wanted—his arm muscles are killer—he thinks romance will make him lose focus and ruin his career plans.

By accident, over Christmas break my friends discovered I'm Wingai. I had invited them over for a movie and game night, giving Bree the details to disperse. She misheard the time, and they showed up earlier than I expected, catching me with my wings out. To my surprise, they didn't scream and run but demanded an explanation. Because I couldn't erase their memories, I divulged what I knew about myself.

I kept my wings out and showed them my talons, similar to an eagle's. I explained about my heightened eyesight, hearing, smell, and strength—twice that of a human. I told them about my extended life span and how I'd still appear young even when I turned fifty. Mom never gave me an exact timeline, but I gathered we lived about a hundred and fifty years over that of a human. I healed quicker—not instantaneously, but faster than a human. Also, I never seemed to catch the colds and viruses that circulated.

My friends then asked about what other kinds of supernatural beings are out there. "Mom once told me there five groups of shifters—people that can transform into an animal. Wingai, Bears, Wolves, Foxes, and Mountain Lions. I haven't met any in real life, though."

"What about vampires or witches?" Bree asked.

"I don't think so, but you never know." I shrugged, emphasizing my lack of knowledge of the paranormal world.

Like Josephina, they accepted me and promised to keep my identity a secret. Bree was mad that I hadn't planned on ever telling them. But when posed with the question of how she thought the general public, or even the rest of our classmates, would react, her hurt lessened. "I'd totally be more freaked out if I hadn't gotten to know you first," she said.

Ben and Jack agreed.

Jack said, "We have enough problems with equality and race among humans. Throw in a bird-girl, and it'd be insane."

Ben lifted his hands, making a frame. "I can easily picture you strapped to a table in some lab getting experimented on. Or maybe you'd belong to one of those traveling circuses." He cleared his throat, putting on the air of an announcer. "Azure, the Wingai Wonder!"

The relief I felt then swamped me like a tidal wave. I nearly cried. Since finding out, our friendship has only strengthened. We're a bona fide quartet. I love it.

Bree hands me a coffee cup. "Double chocolate, extra whipped cream."

"You're a lifesaver." I take a small sip, savoring the chocolaty goodness.

She chuckles. "That's what besties are for."

Jack's blue eyes survey me over the rim of his white cup. Lowering his drink, he says, "Bad night or something?"

"Is it that noticeable?" I ask.

Jack shrugs. "Just seem on edge is all."

"It's finals. We're all stressed," Ben says with a small laugh.

Bree grins, her smile infectious. "If it's Mr. Piper's test you're all worried about, don't be. He's out for the morning with an emergency vet appointment for his dog. She got into something and started throwing up all over the place. So Mr. Piper won't be able to pelt us with the hard questions. We're getting Mrs. Vallence, and you know she doesn't really care about academics. We'll all get automatic passes."

Bree's father, Mr. Ashlander, rules McMinnville High as principal. Bree's ability to produce reliable information on teachers and school events makes her a class favorite. How I gained the coveted spot of best friend is a pure mystery to me.

"What a relief," Ben mutters. Jack nods.

The bell rings. I fall in step with my friends as we make our way inside. A boy brushes past in a cloud of Axe body spray. I cough through the acridness. "All those hours studying wasted. Too bad we can't take them back."

"I know, right?" Bree flicks her brown curls over her shoulder.

We hurry to math class down first hall. As I slide into my assigned seat, Mrs. Garrett stands. She launches into a speech about the merits of math in our future. "Math is an ally, and should remain with you as you go off into the world . . ."

Her voice is so monotone, I can't help but tune her out. My gaze falls on the laminate desk in front of me. Pen and eraser smudges dot the table. In the upper right-hand corner, a heart with the letters R and L has been drawn in Sharpie. I'm slightly in awe that this will be the last time I sit here.

When Josephina became my guardian, I decided I'd had enough of hiding out at home. I hid my wings and talons until Josephina had faith in my control. Mom made me learn years ago to manage the discomfort until it didn't bother me anymore. Later, I took evening flights to expel the energy I built up. Then I pleaded with Josephina to enroll me in public school.

She peppered me with questions, her worry charging through like a white knight. "What if someone finds out you're Wingai? What if you lose control and your wings pop out?"

"They won't. I promise." I grabbed her hand, infusing my tone with patience.

"What are you going to say if someone pats your back? They'll feel the ridges." Josephina eyed my back with pursed lips.

"Old injury from the car accident," I readily replied, hating to use the moment that took my mother's life. Still, it provided a quick answer for my ridges. "Same for these scars." I gestured to my arms.

"And your claws?" she asked, pointing to my hands.

"I've practiced," I said calmly. "They won't come out on their own."

Josephina held her breath my entire sophomore year, but nothing significant happened. I made a few friends and settled into a routine—school, homework, and evening flights. Controlling my wings had become second nature, and my socializing skills had elevated.

A surge of energy brings me back to the present. I stiffen and press my back tight against the chair to keep my feathers in place. My fingertips sting. *What the heck?* Worry settles in. Why am I suddenly having all this trouble?

Bree nudges my arm. Her eyebrows raise in question. I flip open my notebook and scrawl a note. *W. control.* With a sympathetic expression, Bree hands me a piece of spearmint gum.

I duck into a bathroom between classes. The pulsing in my wings is now a constant thrum. My worry morphs into fear. I skirt past the junior exiting the handicap stall and yank the door shut, sliding the lock in place. I remove my shirt. My bra strap rests just below the ridges. I release my wings. Due to lack of space, the ends smush against the walls. Still, the relief is instant, like jumping into a pool on a scorching day. I exhale slowly, grateful for the reprieve.

A sudden gush of adrenaline crams into me. My wings flap vigorously, lifting me a foot off the ground. Full-blown panic erupts. No, not here!

"Where's that noise coming from? Is there a bird in here?" I hear a girl ask.

I shove my fist into my mouth to keep from crying as I retract my wings. They ache something fierce. With trembling hands, I pull my shirt on.

Another girl speaks with exasperation. "You're inhaling too much perfume."

"Joey loves it," the first girl defends.

I wait until I hear retreating footsteps before I exit and wash my hands. My reflection through the lipstick-smeared mirror shows flushed skin and anxiety-ridden blue eyes. I tighten my blonde ponytail, praying no one notices. I dart into English as the final bell rings, breathless from my speed walk.

During lunch, Bree, Ben, and Jack follow me to my cherry-red 1973 convertible Super Beetle, Lady Bug. Not exactly an original name, but it fits. For years Josephina let the bug lurk under a cover in her garage with eventual plans to fix it up. She gifted it to me on my sixteenth birthday, and I've spent the last two years refurbishing it.

"Oh my goodness, these seats are amazing." Bree's eyes are wide with delight as she runs her hands along my new addition.

"Josephina got a great deal off eBay." I grin, careful not to annoy Bree with car talk. I'm extremely passionate about my bug and can easily get carried away.

I head to Dairy Queen for milkshakes—Jack's pick. A warm breeze blows through my hair. My back itches like crazy. I squirm in my seat.

Ben notices. "Something up with your wings?"

I exhale my frustration. "They don't want to stay put. I've been fighting them since last night. I have no idea why. I would've stayed home if it wasn't finals. They're seriously starting to freak me out."

"Could you be getting sick or something?" Jack asks.

I shrug.

"I think it's time you seriously consider going," Bree says from the back seat.

Josephina has been pushing me to take a road trip to find other Wingai after graduation. We both believe Mom left out some pertinent details concerning the nature of my race. However, I'm not comfortable leaving Josephina alone for what could be a long wild goose chase. What happens if she has another stroke and no one's there to help her? I can't risk it.

Another round of energy surges through me. I may have to go after all. "Yeah, maybe," I say as I park and cut the engine.

I reach for the door latch when an electric-blue convertible Porsche claims the parking spot beside mine. I pause, my attention shifting to appreciate the fine machinery. Had it been any other kind of sports car, I wouldn't care, but Porsche and Volkswagen go hand in hand. I'd never trade my beetle—we are a package duo—but I saw no harm in looking.

Jack laughs. "Oh no, Azure's hooked."

"On the car or the hot driver?" Bree giggles.

"Seriously? I'm sitting right here," Ben says with mild irritation.

My eyes snap to the owner, an embarrassed smile on my lips. Bright sea-green eyes framed by dark lashes meet mine. Pure fire races through my wings and into my heart. I slam my back into the seat to hold them in place.

I start the car again and back out. "Drive-through," I choke through waves of fear.

"What's wrong?" Bree, Jack, and Ben ask, their tone inflecting concern.

"I just about lost control!" I pull up to the intercom and make everybody order.

"Because of the Porsche guy?" Bree asks while I fork over the cash.

"I think so." I glance in the rearview mirror at her, unsure. A giddy, lightheaded feeling overtakes my senses as I imagine showing my wings to the guy in the Porsche. I'm horrified. "All I know is that I looked at him and then my wings nearly exploded free."

Bree gasps as a thought occurs to her. "Maybe he's Wingai like you. We should meet him."

"Bree! I nearly exposed myself in public!" I cry, my body trembling from the experience.

The drive-through window opens up. A lady hands me a tray of drinks and several bags. "Here you go."

"Thanks." I give everything to Jack to divvy out.

Rolling forward, I glance at the parking lot on my left. The Porsche hasn't moved, nor has the driver. Sea-green eyes send a double jolt of unwanted fiery adrenaline. I punch the gas.

CHAPTER TWO

CERIL

I breathe harshly. My hand moves to my heart to rub out the intense spasms. I doubt it'll help, but I can't stop myself from doing it. My wings press against my back in a steady rhythm, pushing on a door that I won't open. Their displeasure at being confined eats at me.

Holy feathers, I've found her! My mind implodes with the discovery. My shoulders sag with relief. My eyes sting from the weight of uncertainty lifting off my chest. *I have a match.* A laugh escapes my lips as this knowledge gives way to happiness. *I'm not broken or undeserving of a mate.*

I grab my cell from the passenger seat and call Dad. I'm eager to share the good news. The phone rings twice before he answers.

"Hey, Ceril, how's your search going?" Fingers click against a keyboard. He's put me on speaker while he works. Typical.

I open my mouth, but nothing comes out. I clear my throat and try again. "I found her."

"You what?" A fuzzy jostling tells me he's picked up his phone. A chair rolls against the hardwood.

"I found her," I repeat, surprising myself with a level voice.

"Rose!" Dad shouts into the receiver.

"Hey!" I jerk, holding my mobile away from my ear.

"Sorry," Dad apologizes.

I faintly hear Mom's voice in the background. "What?" Her voice becomes clearer as my parents meet. "Who are you talking to?"

"Ceril." Dad's voice practically vibrates with excitement. "He says he's found her."

"What?" Mom screeches in delight. "Did you talk to her? What's her name? Where are you?"

My chest warms. Feathers, it feels good to finally have this conversation. "One question at a time." I chuckle. "No, I haven't talked to her yet. I'm in McMinnville."

"McMinnville," Dad says with interest. "That's only a few hours away. What's a Wingai doing over there?"

"I know, right?" I say.

"What's your plan?" Mom asks.

"Approach and try not to scare her off I guess," I say. I recount how my wings started acting up when I arrived in McMinnville, prompting me to rent a room for the night. "Nothing wants to stay put. I had a serious fight with my wings and talons this morning. Even now, my back and fingers are burning. I almost paraded in front of her like some half-crazed peacock."

"Normal," Dad and Mom say.

"As I drove around, the heart spasms increased until I struggled to breathe through them," I explain. "I figured either she had to be close or I was really losing it. I stopped at a Dairy Queen and parked next to a red Volkswagen beetle. I looked at the blonde driver and discovered my match."

"That's amazing, Ceril," Dad says with delight.

"Did she show any recognition to you?" Mom asks.

"When I first pulled in, she had her eye trained on my Porsche." I swell with pride. "She seemed impressed." Dad laughs. "She didn't even look at me until her friend in the back giggled something."

"Then what?" Mom sounds breathless with anticipation.

My fingers curl around the steering wheel. "Her eyes widened in terror. She backed out, went to the drive-through, and peeled out of here like the whole armada was chasing after her."

"Oh." Mom sounds disappointed. In the background, I hear my younger brother Jade calling for her. "I've got to go. Talk to your Dad."

"You said she was with others?" Dad asks.

"Yeah." I smile at a passing old couple as they admire my car before stepping inside the restaurant. "Two guys and a girl, human, high school age."

A young redheaded Dairy Queen employee starts washing the windows in front of my car. She makes slow up and down motions with a white rag. Her brown eyes are glued on me with a flirty smile. I cast my eyes to the center console, focusing on my conversation with Dad. I'm not interested in her attempts to catch my attention.

Dad speaks thoughtfully. "Her wings could be giving her trouble too. It's possible she took off to avoid an incident."

I replay the scene of her meeting my gaze, now remembering how she slammed her back into her seat. "That has to be it." I take a breath, unable to remember my expression when our eyes met. Did I glower? Smile? "I have to find her again. I'll check in with you later."

"Okay. Good luck." Dad hangs up.

The girl washing the windows gives me a pouty frown as I start the car and back out. I order a strawberry shake in the drive-through. My stomach is twisty. I'm not sure I could handle food.

I listen to the spasms in my heart for a clue as to where to go. It's the first time I've actually trusted the "homing beacon," as Dad likes to call it.

A few blocks over, I discover her beetle parked at the local high school. I pull into a shaded parking spot next to hers and settle in to wait. I finish my shake, lean back, and close my eyes, breathing slowly through the pounding ache in my back.

My phone chimes—a text from Jade. **You found her.**

Yeah.

Congratulations, bro. I'm really happy for you. Magenta will be furious.

Thanks. I add a grinning emoji. **She knows how this works. She'll deal.** I don't want to give a single thought to Magenta, the possessive crow.

You talk to the girl yet? Jade asks.

No. I'm still unsure how to catch her attention without coming off as a crazy stalker.

Is she hot? Jade adds a query emoji.

Her image is burned in my mind. Light blonde tresses, dark ocean eyes, smooth golden skin, straight small nose, plump pink lips. No makeup, and a simple red blouse. Attraction flares like a bright flame. She's nothing over-the-top like Magenta. Now that I've seen my match, I'm appalled I ever thought her gorgeous. **Magenta pales in comparison.**

Wow! Jade punctuates with a series of grinning emojis. **Can't wait to meet her.**

My thumb swipes across the keyboard. **I've got to talk to her first.**

Good luck. He adds a winking emoji.

I snort as I slip my phone into my pocket. I need all the good luck I can get. Questions about the girl with the VW bug fire on all pistons. I want to know everything about her. I contemplate rifling through her glove box for information. I could probably get a name off registration or insurance papers. I dismiss the idea when it occurs to me that I could accidentally blurt her name and creep her out. I need her to like me, not mace me.

Should I walk up to her with flowers? "Hi, nice to meet you. I'm your match. Will you be my partner for life?" I rest my forehead against the steering wheel. *Feathers.* I'm awful at this. A new thought occurs to me. What if she doesn't even know what a match is? It's plausible since she's living among humans.

I lean back in my seat. Perhaps I should try a more casual approach. I picture a relaxed posture, maybe hands in pockets or resting openly at my sides. "Hey, what's a Wingai doing out of her nest?" Because seriously, I can't figure it out.

I don't know of a single Wingai who would want to leave Soaring Heights or Mountain Hollow, our two small towns hidden in the Cascades. They're protected like sanctuaries and banned from the public like Area 51. Wingai have been infiltrating the government out here in the West since the towns' inception to keep it that way.

In Soaring Heights and Mountain Hollow, we walk proudly with our wings out. Most Wingai hate to go a minute with their feathers tucked in. So why would my match be out here, attempting to blend among the humans? Is she in some kind of trouble, or is it by choice?

I run my fingers through my hair and let my talons lightly graze along my scalp. I'm going to give myself a massive headache if I keep questioning the situation. Patience isn't my strong suit. My future is set to take over Soaring Heights as their Lead. At home, Wingai fly over themselves to ensure my needs are met first. Sure, it makes me spoiled and entitled, but every attempt I've made to be treated like a common guy has failed. I've come to accept Soaring Heights doesn't want to see me that way.

I'm not at home now. I may have a chance to present myself to my mystery girl match without getting twittered over in return. My smile morphs into a sigh. Feathers, I hope I don't mess this up.

A mass of students piles out the doors a little after three. I hop out of my car and lean against it while I wait for my match to arrive. The sun beats on my face. My stomach bounces with nerves. I cross my arms, praying I don't vomit.

A curly blonde swinging a Gucci purse whistles at me. "Hottie alert!" She licks her cherry lips. The handful of girls trailing behind her giggle, their eyes salaciously raking me over.

I smirk, allowing my ego to inflate a bit. Humans are so easy to impress. We're gods of the sky, and our features *are* exceedingly fine.

I freeze as my wings attempt a sudden jailbreak. My eyes lock onto my match. She stands near the curb with a red robe draped over her arm. She laughs at her curly brunette friend. My breath catches in my throat. They swap graduation caps.

A tall sandy-haired boy approaches. I briefly remember him sitting in the back seat of the bug. After some sort of goodbye between the girls, the brunette skips into his waiting arms. She plants a sensuous kiss on his lips. *Boyfriend.*

My match watches them for a second, her expression a half smile, half grimace. It doesn't give me much of a clue as to what my chances with her are. She turns around, eyes focused on her purse. She pulls keys out and looks up. She spies my Porsche and then me.

She halts. A myriad of emotions crosses her face: shock, dismay, fear. My stomach clenches. "You," she chokes.

Well, she recognizes me at least. I put forth my friendliest smile, hoping to put her at ease. "Hey—"

"How—how did you find me?" She holds her keys outward, as if planning on stabbing me with them.

I hold my hands up, trying to appear as nonthreatening as possible. "Feathers, I'm not here to hurt you."

She blinks. Her mouth opens and closes. She drops her hand holding the keys. Her head tilts. Her ocean eyes shift, giving them a subtle glow as she surveys me with eagle acuity. "Feathers?"

I duck my head, offering her a small smile. "I'm sorry. I shouldn't curse. It just kind of slips out."

She steps closer and takes a deep breath, her nostrils flaring as she takes in my scent. Wingai smell better than humans, like an open sky with a hint of a floral breeze. She gasps and quietly whispers, "You're Wingai."

A grin forms on my lips. "I'm Cerulean, or Ceril for short." I hold out my hand.

"Azure." She transfers her keys to her other hand and takes mine.

A jolt sizzles through my arm, going straight to my retracted wings. Azure stiffens. She feels it too. Fear flashes in her eyes. I suspect she doesn't know what these feelings mean. She drops my hand as soon as politely possible. I bite my tongue as my heart spasms increase.

"Do you have time to talk?" I glance around the rapidly emptying parking lot. "Preferably somewhere else?" This isn't the place to have a conversation about matches.

"Yes." Her phone rings, a simple pealing chime. "Excuse me." Her eyebrows furrow in confusion as she looks at the number and answers. "Hello?" I take a step back out of courtesy, though I'm still within hearing distance. "Yes, this is Azure."

Body rigid, her face pales. Ocean eyes brighten with alarm. "Is she all right?" She pauses to listen. "You're sure? Oh." She grips the driver's-side door of the bug for support.

Worry drills holes through me.

Tears slide down her cheeks. She switches her phone to her other ear. "I see." Pause. "Yes." Pause. "No, I'm eighteen." Pause. "No, it was just the two of us."

My stomach twists sickeningly as I get the impression somebody close to her just died.

Azure clears her throat. "Of course. No, that's not necessary. I'll be right over to sign the papers. Goodbye." Her hands shake as she ends the call.

"Is everything all right?" I ask.

She jerks, startled. Her phone slips out of her hand. I swoop down and catch it before it hits the pavement. I hand it back to her.

"Thanks." Her voice trembles as she deposits her cell into her purse, then opens her door. "I have to go." She stares at me, her face a picture of regret. I get the impression she still wants to speak to me, but her business takes precedence.

"Wait." I put my hand on her door, stopping her from getting in. "I don't mean to overstep here, but there's so much you and I need to talk about. Can I follow you in my car and speak with you after your business is done?"

Azure takes a second to think it over before nodding. "All right."

"Thank you." I give her my best reassuring smile. Feathers, she needs it.

I hop in my Porsche, grateful Azure is willing to give me a chance despite what appears to be a sudden crisis for her. Here's my chance to start being a support. I pray she'll warm up to me.

CHAPTER THREE

AZURE

I blink rapidly to dispel the tears as I drive. Every breath is a jagged knife down my throat to my heart. The doctor's words bounce around my head. *Josephina. Stroke. Didn't make it.* I spent years preparing for this possibility, yet shock still blossoms like I've been shot.

I look in the rearview mirror and see Cerulean's Porsche right behind me. I can barely believe another Wingai found me. Bree flashes in my mind, saying, "I knew it!" I bounce between marveling over Cerulean's appearance and Josephina's abrupt passing.

I park at Willamette Valley Medical Center. Cerulean slides into the spot beside me. He jumps out of his seat and jogs over to me as I'm getting out. "Should I come inside with you? You look like you could use some support."

I can practically smell the concern wafting off him like a bottle of cologne. Is it brand-name or some cheap knockoff that I'll regret later? Just because he's Wingai doesn't mean I should trust him. I certainly couldn't count on my mother.

But the hospital is a public place with security cameras, so I shrug, not seeing the harm in it for the moment. He falls in step with me as we make our way to the front entrance. I draw in a lungful of breezy summer air before subjecting myself to the chemical aroma of the hospital.

"Azure!"

Four aging women shuffle toward me. Edna, Betty, Maureen, and Phyllis. Josephina's rummy club. They play every Thursday afternoon. They must have been together when Josephina's stroke occurred.

Edna hugs me, leaving silver glitter on my shirt. "I'm so sorry, Azure."

"Poor, sweet Josephina." Phyllis sniffles into a white handkerchief.

Betty says, "We called 911 as soon as Josephina fell out of her chair. The paramedics came, but she passed before they could help." She put her hand on my arm. Her watery blue eyes fill with compassion. "It was quick. I don't think she suffered much."

"Thank you." I try to smile, but my lower lip trembles.

"Is there anything we can do for you?" Maureen asks, wringing her gnarled hands. "Meals?"

I shake my head. "My fridge is chock-full of groceries already, but thank you for the offer." I take a deep breath and let it settle in my chest. "Honestly, I think I'll be all right.

Josephina and I prepared for this. She had her affairs in order, and I aim to see her last wish through."

"No funeral," the women chant.

An unexpected chuckle escapes my lips. "Exactly. Just remember her in your heart and that'll do us good."

The ladies sniff and nod. They knew Josephina as well as I did. It's what she would want.

Phyllis grasps my hand. "She was so excited for your graduation tomorrow. Wouldn't stop talking about it. She loved you as if you were born out of her own womb."

I pat her hand on mine. "I know."

"She'll be there tomorrow in spirit, just like your mama and papa." Phyllis smiles toothily.

"I'm sure of it." I agree.

I get hugs from everyone before they shuffle out the door. Cerulean melts out of the shadows and joins my side. I jolt, having forgotten his presence.

"Sorry," he apologizes.

"It's okay." My wings pound painfully against my back. I suspect Cerulean is the cause of my wing trouble. I straighten my spine. *Not now.*

A college-aged brunette wearing heavy eyeliner and bright red lipstick addresses me at the front desk. "May I help you?"

"I'm supposed to meet with a Mr. Egot to sign papers," I say.

"Your name?" she asks smoothly.

"Azure Tallon."

Cerulean's breath hitches. When I look at him, he lifts his elbow and coughs into it. "Dry air."

"There's a drinking fountain over there." The receptionist points to a pale-green wall next to a bathroom. She focuses on the computer in front of her and clicks the mouse a few times. "If you'll wait over there, he will be out to see you." She gestures to a row of empty blue chairs.

I settle into a seat. Cerulean gets a drink from the fountain, then sits beside me, silent.

My thoughts drift to find a positive, something Josephina always did in the wake of disappointment. I find one thing to be grateful for. My age. I turned eighteen on the second of May. A legal adult in the eyes of the United States. My stomach had lurched when the doctor I spoke to on the phone asked how old I was and whether he needed to call someone for me. I knew he meant child protection services. I shudder. No foster care system for me, thank you very much.

"Here." Cerulean holds out a box of Kleenex.

"Thank you." I take a tissue and dab my eyes.

"Azure Tallon?" An older man with graying hair approaches.

I rise. "Yes?"

"Come with me." He motions for me to follow as he turns on his heel.

I look over my shoulder at Cerulean.

"I'll wait right here for you." He exudes calm friendliness.

"Miss Tallon?" The older man pauses, tired patience in his eyes.

"I'm coming." I hurry to catch up, wondering what Cerulean hopes to gain out of me.

CERIL

Azure freaking Tallon. Hearing her last name shocked me to my feather tips. I couldn't stop my reaction. I hope my lie about a dry throat and visiting the drinking fountain covered me. I don't want to make her suspicious before we have time to talk.

There are three different races of Wingai: Gold, Silver, and Bronze. We differentiate based on the two strips of color on our wings. Within each race we have Common and Tipped. Tipped Wingai have gold, silver, or bronze on the ends of their feathers. This sets them apart as a Lead over the Common Wingai. I am Gold-Tipped.

Golds reside in Soaring Heights, Silvers in Mountain Hollow. We like to live independently because we can't match with each other. Bronze, on the other hand, can match with any color and therefore inhabit both communities.

Azure's last name is of Mountain Hollow origin. It's a royalty name like mine—Hatch—because their lines carry the Silver-Tipped gene. Gold and Silver don't match, but I'm positive Azure is mine. I'm more confused now than ever.

While I wait, I pull out my phone and call Dad.

He answers on the third ring. "Hey, Ceril." His voice is slightly faint. He's put me on speaker. In the background a utensil clatters. Something sizzles in a pan. A knife chops. I caught him preparing dinner, probably with Mom and Jade. We like to make it a family event when we can.

"You talk to the girl yet?" Jade asks.

"Azure Tallon," I say.

"*Tallon?*" Mom, Dad, and Jade cry with surprise.

"Yeah." I push my hair back. "I'm still trying to wrap my head around it. I thought we couldn't match with Mountain Hollow."

"It's absurdly rare, but you can if you're both Tipped," Dad says. "We've seen it happen only a couple of times in the thousands of years we've been established. Have you seen her wings?"

I train my eyes on Azure. She's stiff as a board, listening to the man talk as he shuffles papers. "No."

"What are you doing right now?" Jade asks.

"I'm sitting in a waiting room at the hospital—"

Mom screeches. "What? What happened—"

"Calm down. Nothing's wrong with me or Azure." I hurry to set the record straight, explaining the phone call Azure received and following her to the hospital. "I don't know for sure, but I think Azure is on her own now."

"She's got you," Dad says.

I snort. "We're strangers. I don't think she even knows what matches are."

29

"Make her know you. Be open, friendly, and patient," Mom encourages.

"Do whatever it takes to earn her trust. We need to see her wings," Dad insists.

"I plan to. I don't want to leave her alone if she'll have me. I hope to make a good match out of this." I watch Azure rise and shake hands with the man. "She's coming out of the meeting. I've got to go. Wish me luck."

"Good luck, bro!" Jade shouts.

I hang up.

CHAPTER FOUR

AZURE

I walk out of Mr. Egot's office, clutching the folder with the important paperwork regarding Josephina. The man grated my nerves. He made me produce my driver's license twice, as if he couldn't believe my adult status. Then he talked to me in a belligerent manner, painstakingly explaining each detail of the paperwork and policies as if I couldn't read or didn't have a brain. My educated answers only riled the man further as we went over the expenses. I felt a profound sense of relief that Josephina prepared me for this.

"Hey." Cerulean approaches with a soft smile.

He's still here. My wings push at me. I stiffen at the pain.

Cerulean matches my steps as we exit. "Everything go okay?"

"Yes," I lie. I won't tell him that I suspect Mr. Egot will call child protection services to check out my story. Maybe he hates intelligent blondes.

Cerulean speaks, bringing me out of my thoughts. "It probably doesn't mean much since you don't know me yet, but I'm sorry for your loss. I haven't lost anyone close to me before, but I imagine it's incredibly painful. I'm sorry to see you go through it."

"Thank you," I say, touched by his sincerity.

We stop in front of Lady Bug. He turns his gaze on me. I study his face. Clear tan skin, a finely sculpted jaw, full lips, straight nose, and those powerful sea-green eyes framed by dark lashes. He could easily grace the tabloids with the title of "Sexiest Man Alive." I flush.

"So, about our talk . . ." Cerulean rubs the back of his neck.

I see the need in his eyes, but he seems hesitant to press me, considering my day. Truth be told, I'd welcome a distraction right now. If Josephina were here, she'd be over the moon that another Wingai has found me. "You're a lone duck in a chicken coop," she'd say. "You'll thrive if you fly the coop and make connections with ducks of your own kind."

A white minivan parks next to my bug. Three small kids hop out and stand by the front passenger door while their mom unbuckles a baby. They stare at Cerulean and me with interest.

"We can't talk here," I say. I decide to take a chance on him and hope it doesn't end up haunting me. "Why don't you follow me home?"

His expression brightens. "I'd love to."

Getting in our cars, Cerulean follows me out of the parking lot and down the windy turns of Baker Creek. I turn onto my familiar gravel road and climb the forest-covered hill to home. I park Lady Bug in the garage and grab my things from the trunk. My heart pangs when I don't see Josephina's familiar Jetta. I must retrieve it from Betty's tomorrow.

I step outside, closing the garage door. I walk over to Cerulean standing by his car. He seems impressed as he takes in the towering fir trees and ferns surrounding my two-story home. It's painted white with gray stones paneling the bottom. A red front door adds a pop of color. Two rocking chairs rest on the front porch.

"Welcome to my home," I tell Cerulean.

"No neighbors?"

I smile. "Just wildlife friends. My mother bought this place before I was born. That small house you passed on our way up the gravel hill was Josephina's. When my mom died a few years back, Josephina moved in with me. She gave me her house when I turned eighteen last month. My property in whole is around four hundred acres."

He smiles appreciatively. "It's really great."

Before going inside, Cerulean goes back to his car and opens the trunk. He pulls his shirt over his head, and I avert my gaze. When he walks back to me, he's wearing a black T-shirt instead of dark gray. "Most of my shirts are made with slits in the back for my wings. I keep a few that aren't for when I'm around the humans."

"Nice," I say.

An aroma of beef roast, potatoes, carrots, and spices hits me in the face when I enter. I kick off my sandals into the pile of shoes by the front door and walk into the kitchen. The Crock-Pot sits by the stove, the light flashing over the warm sign. Josephina liked to have dinner already prepared when she went out for rummy club.

Cerulean places a hand on my shoulder. I turn to face him and suddenly can't hold back the tears. His arms encircle me. I sob into his shirt. Through blurry tears I see blue wings expand. They wrap around me in a feathery embrace.

I can't hold mine back anymore. They burst free, ripping through my blouse to meet his. A swell of adrenaline flows through my wings and into my pulsing heart. It snaps me out of my grief, and I push away from him, suddenly afraid. I try to retract my wings, but their resistance is too great. I gasp in pain.

Cerulean grips my upper arms, his touch gentle. "It's okay. Our wings are recognizing each other. Don't fight it and it won't hurt." He brushes his teal and gold-tipped feathers against mine. The fire abates. I let out a shaky breath, allowing my shoulders to relax. "Everything's okay, Azure. You have nothing to fear. I promise."

His wings rub against mine. A soothing warmth spreads into my body through my feathers. I swallow, unnerved. This never happened when my mother's wings touched mine. "How are you doing this?"

His eyes and smile are warm, his tone gentle. "We're matches. All Wingai have the ability to calm their mate."

I back up until my waist hits the kitchen island. "Mate?" My fingertips transform into talons with my alarm. Dang it! Taking a deep breath, I force them to retract. My fingertips sting.

Cerulean shifts his weight as he pushes his hair out of his eyes. "Your mom never told you to expect a match?"

I shake my head. A flash of anger sears my heart for my mother's selfishness. My gaze drops. I rub the scars on my forearms. Mom never cared about preparing me to be Wingai. I spent my time tiptoeing around her meltdowns, trying not to get hurt. She had so many triggers. What the heck am I supposed to do now? Take Cerulean for his word? Trust a practical stranger to explain what my mom didn't?

"Azure." Cerulean's eyes have landed on my arms. His brow furrows, lips hinting at a frown as he takes me in. I still, wondering what he thinks of me. Probably nothing good. I'm damaged.

"I didn't mean to overwhelm you about our being matches. I hoped you knew something about it. I'm sorry." He runs a hand through his hair, giving me the impression he's trying to figure out how to fly through uncertain territory. "I don't want to stress you out even more." He clears his throat. "Perhaps I need to step back, let you get your bearings before we discuss this." He walks over to the Crock-Pot and gestures to me. "Are you hungry?"

Not particularly. But then I think of Josephina carefully dicing vegetables, sprinkling her favorite seasonings with a heavy dash of thyme, and I don't have the heart to refuse. "Josephina would be disappointed if we let her last meal go to waste," I say.

Too keyed up to care, I take a seat and allow Cerulean to rummage through the kitchen. He brings me a steaming bowl of Josephina's stew and a bottle of water. I murmur a thanks.

"Is there anything else you need?"

"No, thank you. Please eat too," I say.

"Thank you."

While he prepares himself a bowl, I take a moment to study his wings and compare them to mine. His wingspan is almost twice the size of mine. Each wing has a strip of gold where it joins his back. I have strips of silver. The majority of his feathers are cerulean blue with gold tips that match the strips at the base. Mine are a darker blue with silver tips. Do the gold and silver signify gender?

"Do they meet your approval?"

I start at the sound of his voice. He looks at me over his shoulder, his eyes bright with amusement. My cheeks heat. "I'm not a good judge." I curse the ignorance my mother left me in.

CERIL

I join Azure at the table. Involuntarily, one of my wings extends to brush against hers. She stiffens. I have the decency to be embarrassed. "I'm sorry." Leaning away, I try to retract, but I meet resistance. "They don't want to mind." I grab a fistful of my feathers and yank. My breath hitches at the burning pain.

"It's okay." Azure reaches out and touches the back of my hand. A spark runs through me at the contact. "You can let them be for now."

I release my wing, and it springs forward to mingle with hers. Azure's lips curve into a small smile, but I see the discomfort in her eyes. Feathers. "I'm sure they're just overexcited to meet you. It'll wear off soon." At least, I hope it does.

"Sure," Azure agrees, but I don't think she actually believes it.

I turn my attention to the food, happy the taste lives up to the smell. Not wanting to scare her with blatant staring, I sneak glances at Azure's wings. They're undeniably gorgeous, and my initial attraction swells. I love the vividness of the silver paired with the deep blue hue. Technically, the shade's a little darker than what her name implies, but I don't think it matters. Some Wingai are sticklers for naming their kids the exact shade of their wings. It's a bit overboard to me.

Azure carefully forks small mouthfuls and chews quietly, a faraway look in her eyes. She tugs on my heart. Already I feel protective instincts I didn't know I had. I want to shield her from her grief of losing Josephina, and from the uncertainty I brought. I want to convey that she can count on me as her match without scaring her off. Dad was totally right when he said finding your match changes you. In the span of a day, I feel like my whole world has shifted, making Azure my primary focus.

The age-old saying "actions speak louder than words" flies through my head and lights a fire in me. Small actions of support sound like a good start to gain her trust.

As the silent meal ends, Azure turns to me. "There's a spare bedroom, if you'd like to stay the night."

She's asking me to stay? Hope blossoms in my chest. "Thank you."

"The sheets might be a little dusty, but the bed should be soft." A ghost of a smile graces her lips. She stands and gathers dishes to take to the sink. My wings lament the loss of contact.

I rise. "Would you like any help?"

"Oh." She hesitates. "No, it's all right. It should take me only a minute."

"How about we make it thirty seconds?"

"Okay."

Azure puts the leftover dinner in the fridge, then washes the Crock-Pot. We make short work of the dishes, washing, drying, and storing them. She chews her bottom lip as she flits about, giving me the impression she's deep in thought.

After wiping down the granite countertop, she says, "I'm sure it's obvious to you that I don't know much about Wingai. My father died before I was born, and my mom refused to talk." Her expression pinches, then clears. "She died in a car accident when I was fifteen. I had plans to search for other Wingai after graduation and get some answers." She takes a breath, and her face tilts up as she studies my face. "But you found me first. It wasn't happenstance that you pulled up to my bug at Dairy Queen, was it?"

"No. I've been searching for you since February." I can't lie. Relationships should be based on truth, respect, trust. I want us to start out right.

"Because I'm your match . . ." Her wings enfold her in a hug, perhaps a nervous, or protective gesture. I struggle not to wrap mine around her again.

"Yes."

Her deep blue eyes pierce me as she takes a seat at the island again. I join her. "What makes you think I am your match?"

"When a male Wingai turns eighteen, an extra sense is activated." I put a hand on my chest. "The heart spasms rhythmically. It speeds up the closer he gets to his match and fades the farther apart he gets. Sort of like a metal detector or homing beacon." I drop my hand.

Azure's eyes are wide with interest as I explain. "Wingai are very close-knit. We keep meticulous census records on our people, and everyone checks in regularly. It's unheard of for someone to part from the community. When I turned eighteen and began a search for my match among the Wingai, I felt nothing indicative." I push my hair back. "These last few months have been confusing and frustrating. I felt I had a match, but no one sparked." I rest my elbow on the table and smile at Azure. "So, I left home and followed my extra sense until it led me to McMinnville. When I saw you, my wings ached something awful to be released, and I thought my heart was going to explode out of my chest. That never happened at home. I knew you were the one."

"I see." Azure tucks a stray hair behind her ear. "I'm aware my mom kept a lot of secrets, but you could be spinning lies and I wouldn't know any better."

I frown. Matches fuel Wingai. What kind of mom would keep that hidden? It's criminal. "It's a vulnerable position to be in, for sure. I truly do mean well, but frankly we don't know each other well enough to trust every word that comes out of our mouths."

"Exactly," Azure agrees with emphasis.

I scratch my chin. "I think the best way to solve this would be to have you visit Soaring Heights. It's only a couple of hours east from here. You could meet other Wingai and see for yourself."

Azure nods. "I'll give it some consideration."

I smile. "Please do. The last thing I want is to deceive you."

Azure rubs her temples and sighs. "It's been a long day. I'm going to rest. The guest room is on the second floor, first door to your right." She stands. "Good night . . . Cerulean or Ceril?"

I like hearing my full name on her lips. With everyone at home calling me Ceril, it sets her apart and makes me feel more connected. "Cerulean is fine."

"Cerulean it is." Her wings enfold her as she turns out of view. I hear her footsteps patter up the hardwood stairs and a door open and close.

I step outside to grab my bag and call Dad. I lean against my Porsche while the phone rings. When he answers, I say, "You were right. Azure is Silver-Tipped."

"Feathers." Dad takes a breath. "Any mention of a family? A woman named Amethyst, perhaps?"

"I didn't get any names. She says her father died before she was born and her mother passed in a car accident when she was fifteen. Her mom kept all Wingai knowledge a secret. Azure didn't know to expect a match." Anger simmers from the injustice. My hand not holding the phone shifts into talons. "I get the impression Azure's mom didn't treat her well. She has scars on her arms that look like she's been slashed up."

"That's unfortunate," Dad says with regret in his voice. "Some Wingai who lose their match become unbalanced.

41

They can be dangerous around others. I've seen it happen before. About four years ago, we had to isolate Auburn for a while when his match died unexpectedly. He destroyed his nest and nearly sliced through his son. He's better now, but not everyone comes out of it."

"Yeah, I remember." All of Soaring Heights had gotten together to get Auburn help. Too bad the same thing couldn't have happened for Azure.

Dad switches subjects. "What have you told her?"

My eyes dart to the second story. A light shines through a sliver between some curtains. "I told her we were matches, but that's it. She's overwhelmed enough as it is. She's not ready to believe everything I say anyway, considering we just met."

"Of course," Dad agrees. "You realize I'm going to have to let Russet know you've found them a Lead for Mountain Hollow. We can't keep her a secret." His voice hardens with his distaste of the Silver Wingai's Acting Lead. "They'll want to send a delegate of their own. I'll need her address."

My wings stretch taut with alarm. "No way. They'll brainwash her to hate me before I've solidified my match." Almost twenty years ago, a crazed human broke into Soaring Heights and tried to blow us up, believing we were an abomination of epic proportions. Mountain Hollow's Lead— who I suspect was Azure's father—came to help de-escalate the situation, and he, along with the human, lost his life in the process. Since then Mountain Hollow has been without a Silver Lead, and they blame their misfortune on us.

"Ceril, think of the consequences. Withholding Azure could give Russet the incitement he's looking for to attack us." Dad softens his tone. "You know I would love nothing more than to give you time to create a relationship with Azure, but as Lead Wingai of the Gold, I have to consider the safety of our people."

"Give me one day," I plead, knowing I can't ask for anything more. "Azure's set to graduate from the local high school tomorrow. She should be allowed to close that chapter of her life first."

"All right," Dad concedes, "but I expect a text with an address tomorrow."

"You'll have it," I promise.

CHAPTER FIVE

AZURE

I wake to the sound of my phone chirping. I reach for it on my nightstand and unplug it from the charger. The text is from Bree.**Happy Graduation Day! Don't forget practice at 9. Nails and hair at 10:30. We've got to look our best as we cross the stage with our diplomas.**She adds a winking emoji.

I sigh and let my fingers swipe across the screen. **Can't make it to either.** I accidentally hit send before I finish typing out the full message.

Bree responds two seconds later. **WHY?**

A twinge of guilt snakes across my stomach. I should have texted her when it happened, but I got too caught up in grief and with Cerulean.**Josephina had a stroke at rummy club yesterday. She died. Could you tell your dad?**I insert a crying emoji.

I wait about twenty seconds for her to text back.**OMG! I'm so sorry. Do you need anything? I'll skip practice and come over if you want.**A minute later she sends another text.**Dad says you don't even have to go to graduation. He'll give you your diploma.

I grumble at the autocorrect mistakes as I answer.**Thanks, but I'll be okay. I've got a morning filled with getting affairs in order. I'll be pretty distracted. I'm still going to graduation, promise.**Josephina would be disappointed if I didn't walk across that stage. She wouldn't want her death to hinder my plans to have a normal high school experience.**There's more I need to tell you, but I'll wait till tonight when I'm not so busy.**

Okay, girl. I'm here if you need me. XOXOXO.

I set my phone down and stretch. Taking a deep breath, I detect eggs, sausage, peppers, and onions in the air. I climb out of bed and pad down the stairs to the kitchen to investigate.

I hang in the doorway and watch Cerulean slide a perfect omelet onto a plate. The events of yesterday come flooding back. *Wingai. Match.*

Wings retracted, he's dressed in dark fitted jeans and a navy T-shirt that hints at a sculpted chest underneath. His dark brown hair, on the longer side of short, seems artfully mussed. He'd make a fortune modeling.

He flashes me a knowing smile. "Hey."

My face heats. "Hey."

"Do you like eggs?" he asks, holding up the omelet.

I nod. He places the plate on the edge of the island and pours me a glass of orange juice. "Enjoy."

"Thank you." I take a seat and pick up the fork. I can't remember the last time I had something other than oatmeal for breakfast. I gasp in surprised pleasure as the flavor hits my tongue. "Oh, this is good." I plunge my fork into the omelet with renewed vigor.

Cerulean grins. My stomach flips. He retrieves a plate for himself and sits beside me. His eyes trail to my exposed wings with something akin to satisfaction. It abruptly occurs to me that they're not giving me any trouble, despite sitting right next to Cerulean. Unnerved, I hop off the stool and bring my wings to my face to check.

"What the—" I yank on a wing to bring it closer, ignoring the strain. I seize with fear. I see gold coloring in my feathers, making some sort of swirly, intricate designs. A tattoo on my feathers? "Cerulean—"

"Don't panic." Cerulean puts his hand on mine clutching my feathers. "It's normal."

I shake my wing at him. He drops his hand. "This wasn't here yesterday! What have you done?"

Cerulean speaks in gentle tones. "Calm down, Azure. It's not going to hurt you." He smiles. "When we meet our match, our wings take on their color. Mine changed too." He takes his shirt off and releases his wings. He shields his bare chest, allowing me to see the silver now coloring his feathers in the same arrangement. "Each design is unique to the match. It's to show all Wingai that you are taken." He retracts his wings and puts on his shirt.

I let out a gasp of indignation as I hide my wings. "Taken? I don't even know you!" Cerulean opens his mouth, but I hold up a finger. "Shh!" I dart to the kitchen window and peek through the red curtains, certain I heard a car on the gravel drive.

A blue Ford with a government license plate stops in front of my garage. A decal on the side reads, "DHS." I spy a forties-something lady with a clipboard and groan. Stupid Mr. Egot. I whirl away and race up the stairs to put on decent clothing.

Cerulean's concerned voice comes through my closed door. "Azure, why is a lady from the DHS here?"

"Mr. Egot," I hiss, shimmying on a clean pair of jeans.

"Who?" Cerulean asks.

I slip on a dressy blue shirt and let my hair down, raking my fingers through it quickly. "The man I talked to at the hospital didn't trust me." I snatch my phone and shove it in my pocket. I nearly run into Cerulean as I open my door. He grabs my upper arms to steady me. The doorbell rings. "We're not hiding anything. If she asks about your presence, say you're a friend helping me through the grieving process."

He shrugs. "It's true enough."

I sail down the stairs, then take a few breaths to calm my anger and nerves. I answer the door. "May I help you?"

"Azure Tallon?" the lady asks.

I nod.

"I'm Dorothy Halifore. I work for the DHS." She hands me a small white card with her information on it. "I come on behalf of McMinnville High School. The school counselor, Mr.

Franklin, informed me you had a death in your family yesterday. Is it all right if I come in?"

Whoa, not Mr. Egot? Principal Ashlander must have called Mr. Franklin right after Bree told him. He was quick. I open the door wider. "Sure."

I show her to the living room. A dark wood coffee table separates two charcoal-gray couches. End tables grace each side of the sofas with silver lamps residing on them. Two recliners occupy opposite corners of the room. A gray stone fireplace takes center focus on the back wall. A flat-screen TV hangs over the mantel. "Please have a seat."

Dorothy settles on the end of a couch. I take the opposite one. In full view of us, Cerulean stands in the kitchen wiping down the stovetop.

Dorothy eyes me. "Mr. Franklin asked if I'd stop by for a quick welfare check and bring you some pamphlets with information that may assist you. Government programs and such." She waves a hand. "It's not easy to start adulthood on your own. We want you to know there's help available."

"That's kind of you. Thank you." I take the folder she holds out.

"You're welcome." She smiles briefly before her eyes become scrutinizing. "Are you doing okay?"

"Yeah, I'm all right." I sigh, knowing I need to be real here to assure Dorothy so she will leave. "Josephina was eighty-four. Her ministrokes were happening more often. The doctor said she was living on borrowed time. We put plans together. I have a list of who to contact. I just need to get started."

"That's good," Dorothy says. "And I see you have a young man to help." Her brown eyes rest on Cerulean loading up the dishwasher.

"Yeah, he's a good support," I say with some confidence. "I couldn't do this without him." Better let her think we're together.

Dorothy's lips twitch in amusement. She stands and smooths her button-up blouse. "It sounds like you have everything in order. Thank you for your time."

"No problem." I show her out and wait on the porch until she drives down the hill.

My phone chirps. I read a message from Jack. **Bree just told me! I'm so sorry! You okay? Anything I can do?**

Am I okay? Not in the slightest. But no one needs to know that. **Thanks. I'm okay. Josephina prepared me for her death a long time ago. I'll see you at graduation tonight.** I throw in a smiley face for good measure.

I'm here if you need me. See you tonight.

CERIL

The morning passes slowly while Azure settles what she can of Josephina's affairs over the phone. She paces in the office while holding her cell up to her ear. She wears a tight expression, back and shoulders stiff. I resist the urge to touch her, loosen her up with a shoulder rub or something. I'll probably get a slap in the face if I make any perceived advances.

Instead, I sit in a black recliner wedged in the corner of the room. I make a note of Azure's address in my phone and then play Angry Birds. Twenty levels beat so far.

"I'll see you soon. Goodbye." Azure slips her cell into her pocket, closes her eyes, and rubs her temples.

I take this as a cue to speak up. "Everything okay?"

She drops her hands. "It's just a lot."

I stand. "What can I do to help?"

"I have to stop by the mortuary, then go to Betty's to pick up Josephina's car. Would you mind driving it home for me?" she asks.

"Of course," I say, grateful to be able to do something.

Azure starts up a conversation on the drive into McMinnville. "Tell me about yourself. Do you have any brothers or sisters? Pets?"

I smile, pleased she's asking questions to get to know me. "I have an older sister named Scarlett. She's married to her match, Midnight. They're expecting their first child at the end of July. We're really excited for them. I'm looking forward to being an uncle."

Azure smiles briefly at me. "That's great."

I can see she genuinely means it, and my heart warms. "I also have a brother. Jade's a year younger than me and my best friend."

"That's cool," Azure says as she slows to a stop at a red light.

"I'm blessed." I grin. "What about you? How much did Josephina know about your being Wingai?"

"Josephina knew everything I did. My mom slipped up and accidentally drifted too far onto Josephina's land," Azure says.

"What about your friends I saw you with?" I ask.

An embarrassed expression crosses her face. "They know too. It was a mistake on my part." She laughs, her tone brittle. "I guess I'm worse than my mom because she had only one person find out and I had three." She proceeds to tell me about a miscommunication over winter break that resulted in the exposure. "I totally expected our relationship to go south. Most humans don't accept anything out of their realm of normal. But luckily our friendship was strong enough to trust each other. Now we're friends for life." She smiles brightly.

I'm surprised. Soaring Heights doesn't have her kind of success stories with humans. We don't take chances on them. If one found out, they'd be given a mind-erasing drug or quietly taken out. But I don't think I should tell her that yet, so I just say, "that's great."

We stop at the mortuary. The place gives me the shivers. The workers here deal with dead people daily. I hang in the shadows while Azure speaks with the proprietor, signs some papers, and sets a date for when she can pick up an urn.

She steps outside, and her eyes crinkle and lips pinch in a frown as a bit of emotion shows through. "On to Betty's."

"Do you want me to drive?" I ask.

"No, I'm all right." She gets in the driver's seat.

Five minutes later, she parks behind a newish white Jetta at a gray one-story house with blue shutters. Two red Fords are stationed in the driveway.

A man with salt-and-pepper hair, a beard, and a paunch belly opens the door. He meets us on the walkway with Josephina's things: a brown purse and a black coat. "Mom's lying down. She's been crying about Josephina off and on all day." His brown eyes find mine. "I see you got yourself a young man to drive the Jetta."

"Yes, I did." Azure smiles. "Tell Betty I wish her well, and thanks, for everything."

The man nods. "I'll let her know." He returns to the house.

Azure fishes around Josephina's purse and hands me a set of keys. "Drive safe."

"Always," I say.

CHAPTER SIX

AZURE

I take measured breaths, holding tears at bay as I drive home. My mind slips into a memory.

"Don't hold no funeral or nothing when I die." Josephina pointed a chocolate-covered wooden spoon at me. "I hate the idea of people crying over a casket." She shuddered as she stirred the chocolate fudge brownie mix. "I want to be cremated and my ashes spread with the stars over the property."

"Do we really need to talk about this?" I asked, my stomach queasy. I focused on the chocolatey goodness.

Josephina poured the batter into a pan and shoved it in the oven. "Of course we need to talk about this. I'm eighty-four years old. You heard the doctor. Those strokes are just going to keep coming, and one day one will take me. Now I hope to see you through high school, but no one but the angel of death knows when my time is up."

"Yes," I agreed reluctantly.

Josephina's wrinkled hands covered mine. "I've talked with my lawyer, and I've got everything set up. He's written down my wishes and put them on file with the proper people. There'll be life insurance money, and you know I've got some set aside for the immediate costs in a separate fund. You don't have to worry about anything."

I smiled lopsidedly. "You'll still be taking care of me from the other side."

Josephina smiled wide. "Yep. Now about my clothes . . ."

I blink out of the memory, momentarily surprised to see I made it home in one piece. Muscle memory. I use my phone to check the time. Four hours till graduation. I set an alarm to remember.

Cerulean hands me Josephina's keys as I get out. "What's next?"

"Are you sure you want to keep hanging around?" I ask instead. "I'm not the greatest company." I don't want him to feel obligated to stay here because of what I'm going through.

Cerulean doesn't skip a beat. "You're my match. I want to spend every second with you, regardless of what we do."

I flush under the intensity of his sea-green eyes. I won't say I don't enjoy his attention, but I'm not sure I need or am ready for it right now.

Cerulean takes my hand in his. I stiffen. He sighs. "Look, I know you're dealing with a lot. This is obviously not the right time to charm your feathers into the clouds, as much as I'd like to. I think you could use a friend more than a romancer. So that's what I'm going to be—if you'll let me."

I let out the breath I didn't realize I held. "I'd like that."

He grins. "Me too. How about I make you lunch and you let your wings stretch a while before you tackle your next thing?"

"Graduation, but I've got a few hours before then," I say.

"Perfect." He leads me inside and has me sit in one of the recliners in the living room. I lean back and put my feet up, appreciating the moment to breathe. I purposely let my mind drift. Cerulean pulls me out of wandering nothings with the announcement of lunch.

"I noticed you have twenty jars of spaghetti sauce in the cupboard. I'm assuming you like pasta." He raises an eyebrow, his face amused.

I laugh. "Guilty." Sitting down at the table, my mouth waters at the spaghetti and garlic toast. "This looks really wonderful. Thank you."

A pleased smile graces Cerulean's lips. "It's my pleasure."

I'm unnerved at how easily I'm letting him insert himself into my life. I need to get to the bottom of this match thing before he charms me further. I twirl my fork around the spaghetti. "So about this match thing . . ." I pause, unsure how to proceed or what I'm really asking.

Cerulean takes a sip of his water. "Are you sure you want to get into this?"

"No" escapes my lips before I can stop it. "I mean, yes." I shovel a bite into my mouth to stop myself from saying no again.

Cerulean chuckles. "I sense some indecision."

"Maybe—" My phone rings. "Excuse me." I glance at the number, recognizing it as the life insurance company. I had left a voice mail earlier. "I have to take this." I leave the table to answer it.

Business dominates almost the rest of the afternoon. I feel like a tennis ball bouncing back and forth as I get transferred between departments as they verify my claim. When I finally put down my phone, my alarm pops up for graduation. I swipe the screen to shut it off.

Cerulean cracks an eye open from his place on the recliner where's he's been leisurely catnapping. "All done?"

"For now." I sigh, rubbing my temples. "I've got to get ready for graduation. Would you like to come?"

Cerulean smiles warmly. "I'd love to."

I take a five-minute shower, then slip into dressy black pants and a ruffled navy-blue top with a high back and a V-neck. Bree picked the outfit on our recent shopping excursion. I shove my feet into black flats and run a brush through my hair. I apply a smidgen of makeup: eyeliner, mascara, lip gloss. I prefer understated beauty over attempted Instagram model.

Cerulean leans against the stair banister, phone in hand, as I descend. Looking up at me, his eyes grow into the size of dinner plates. He drops his cell. It lands with a thud on the hardwood. "Whoa."

I gesture to my top. "I promised Bree."

He swallows. "Feathers, you're gorgeous." He darts down to retrieve his phone, an embarrassed smile peeking around his lips.

My heart beats faster as my wings threaten to break free.

CERIL

We take my Porsche. On the drive, Azure studies the inside of my car, eyes critical but lips curved in a pleasing smile.

"Do you like it?" I ask.

"Not as much as Lady Bug, but it's very nice. Comfortable," she says shifting in her seat. "Porsche and Volkswagen kind of go hand in hand. Porsche motors can be used in Volkswagens."

"Ah, they're matches," I say, braking at a stoplight. I glance at Azure to see a faint blush on her cheeks. Adrenaline spikes through my wings into my heart. I straighten, tamping down the urge to release them. I picture my brother's sports car. "I suppose if I drove a Camaro . . ."

"I wouldn't look twice," Azure answers with hard conviction.

I laugh. "Feathers, Jade will be crushed. He loves his Camaro."

Cars line the streets around the high school. I suspect the parking lot is just as full. I stop multiple times to let families cross the street. Many carry gift bags and bouquets. I make a mental reminder to get something for Azure later.

I take the place of a white car pulling out along the side of the road adjacent to the school. Azure rummages through her purse and hands me a red ticket.

Stepping out, she dons her robe, cords, and cap. "How do I look?"

I can't stop myself from grinning. "You're a vision in red." She laughs.

We head to the stadium, joining the throngs of people going the same direction. Azure leaves me at the end of a long ticket line. She gives me a tentative smile. "Thanks for coming."

"I'm happy to be here." I consider it an honor to support my match.

I watch her dash off while I move steadily through the line. A mother in front of me carries a little girl no older than two. The toddler grins at me, holding out a small stuffed unicorn with rainbow hair.

I smile at her. "What a pretty pony."

The little girl giggles. The mother looks over her shoulder at me and smiles briefly.

My phone buzzes as I near the ticket booth. I read a text from Dad. **I'M WAITING.**

Feathers, he's not playing games. This isn't the first text he's sent me today, but it's the only one that gives me pause. I don't care to be the object of his anger. With a heavy heart, I give him Azure's address. I figure I have a couple of hours before the house comes crashing down.

He responds immediately. **Thank you.**

"So not welcome," I mutter, shoving my cell into my pocket. Handing my ticket over, I turn my attention to the event before me. Tons of humans celebrating in one place. This should be interesting.

AZURE

The senior class congregates on the far side of the stadium, just out of view of the main seats. In a hurry to reach my spot in the alphabetical line, I give Bree a passing wave. With the last name of Ashlander, she stands near the front behind the Abbleton twins. Relief shows on her face. "I'll find you after," I tell her.

"You better!" she shouts.

"Azure!" Jack pulls me into a hug as I step into my place. "I'm so sorry for your loss."

"Thanks, Jack," I say. He gives me a squeeze, then lets go. "How are you holding up?" His eyes roam over me.

I take a breath and exhale. "I'm all right," I answer, surprised by the genuine emotion. At Jack's dubious expression, I put a hand on his arm. "Really. I've been expecting this for a while. Josephina did her best to prepare me for it." I smile. "I'm better off than most eighteen year olds. I'm not in jeopardy of losing my home or anything. Josephina's life insurance money and my trust fund should keep me going for several years."

Jack grins. "So you're really a middle-aged lady hiding under the guise of a teenager. I can only hope to be as set up as you when I'm thirty."

I laugh. "You're gonna make millions playing baseball. You'll have three mansions and an island!"

The principal's voice rings over the loudspeakers. "Ladies and gentlemen." The band plays a fast, welcoming beat, drowning out his voice. Our senior class marches into view to a cheering crowd on their feet.

I see Cerulean standing in the second row. A proud smile stretches across his face. My heart pulses, sending energy straight to my wings. I drop my gaze, again unnerved at how easily he affects me. Tendrils of fear wrap around my heart. I don't think falling under his spell is a good idea right now.

The first hour of the ceremony drags as students and faculty give nostalgic speeches. A slideshow of our greatest moments—homecoming, assemblies, our basketball championship win—flashes across a white screen. Then Principal Ashlander rises and starts reading the names. Jack and I, and somewhere in the middle Ben, cheer loudly as Bree strolls across the stage. We chuckle when her dad gives her a bear hug, emotion clear on his face.

In seemingly no time, I stand near the steps to the stage behind Jack.

"Jack Tager," Vice Principal Roberts calls.

"Yeah! Go, Jack!" I clap loudly.

He flashes me a grin over his shoulder.

"Azure Tallon," Principal Ashlander reads.

My heart pounds as I climb the three steps, walk to the middle of the stage, and accept my honors diploma. Principal Ashlander gives me an unexpected hug. "Congratulations, Azure. I'm so happy you could be here despite your loss."

I smile. "Thank you."

A horn rings from the stands. "Azure!" I look out and burst into a fit of giggles. Betty, Phyllis, Maureen, and Edna surround Cerulean. Edna carries the horn. Betty, Phyllis, and Maureen hold a painted sign that reads, "Congratulations, Azure!"

When the last student, Lacy Zindar, returns to her seat, Principal Ashlander speaks into the microphone. "That concludes our graduating class—" Again his voice gets lost in the roar as we throw our caps into the air.

Relief and joy enter my heart. *Graduated.*

Pandemonium descends as families and friends walk onto the field to meet their students. I dance around people, searching for Bree in the fading light. She finds me first. Our caps collide as we hug. She speaks a fast litany of words. I catch a few. ". . . tragic . . . sorry . . . here."

I grip her shoulders. "Slow down. I can't understand you."

"Sorry." She chuckles. "Are you coming to grad night?"

"I can't—"

"Why not?" Bree cries with dismay, stopping me from explaining. "You need a night of fun to take your mind off everything."

"Bree!" Ben wades through a large family to reach his girlfriend's side. He notices me. "Azure, I'm so sorry for your loss. You okay?"

I nod. "I'm managing all right."

"My parents want a picture of us together," Ben tells Bree. "I'll be right back with them." He kisses Bree's cheek, then melts into the throng, calling out for his family. I doubt they'll hear him amid the noise.

Bree watches Ben for a second before turning her full attention on me, her expression serious. "Azure, I really don't think you should be alone."

Cerulean emerges out of the shadows and wraps an arm over my shoulder. "She's not alone. She has me."

Bree's brown eyes nearly pop out of her face. "Porsche guy?"

Cerulean laughs. "I'm Ceril." He holds out his hand.

Bree shakes it slowly, and her eyes dart to me questioningly.

"He's the cause of all that trouble I had yesterday," I tell her, motioning to Cerulean with a tilt of my head.

Bree squeals. "Oh my gosh, I was right?" I nod. "Ha, yes, I knew it!"

"Now's my chance to get answers," I say.

"Totally," she says with exuberance.

Ben returns. He looks at Cerulean with a raised eyebrow. "Porsche guy?"

Ben's father, a tall, slim man in a business suit, approaches. "Come on, Ben, the light's fading." He waves his phone.

Bree glances at Cerulean, winks at me, then allows Ben to tug her along. "Text me!"

I shoulder my way through the people, Cerulean at my side. "The girls asked me to give you their best wishes. They didn't want to brave the masses."

"The *girls*?" Since when has anyone referred to the eighty-year-olds of the rummy club as girls?

Cerulean shrugs. "They insisted I call them girls when we sat together."

I snort. Apparently old women are susceptible to him too.

I breathe easier the farther we get from the stadium, inhaling the scent of freshly cut grass. My pace slows from a rush to a casual walk. Twilight's in full swing, and stars appear in the clear sky. It's a warm, beautiful night. Josephina would have liked it.

We stop at Cerulean's Porsche, and curiosity overtakes me. "Can I take it for a spin? I've never driven a sports car."

He hands me his keys. "Go for it."

CHAPTER SEVEN

CERIL

Azure doesn't say a word until we stop in front of her house. She spends the entire drive eyeing my car like a lover undressing secrets. Envy spills and bubbles through me like an erupted volcano. I want her to look at me that way, to need me for more than information about the Wingai. Someday, I hope.

"Thanks for letting me test-drive. It's a great car." She hands me my keys.

"Does it sway you even a little from your bug?" I ask.

"Maybe a little," she admits with a small chuckle. "It's a smooth drive."

My phone vibrates as we're heading inside. I pull it out.

Scarlett sends me a few angry emojis. **Why didn't you tell me you found your match?!**

Feathers.

"Hey, I'm going to change. Then I thought maybe I'd take a night flight, if you'd like to join?" Azure asks.

I don't hesitate. Any time spent with my match is valuable to me. I want to forge a real connection with her. "I'd love to." I tug at my shirt. "Guess I better change too."

"Meet me on the porch in ten." Azure dashes up the stairs.

Taking her lead, I go to the spare bedroom and change my shirt. I groan with relief as I release my wings. My heart spasms, reminding me of Azure's closeness. Feathers flap with accumulating energy.

I snap a picture of my wings with the match design and send it to Scarlett. **You get first pic.**

She responds thirty seconds later. **OMG, SILVER?!**

I read another text, this one from Jade.**Heads up, Dad is stressing hard-core about your match. Entire case of Cherry Vanilla Coke gone.**

Feathers. I respond to Jade. **Do you know if he's told Russet yet?**

They spoke via video chat a few hours ago. Hey, how come Scarlett got first pic? What happened to bros before sis?

I neglected to tell Scarlett I found my match. She deserved first pic.

Free pass this time, then, Jade says with a smile emoji.**Sis just walked in with Midnight, wanting answers about your match. Dad's reaching for a second case of Coke.**

Not good. I scroll through my contacts and call Dad. I need to hear what he's done. The phone nearly goes to voice mail before Dad answers. "Hey, Ceril." I detect a small strain in his voice. It sets me on edge.

"You spoke to Russet?" I ask.

In the background I hear Scarlett urge, "Put him on speaker!"

Dad obliges. "Is Azure with you?"

"No, I'm in the guest bedroom. We're going on a flight in a minute. Did you speak to Russet or not?" I press.

Dad sighs. "Yes, I did."

"And?" Scarlett, Jade, and I say simultaneously.

"I explained the circumstances. Russet thanked me for bringing this to his attention and then cut our communication. I've kept the peace intact. However . . ." Dad takes a breath. "I don't know what he's planning to do with the information."

I swear. My wings unfurl, stretching with the stress pumping through my veins.

"Did you get any sort of read off Russet?" Scarlett asks Dad.

"Other than initial surprise, no," Dad says. "I'm sorry, Ceril. Russet, as usual, wasn't interested in coming to a mutual agreement with me. At the very least, expect a delegation. Russet will want to verify my claim."

I push my hair away from my face. "I haven't had a chance to explain anything to Azure yet. I better start preparing her." No wonder Dad's going through cases of Coke. Being left in the dark about Russet's intentions is like getting kicked out of the nest with no warning.

"That's a good idea," Dad agrees.

"Do your best to solidify your match," Mom says. "Don't let Russet sway her from you."

Anger seeps into my tone. "She's just lost her guardian. Azure's in no position for any of this."

"Do what you can anyway," Mom encourages.

"Right." I try not to sound sarcastic, but I know a lost cause when I see one.

"I'm sure it will work out, Ceril," Scarlett says with forced enthusiasm.

"Yeah," Midnight adds, no doubt prompted by Scarlett. "Destiny is never wrong. Azure's your match for a reason."

"Thanks, guys." I realize my ten minutes are probably up. "I better go."

"Keep us posted," Dad says.

"Will do." I end the call.

AZURE

I sit in Josephina's favorite rocking chair on the front porch while I wait for Cerulean to come down. Every night she would sit here and talk to her husband Max. He died of cancer twenty-three years ago. They were unable to have children, and Max was all she had for many years. I like to think of her at peace, reunited with him now.

"Max loved motorcycles," Josephina said to me once, her eyes closed in remembrance. Her feet propelled the rocking motion of her chair. "He had his eyes set on some fancy red Harley with a sidecar." She chuckled. "He could've told you all the specs like you can with Lady Bug. We planned to take a trip around America when he retired from the steel mill." She sighed, her old age showing in the tired lines of her face. "Then the cancer struck. I told him we'd take that ride when he got better, but he didn't, so he made me promise we'd ride the heavens."

"Ride that Harley with Max in the heavens," I whisper to the rocking motion of the chair.

Cerulean steps out, closing the front door softly behind him. His wings rest naturally against his back. The gold and silver gleam under the porchlights. My feathers twitch with an urge to touch his. "Sorry to keep you waiting."

"It's fine." I stand, wiping a few unexpected tears off my cheeks.

He embraces me, his wings folding around me. "You look like you need a hug," he says softly.

His feathers send a calming warmth into me. I rest my head on his chest, taking the comfort he offers. He smells like home, the smell of earthy pine and moss. His heart pounds underneath my ear. The stress and grief melt away with his touch. "Thank you," I whisper, looking up at him.

"You're welcome." His eyes smile into mine. The air charges around us. My gaze unexpectedly drops to his lips, and I wonder what it would be like to kiss him.

As if reading my thoughts, Cerulean bends his head to touch mine. His thumb rubs my cheek in a comforting gesture. I'm tempted to close the gap between us just to feel something different, experience something new.

We spring apart at the sound of tires on gravel. My wings retract faster than I can blink. I shade my eyes against approaching high beams. Two fancy silver SUVs stop behind Cerulean's Porsche.

"Feathers!" Cerulean curses.

I glance at him. Wings hidden, he wears a hard mask of anger. I shiver with alarm.

The doors open on both vehicles. I count eight people stepping out. Subconsciously, I find myself stepping closer to

Cerulean as they advance. He takes my hand and squeezes. I inhale deeply, catching the unique scent of Wingai.

As the light from my porch descends on them, I notice three are women and five are men. All have youthful appearances. They wear black uniforms with silver wings and the letters SG embroidered on their left breast. Handguns rest on utility belts that would rival a police officer's.

I stiffen in fear.

One of the men places himself in front of the others. His wavy blonde hair curls around his ears. He has smooth features, bright blue eyes, a slight curve in his nose, thin lips. I sense strength behind his lean build. He stares at Cerulean with recognition. "Ceril." His voice is deeper than I expect.

"Sky," Cerulean acknowledges.

Sky flicks his eyes to me. "Azure Tallon?"

How does he know who I am? I clear my throat to find my voice. I go for smooth professional. They're on my property, but they have weapons. "May I help you?"

"I would prefer to discuss my business in a more secure location." He gestures to my house. "May we come inside?"

I can't say no. There are way more of them than me. Still, I glance at Cerulean, seeking approval since he knows them. He nods.

"Yes."

"Thank you." Sky smiles briefly, obviously aware of my reluctance.

I pull my hand free from Cerulean's and head inside. The others follow silently. I move into the living room and stand in front of the fireplace. As the others file in, I gesture to the furniture. "Please have a seat."

Cerulean takes a position at my side. Sky also stands close. He situates slightly to face me but also to stay seen by the others. They occupy the couches and recliners and turn their silent attention on me.

Sky takes a quick sweep of the room with his eyes, nods to himself, then speaks. "I'm Sky Winter, Commander of the Silver Guard." He gestures to his comrades. "This is my team. We come on behalf of Russet, our Acting Lead, to verify that you are one of us."

"Wingai," I state.

Sky smiles briefly. "Yes. May I see your wings?" His team leans forward in anticipation.

I hesitate, worried he may want to do something to them.

Cerulean correctly interprets my pause. "It's okay, Azure. They just want to look." He steps back to give me space and smiles at me in encouragement.

I stretch my feathers taut upon release. Multiple gasps hit my ears. Most of Sky's team rise, eyes bugging out of their heads. Their shock unnerves me. Are my wings broken or unnatural?

Sky circles and assesses me. He turns to Cerulean. "Ceril, your wings."

Cerulean reveals his. Another round of gasps goes through the team. Everyone is on their feet now. Cerulean joins my side, allowing his feathers to mingle with mine. I'm grateful for the calm he infuses.

"It appears the claims are true," Sky says almost to himself.

"We have no reason lie," Cerulean's voice and expression are firm.

Sky quirks an eyebrow but doesn't comment. He turns to his team. They nod at him in some unspoken agreement. Sky's blue eyes fall upon me. "As Commander of the Silver Guard under the direction of Acting Lead Russet, I am placing you under my care. You are to come with me and my team to Mountain Hollow to be integrated into our community."

I retract my wings. "Excuse me?" I stare at him blankly while I try to process his words.

"It is against our law for a Silver Wingai to live outside of our Acting Lead's jurisdiction. We do not belong with the *humans.*" Sky spits the word out. I take offense. "Pack a bag and we'll be off."

"No." Every fiber of my being tells me this is a bad idea. "I'm not going anywhere with you."

"You do not want to make this difficult," Sky says, undeterred. He addresses his team over his shoulder. "Honey, Ivory, find Azure's room and pack a bag for her." Two of the women leave.

Cerulean steps in. "Azure is my match. She should be under my care."

"You have no rights until your match is confirmed and sealed," Sky recites as if reading from a law book.

"Under Gold law, I have the right to be with her," Cerulean snaps back.

Sky doesn't back down. "Azure is Silver. Our rules apply over yours."

I cross my arms and inject steel into my voice. "I am an adult. No one has claim over me."

Everyone in the room shakes their head at me.

"Wingai do not follow human practices." Sky sounds like he holds a serious grudge against humans.

Cerulean argues. "Azure is not ready to be thrown into Wingai society. She needs to learn a little more about us first. Give me another day with her, and I'll take her to Mountain Hollow."

"I'm not going anywhere!" I shout while Sky says, no.

Sky's team blocks the way to the door. Running would be fruitless. I inch away from Sky and Cerulean and pull out my phone. My throat is dry. I swallow and gulp in Wingai-scented air. I dial 911 and hold the phone to my ear. It rings once.

"911 services. What is your emergency?" a woman speaks, her voice calm and cool.

I surprise myself with an even tone. "I have intruders in my home."

Cerulean swivels around and stares at me with shock and dismay. Sky curses.

"What is your location?" the woman asks.

Sky rips my phone out of my hands. He ends the call and hands it to a male team member. "Disable tracking." He grabs hold of my arm. "Time to go."

"Let go of me!" I try to wrench my arm free, but his grip is too tight. I shift my hands into talons. Quick as lightning, Sky does some sort of twist with my hands. I gasp in surprise as my nails retract.

"Get your hands off my match!" Cerulean reaches for me.

Sky throws his arm up and blocks Cerulean while simultaneously pushing me into his team members. The burliest one scoops me up and heads for the front door. I twist and squirm, but the man's grasp is iron tight. The others swarm, ensuring Cerulean has no chance to get to me. Burly Guy sets me inside the back of the first SUV into the waiting arms of another male team member. This man has spiky brown hair with the tips dyed crimson. Burly Guy then gets in, sandwiching me between him and Spiky Red. I sink into my seat as Sky starts the vehicle and punches the gas.

Anger and fear flow through me like a fast-moving river, heating my skin and tightening my chest. This is not how I intended to find my answers. Are all Wingai just as crazy as Mom was?

CHAPTER EIGHT

CERIL

As the two SUVs drive off, I dash back inside Azure's house. I run to the spare bedroom and grab my bag. On my way back outside, I quickly turn off all the lights and lock her door. Hopefully if any cops show up, they'll think she's out visiting for the night. I throw my bag in the passenger seat and shove my key into the ignition. My tires spin as I peel out.

I grip the steering wheel so tightly my hands cramp. My body is on fire with rage. If Russet were in front of me, I'd pummel him to dust. How dare he order the Silver Guard to take Azure from me.

As I enter the main city of McMinnville, I see a police car, lights flashing, heading toward Azure's house. What a freaking mess this has turned out to be. I push the button to bring the canopy up. I roll up my windows, shutting out the cool summer wind.

I activate the car's Bluetooth. "Call Dad."

"Calling Dad," a detached female's voice says through the speakers.

Two rings and Dad answers. "Hey, Ceril."

I slow to a stop at a red light. Every delay adds more frustration. "I'm going to kill Russet." I seethe.

"What happened?" Dad's tone goes from tired to sharp.

"He sent the Silver Guard and kidnapped Azure!" I shout.

"What?"

The light turns green. I hit the gas, lurching ahead of the red truck in the lane beside me. "Sky showed up with his elite team, made Azure and me reveal our wings, and then demanded Azure leave with them to Mountain Hollow because she's not authorized to live among humans. They scared her so bad she dialed 911."

"Police?" Dad's voice rose several octaves. "Ceril—"

"Sky cut off Azure's communication before she gave much info, but I saw a patrol car heading toward her house as I came into McMinnville," I say. "Azure's friends know I was with her. I could be implicated in a missing person's case."

Dad mutters a stream of curses.

Anger fuels my voice. "Sky refused to negotiate. His team literally hauled Azure out of her house, shoved her in the back of an SUV, and took off. They blocked me from getting near her. Under Silver law—"

"You have no rights until your match is confirmed and sealed," Dad finishes.

"Azure is on her way to Mountain Hollow, completely unprepared, probably scared out of her mind—and I'm not with her." My throat constricts with emotion. My heart spasms in pain, screaming at me to find my match. The longer I'm away from her, the more it will continue to hurt until our match is sealed.

Dad lets out a stressful sigh. "Come home and we'll get this sorted out together. Do not bang down the gates of Mountain Hollow without me."

"Fine." I'm sensible enough to know I'll have an easier time taking Azure back with Dad by my side. "I'll be home in an hour and a half."

"I'll be up," Dad says.

Merging onto the interstate, I press on the gas.

AZURE

The SUV has an overwhelmingly masculine scent. A mixture of spicy colognes and natural man. I've never been in a vehicle with this much testosterone. It's unsettling. I keep my arms wrapped around my torso and my legs pressed together to avoid contact with Burly Guy and Spiky Red.

Sky eyes me from the rearview mirror. "Relax, Azure. You're not in danger."

"Excuse me?" I have a mind to knock him upside the head. Perhaps if we crash, I can escape. Or die, if the accident is too bad. That thought stops me from acting out.

The man in the passenger seat rubs the auburn stubble on his chin. "We're all gonna get fired when she's properly placed."

Sky rolls his eyes at him. "We're not going to get fired, Cider. There's no one better than us."

Cider shakes his head. "There are going to be repercussions somewhere. Fire and brimstone raining down on our heads."

Spiky Red speaks up. "Don't be so doom and gloom, Cider. Nothing is established yet."

Burly Guy nods. "As soon as we hand her off to Russet, it'll be mission accomplished for us. Any fire and brimstone happenings will be dealt with by him."

"He'll deal with it by sending us out," Cider retorts.

"Enough," Sky says sternly. "What will happen will happen." He turns on the radio. Elvis Presley croons through the speakers.

Spiky Red complains. "We're in the human world. Pick something modern."

Cider turns the dial to an eighties station. "Girls Just Want to Have Fun" blares. Burly Guy, Sky, and Spiky Red groan. The men proceed to squabble like freshman girls until they settle on a country song I've never heard before.

Spiky Red reaches into a bag under his feet and retrieves snack-sized bags of Chex Mix. He passes them out to the men, then turns to me. "Want one?"

He wears such an open expression, I grudgingly take it. "Thank you . . . ?" I can't exactly call him Spiky Red.

"Crimson," he supplies. "And that's Onyx." He gestures to Burly Guy, who flashes a grin. "You know Sky, and that's Cider." Sky keeps his eyes on the road. Cider turns in his seat to smile at me. Crimson sounds hopeful. "We don't have to be enemies."

"Friends don't kidnap someone against their will," I answer.

Sky flicks his eyes to the rearview mirror. "You are Wingai. You belong with us, not the humans."

82

"I decide where I belong," I say. "You're making a bad case for yourselves by forcing me to go with you."

"That wasn't our decision to make," Sky says. I can't tell if he was in support of it or not, but he certainly followed through.

"We're just the errand boys." Onyx sighs.

Crimson and Onyx cover the side windows with their bodies. Staring ahead, all I see is a line of red taillights and headlights from oncoming traffic. Eventually, the number of cars ahead of us lessens. Sky takes us past glittering city lights and onto a forested two-lane road.

"Almost home," Onyx murmurs while staring out the blackened window.

Crimson squirms. "Finally. My wings are stifled."

"You having trouble, Crimson?" Sky inquires.

Crimson straightens. "No."

"Are you sure?" Sky persists. "We can go another round of restraint training."

"I'm good, I swear." An edge of panic laces Crimson's tone. The men chuckle.

We come to a stop in front of a large metal gate with the name "Mountain Hollow" welded over it. A young man steps out of a small post and approaches the vehicle. Sky rolls down his window. They speak in low murmurs, nothing I can hear. The guard returns to his post, and the gates open. Sky drives through.

Cider turns in his seat to see me. "Welcome to Mountain Hollow."

Adrenaline heats my body. The car is suddenly stifling. I feel sick to my stomach. A panic attack? I can't afford to be weak right now. I shut my eyes and take quiet, slow, even breaths. I push the anxiety back until I'm confident I can function.

When I open my eyes, Crimson asks, "You okay?"

"I'm fine."

Sky parks. "We're here."

"About time," Onyx mutters. Getting out of the SUV, he reaches back in and takes me by the hand. I scramble out before he drags me.

I stifle a gasp at the mansion before me. Many outside lights illuminate three stories of multicolored gray stone and white siding, a ton of windows, and several balconies.

"Come on." Onyx tugs on my hand.

I stumble onto a cobblestone path lined with roses, dark green shrubbery, and minilights. Two stone Wingai—one male, the other female—adorn the cement steps leading to black double doors. Sky rings the bell. His team huddles around me.

Both doors are thrown open by a young but well-built man. His dark hair is just long enough to touch his ears and ruffled. Cool gray eyes gleam under thick eyebrows. His nose is thin, lips plush but not overly so, jaw slightly angular. He's wearing a white button-up shirt with the collar undone and dark jeans. Wings protrude out of his back. A dark yellow match design weaves through maroon feathers with bronze tips.

"Sky." His voice is warm in welcome.

Onyx prods me forward as Sky turns to me and places a hand on my shoulder. "Azure Tallon, as you have requested."

This must be Russet, the Acting Lead—whatever that was. His eyes take me in head to toe. "You're the spitting image of your mother." Murmurs of agreement go around the team. My insides clench. Russet opens his arms. "Welcome to Mountain Hollow, Azure Tallon. I'm Russet Seed, Acting Lead for Silver Wingai. Please come in." He steps back to allow us entrance.

I don't move. With a barely distinguishable huff, Sky steers me inside. My first breath feels like I've inhaled a rose and hyacinth garden. The smell coupled with the opulent entry hall—shiny white tile, two sweeping staircases, silver banisters, crystal chandelier, and paintings of birds drawn in silver—disconcerts me.

Russet addresses Sky's team. "Go help yourself to some of Marigold's cookies while I speak with Sky and Azure."

Faces light up. They thank Russet warmly and head deeper into the house. Russet proceeds down the hall. Sky pushes me to follow.

We enter a large room. Bookshelves line an expansive wall behind a massive cherrywood desk. Placed strategically around the room are several white couches and chairs with small cherrywood end tables nearby. Another crystal chandelier graces the ceiling. My insides frown. Everything about this mansion is too much for my tastes. There's nothing homey here. I want to go home.

Russet sits behind his desk. Sky directs me to a white chair on the other side and lightly nudges me into it. He takes the adjacent seat.

Russet turns his attention to Sky. "How was your forage into the realm of humans?"

Sky reports on my retrieval. Russet's eyebrows raise with interest at the mention of me trying to call the police. Sky assures him he had my phone dismantled and us out of there before any trace could be found.

Russet smiles. "Excellent. It sounds like your team did well."

"Thank you." Sky smiles with pleasure.

I scowl.

Russet drops his gaze to me. "Azure Tallon," he says slowly, rolling my name around his tongue as if tasting it. "When Emerald told me of your existence, I thought perhaps he was playing a cruel joke. Gold Wingai are not always trustworthy, you know. Still, it begged checking out, and here you are. It's shocking really."

I couldn't contain my anger any longer. "What's shocking is your treatment of me. How dare you steal me from my home. I haven't done anything to deserve this."

Russet doesn't bat an eye. "On the contrary, it is against our law for a Silver Wingai to live outside of Mountain Hollow without my approval. Since I never gave it, that makes you a criminal. Taking you was perfectly within my rights."

My voice rises in pitch. "A criminal? You can't be serious."

"Dead serious." He leans forward and rests his folded hands on the desk. "Now, since you weren't aware you were breaking any laws—"

"I didn't know any Wingai until yesterday!" I exclaim with irritation.

Russet's lips twitch in a hint of a smile. "Yes, for that reason I'll pardon you from this transgression." He leans back in his chair. "Tomorrow we'll bring you up to speed on all things Wingai to ensure it doesn't happen again."

"Doesn't happen again," I repeat dumbly. "You mean I can't go home."

"Certainly not." Russet acts like my desire to return to my house is ludicrous. "Mountain Hollow is your new home now."

I stand. Sky rises as well. Waves of heated rage flow through my body. My wings threaten to unfurl. I straighten. "No."

Russet gets to his feet. He presses his hands on his desk as he leans forward. "As of this moment, you don't have a choice. Wingai do not belong with *humans*." Like Sky, he makes the word sound dirty, like he's talking about clogged toilets. Sky nods vigorously. I find it insulting.

Russet's harsh tone softens. "With time, you'll understand what I'm doing is in your best interests. I'm sure you'll grow to love it here, as I have."

"I doubt it," I mutter under my breath while giving him my best glare.

Russet steps away from his desk. "It's late. A good night's rest is sure to restore your mood. Let me escort you to a room."

"I don't want a room," I protest as Sky takes me by the arm, forcing me to stumble along with him after Russet. Further demands for answers fall on deaf ears.

Down the hall and up the stairs, Russet opens the first door on his right. He flips on the light. "This should work quite nicely for you."

I step inside. The room is decorated in shades of red and dark wood. I see a queen-size bed, double nightstands, a long dresser. A desk and chair rest near a window, red shades drawn. An open door reveals a small bathroom.

Russet gives me a devilish grin. "We'll chat in the morning." He shuts the door, leaving me inside. I watch as the doorknob rattles, alerting me he's locked it from the outside. I run to the window and throw the shades open. Decorative bars cover it.

I'm trapped.

CHAPTER NINE

CERIL

I park my Porsche in our garage and head inside. Dad sits in his favorite recliner in the living room clutching a can of Coke. A baseball game plays on the TV. Seeing me, he grabs the remote and turns the TV off. His green eyes settle on me. "Good to see you made it home safely."

"Let's go get Azure," I urge.

Dad holds up a hand as he stands. "Wait a minute. We're not going to get anywhere tonight. It's late. Mountain Hollow would never let us in. I suggest we try first thing tomorrow morning. Say, nine o'clock?"

I huff. I don't want to wait. I want Azure with me. Every second she's away sends pain shooting through my heart.

Dad puts his hand on my shoulder, reading my expression. "I know it hurts, but I promise we'll do everything we can to get her tomorrow."

I let out a breath. "Fine." I need Dad by my side if I'm ever going to get Azure.

I see relief in his eyes as he lets go. I appreciate the trust he has in me. "Go get some rest if you can."

"Right," I say.

Turning around, I trudge up the stairs to my room. I release my wings, relieving some of the tension I carry. I plop onto my bed and grip my forehead, exhausted and stressed. A random flash of fury shoots through me, and I inhale sharply. What was that? Azure? But we haven't sealed our match yet.

Our first kiss done of mutual will and desire seals our match and declares us mates for life. When that happens, we unlock special abilities. When our wings touch, Azure and I will be able to share thoughts and emotions and soothe. Males gain the power to protect their matches with camouflage and mimicking. Females can project their emotions onto their mate without the need for contact. If Azure were in danger and scared, she could transmit that feeling to me. Then I would use my tracking sense to find and defend her from whatever threat she faced.

I'm upset, but that rage definitely didn't feel like me. Could our match be strong enough for Azure to cast her feelings before we've sealed it? I make a mental note to ask Dad.

The next morning, close to nine, I pace the front porch, waiting for Dad. I've been ready to leave since sunrise. I flex my hands as I walk, shifting my nails into talons and back again. If we don't leave soon, I'm going without him.

Dad approaches, keys in hand. Finally. "You ready?" he says. His emerald wings are stiff in anticipation.

"Let's go." I follow him out the door.

Mountain Hollow is situated five miles behind Soaring Heights on a private marked road. Before this feud between our people, we enjoyed the proximity and traveled back and forth regularly. Especially Bronze Wingai who have family in both communities, since they can be matched to a Gold or a Silver. To the government, the two cities are one slab of protected land barred from the public.

A fifteen-foot-tall steel fence encloses Mountain Hollow. Trees and shrubs create a second barrier, making it nearly impossible to see inside. Security cameras dot the fence, with multiple twenty-four-hour teams watching for outsiders. The place is locked down similar to a high-security prison, though I've never heard a Silver Wingai complain about it.

"Did you tell Russet we're coming?" I ask Dad as he stops in front of the gate.

"No. I don't want to give him a chance to turn us away," he answers.

Apple, their day guard, steps out of the post.

Dad rolls down the truck window. "I have business with Russet."

Apple surveys us with suspicion, his hand on the gun resting on his hip. I fight against an eye roll. I swear they hired the twitchiest Wingai alive. Dad wears a pleasant smile, showing patience that I don't have. After what feels like an eternity, Apple nods. "Proceed." He opens the gate.

91

To their credit, Mountain Hollow doesn't feel like a compound inside. In fact, it's much the same as Soaring Heights. Driving down their main street, I see a bank and coffee, antique, and jewelry shops. A grocery store offers a sale on steak and strawberries. We drive by lawyer and real estate offices and some restaurants.

Dad turns left, passing a grassy park with a large play structure. Three children swing on the swings, tiny wings fluttering. A little boy with orange feathers jumps off the top structure and flies around in a circle before dropping down.

Finally Russet's house comes into view. My heart spasms increase at Azure's closeness. Feathers, I can't wait to see her.

Dad parks and then turns to me, a serious glint in his green eyes. "Let me do the talking."

"Fine."

We stride up the rose-lined path to the front door. Dad rings the bell, then shoves his hands in his pockets, exuding calm. I shift my weight from side to side and flick my wings as energy accumulates.

"Steady there," Dad says.

"I'm trying," I answer, working hard not to fidget.

Russet's housekeeper answers. She tucks her green wings close as though she might be susceptible to something nasty. Stupid prejudices. "Lead Emerald. How may I help you?" Her expression is as cool as her voice.

"I must speak with Russet," Dad tells her.

"I'm sorry, Russet has a full schedule today. I'm told no visitors." She looks pleased as she says it. No dirty Gold Wingai stepping onto her polished floors.

Dad speaks with authority. "I'm not some common Wingai. As Lead I demand to be seen."

Her mousy face pinches. "I will see if he's available." She motions for us to come in. We step into the entry hall. "Please wait here." She dashes off. I'm glad to see her leave.

A couple of minutes later, Russet strolls down the hall. "I expected I would see you today."

I ball my hands into fists to stop them from shifting. I step forward. "I want to see Azure. *Now.*"

Russet's gray eyes flash at the hardness in my tone.

"Ceril," Dad says sharply.

I know I promised Dad to let him do the talking, but at this moment all I care about is seeing Azure. She is the only thing that matters to me. Dad places a heavy hand on my shoulder, obviously trying to keep me in my place.

"I would like to meet my son's match. May we visit her?" Dad asks.

"Not today," Russet says. "Azure is in the middle of training. I don't want her out until she comprehends what it means to be Wingai."

My wings unfurl, knocking Dad aside. "I am her match. You can't keep me away from her!"

"Yes, I can. Azure is not fit to be among other Wingai, especially Gold." Russet's smile is on the verge of a sneer. "She is too humanized. She must be properly incorporated into our ideals and lifestyle."

"Surely that would go easier with her match by her side?" Dad says.

"I think Ceril will distract her," Russet says flatly. "Your Gold ways will confuse her with ours."

"Our ways will have to mix," Dad counters. "Azure is matched to a Gold."

"Perhaps," Russet concedes, "but not yet."

Sky, Cider, and Onyx step into the hall and approach.

Russet smiles. "I'll contact you when she's fully instructed." He turns to go.

"How long will that take?" Dad asks.

Russet pauses and shrugs. "No telling. Azure must denounce her human lifestyle. That won't be easy for her."

I haven't known Azure long, but I know she isn't going to be ready for that anytime soon. Perhaps never.

"Will you please see our guests out?" Russet asks his guards.

They glance at us and nod. Russet retreats down the hall, grinning like the pompous jerk he is.

I'm not ready to let this go. I plant my feet. "I'm not leaving until I see Azure."

Dad grabs hold of my arm. A peek of talons digs into my skin. "Ceril, we're going." His tone and expression are hard as granite. I know not to disobey that voice, but right now, I don't care. I'm about to tell him as much when he lowers his voice.

"This isn't over." I see fire in his green eyes. He's just as angry as I am. My gut tells me to listen to him.

I address Sky. "One matched man to another. If you see Azure, please tell her I'm not giving up on her."

Sky nods. For once I don't see coldness in his eyes. I swivel and stride out the door, hoping but not banking on Sky delivering my message.

Despair sinks its talons in me as I climb in the truck. My chest aches something fierce. I pull my drooping wings in close. After so many months of searching, only for her to be ripped away like this, is pure agony. I resent telling my family I discovered her. One day with her wasn't enough.

Dad doesn't speak as he drives out of Mountain Hollow, but he shoots me furtive glances with deep-rooted concern.

I suck in a sharp breath as I experience another flash of what I think are Azure's emotions. Sorrow and something else . . .

"What is it?" Dad asks, his momentary gaze piercing.

"Azure." The feeling hits me again, and my stomach drops. Hatred and shame. It's raw and deep. She carries demons in her closet.

"You can feel her?" Surprise colors his tone. "You haven't sealed the match."

"It's random and lasts only a moment," I tell him.

Like Mountain Hollow, Soaring Heights also has a gate manned by a guard twenty-four hours a day, although our gate isn't nearly so compound-ish. It's half the size and more decorative, with wrought iron arches and vines and a security camera here or there.

Almond pokes his head out of his post and waves us through, a welcoming smile on his face. Dad drives the mile and a half through a pure Douglas fir and pine forest into Soaring Heights.

He slows to a stop to allow a mother and two children to cross the street to the library. Recognizing us, they grin and wave, prompting us to respond in kind. As Lead and future Lead, we have a face to present to society.

As we get going again, Dad asks, "What emotions have you felt from Azure?"

"Dark ones. Rage, hatred, shame," I say.

Dad doesn't let up. "For her current situation?"

"I don't think so." I think of the raised skin on Azure's arms. "The scars I've seen on her paint a telling picture."

"Hmm." Dad's expression is troubled. Probably not half as disturbed as mine.

Dad pulls in front of the garage and cuts the engine. Angry and defeated, I don't want to go inside the house. I'm not in the mood for everyone's pity. I had enough of it this morning when Jade and Mom tried giving me a pep talk, which went right over my head.

Dad puts a hand on my shoulder. "We're not going to let this slide."

"I don't think Azure will ever denounce her human lifestyle. She's too invested in it," I say with certainty. "If

Russet holds to that, I'll never get his approval to see her. Those lessons he's giving her will teach her to hate me. She'll never want me as her mate. Our match won't get sealed."

"That's not going to happen." Dad's green eyes light with fire again. "I'm calling in the Flock. We're going after Azure."

I raise my eyebrows in surprise. "I thought you were trying to avoid war."

"I am." Dad's expression becomes enigmatic as he explains. "I believe everyone in Russet's household is on lockdown, not to speak a word about Azure. Russet will want to make her completely dependent on him before she is revealed to her people as Silver Lead."

I rub my jaw. "You think Russet is that power-hungry?"

"It's possible," Dad says. "He's had complete control of Mountain Hollow for almost twenty years. He might not want to give it up."

"So what are we going to do?" I ask.

"We free her and reveal your match to all Wingai," Dad says. "There will be an immediate shift in leadership as Mountain Hollow recognizes her as their Lead, and Azure can call off any attack Russet may have ordered."

Hope flares in my chest. If this works, we could get Russet off our backs for good. "Let's do it."

Dad grins. "I thought you'd agree."

CHAPTER TEN

AZURE

Sun streams through the white gauzy curtains. I lie on the bed, ankles crossed, my wings wrapped around my bare shoulders. A chill I can't seem to chase has crept into my bones. I've been suffering surges of adrenaline and heat. I can't make sense of it. I wonder if the police ever made it to my house. If they saw I wasn't home, would they try to contact any known associates? What would Bree, Ben, or Jack say?

Footsteps stop outside my door. The knob jiggles. I climb out of bed, retracting my wings. The door swings open to reveal a young woman carrying a breakfast tray. She has short brown hair and matching eyes. Her face is rather pointed with a pert nose and small lips pressed tight. She wears black dress pants and a black and white polka dot blouse on her tiny frame. Mint green wings with a lilac match design protrude out of her back.

"Good morning. My name is Fern. I am the housekeeper." She introduces herself in a professional voice lacking warmth. She places the tray on the desk and retreats closer to the door.

"Excuse me, Fern." Crimson sweeps past her. "Brought your bag." He drops my black duffel onto the bed.

"Thank you." It's hard not to be nice when he's trying to be friendly and pleasant.

"Chin up, Azure. You'll be happy here before you know it." He grins encouragingly before darting out.

"He's right, you know. Mountain Hollow is the best place for you." Fern smiles, but it doesn't look particularly natural. I doubt she does it often. "I'll be back in about a half hour to escort you to Russet." She locks the door after she leaves.

I'm all for rebellion, but refusing to eat would be silly when I need my wits about me. I shovel the pancake, sausage, and scrambled eggs into my mouth, then wash it down with orange juice. Next, I unzip my bag, curious to see what they packed. I pull out my black purse, surprised they brought it. My wallet, lip gloss, hair ties, and crumpled receipts are all in there. Everything but my phone. I don't expect to get that back. Setting that aside, I find the essentials in clothing and toiletries and head to the bathroom to dress.

The dark-blue T-shirt has two ragged holes in the back. I put the shirt on and twist, using the mirror as best I can to see. My talon-slashed shoulder blades, courtesy of my mother, are exposed while the rest of my back is covered. There's nothing pretty about it. I go back to my bag and discover every shirt has had the same hack job. Just great. I keep my hair down, grateful it's long enough to hide most of the mess.

I grab my wallet and slip my driver's license, debit card, and forty dollars into my pocket. I want to be ready if I do get the chance to escape.

I catch Fern making a face at my top when she reappears. It really is awful. Her eyes zero in on the scars on my forearms, and her expression tightens. She quickly smooths her features and asks delicately, "Won't you feel better with your wings out?"

"No." Though they would hide the butchered work better than my hair, I'm not comfortable enough here to leave them out.

"Right this way, then." Fern leads me down the stairs and into the same office Russet and Sky took me to the previous night. She leaves me.

Russet chats quietly with a woman sitting on the edge of his desk. Her flaming red hair and freckled face grab my attention. Her silver-striped wings are a bold dark yellow with bronze swirls and arcs. Russet's match. She and Russet turn their gazes on me.

"You weren't kidding about her appearance," she says, her light-green eyes widening. "She's nearly a perfect clone of Amethyst."

My mother was a mental case. I hate being compared to her and resent her inability to speak about these people. Based on the reactions I'm getting, they clearly knew each other well.

The lady hops off the desk and strides to me, holding out her hand and wearing a bright warm smile. "Hi, I'm Marigold. It's so wonderful to meet you."

I shake her hand and manage a small smile. Her gaze softens. "I'll leave you to it." She returns to Russet and presses a quick kiss to his lips. "Come find me when business is over."

Russet smiles lovingly at her. It's a look I didn't expect to see on his face. "Always." He flicks his gray eyes on me, gesturing to the chair before him. "Have a seat, Azure."

I reluctantly sit.

Russet leans back in his chair and settles his gray eyes on me. "I think it's about time we shed some of your ignorance. For the moment, I will play the role of teacher and explain what you need to know about being Wingai."

I cross my ankles and fold my hands, situating myself to be more comfortable. Despite not wanting to be here, I do need to learn about my race. My mother's not here to hold me back.

Russet smiles when he sees he has my complete attention. "First off, we are not related to angels. If there is a being of higher power that employs people with wings, I cannot be certain."

"I never thought I came from angels or demons or fairies." Mom once told me to liken ourselves to birds, and I stuck to that.

"Good." Russet takes a breath. "There are three different races of Wingai: Gold, Silver, and Bronze. You can tell the difference based on the two strips of color on their wings. Within our races we have Common and Tipped."

"Tipped?"

"Those with bronze, silver, or gold on the ends of their feathers." Russet extends his wings, emphasizing his bronze tips. "Tipped are rare among us."

"How rare?"

The corner of Russet's mouth lifts. "You are the only Silver-Tipped Wingai currently in existence."

Surprise flits through me. "The only one?"

"The only one," Russet repeats. He clears his throat. "We all share the same wing structure, as you can see." Russet waved at himself. "Silvers are faster. Golds have better stamina—meaning they can fly for longer without rest. Bronze are a toss-up. Some are fast fliers, and others have better stamina.

"Our bodies are superior to humans'. We can lift double the amount humans can. For us, their diseases and colds are practically nonexistent."

I'd already noticed that. Josephina seemed to catch at least one virus over the winter and early spring. Despite our close contact, I'd never get it.

"We heal faster," Russet says.

But still scar like a human.

"We aren't without our own set of problems, though. Molting disease, for one." Russet waves his hand airily. "But our physicians are very adept at handling these things."

"That's good," I say. I've never been to a doctor for myself before. I couldn't risk it, no matter how many slashes my mother inflicted. Must be nice to go to a Wingai doctor and not have to worry about being different.

"How old do you think I am?" Russet asks.

"You could be twenty-five or eighty," I say without skipping a beat.

Russet smiles. "Close. I'm seventy-nine. Average lifespan for us is two hundred seventy-five to three hundred."

"I knew it was longer than humans." One of the few bits of knowledge Mom imparted.

"Much longer," Russet agrees. "This is one of the reasons we stay in our communities. It would not bode well to have the humans notice we're not aging along with them."

"Yes." It pangs me to think I will outlive my friends.

"There is one exception to our aging process. Menopause. Wingai females lose their ability to reproduce around fifty years old. It's not easy for a Silver Wingai female to get pregnant, so think sooner than later." Russet leans forward and rests his elbows on his desk. His expression turns contemplative. "Have you ever been romantically involved with a human?"

I speak firmly. "No. I've never aligned myself with anyone."

A corner of Russet's lips turns up. "Good. There's more about being Tipped you need to know. Tipped wings are genetic, passed on through a few select families. For Silvers and Golds, there can be only one for each generation. For Bronze, two."

"Why?"

"Because Tipped are Leads," Russet says like it's obvious. "There needs to be only one president and one vice president to speak for each generation."

"What about that other place? Soaring Heights?" I ask, thinking of the home Cerulean mentioned.

"Emerald Hatch, Ceril's father, is Lead over the Gold and Bronze in Soaring Heights," Russet answers. "Because Ceril is Tipped, eventually he will take his father's place. Your father was Lead over Mountain Hollow before his untimely death. His role now falls upon you."

I struggle to get the words out. "You're saying I'm supposed to . . . rule over Wingai?"

Russet smiles. "Over the Silver and Bronze in Mountain Hollow, yes."

I put a hand to my forehead, and my other arm wraps around my torso. My stomach churns. My heart rate speeds up. The room is suddenly a hundred degrees.

Russet reads my rejection. "You don't have a choice in the matter. Once I reveal you to the Wingai and Shifter Council, they will recognize you as Lead whether you want them to or not. One look at your wings and they will cease to come to me with their problems. They'll turn to you."

He can't hold me hostage if I'm in charge. "Then reveal me."

Again, he accurately reads me. "So you can fly out of Mountain Hollow? I don't think so." I glower at him. "You need to understand your importance before you take over."

"Then go on." I wave my hand. The sooner he's explained everything, the sooner I can plan my escape.

Russet shakes his head at me, but he continues. "At birth all Common Wingai must be recognized by their Lead, or Second in the case of the Bronze. Tipped do not because they are born recognized by themselves. This is done by touching your wings to theirs. An energy transference will occur." He leans forward, and his voice seeps with importance. "This step is crucial to our survival."

"Why?" I ask.

"If a Wingai is not recognized by their Lead or Second, their wings will not have the power to acknowledge a match. They will be matchless," Russet says gravely.

"Is that so bad?" I ask.

"Only matched couples can reproduce within the limited window we have. No matches means our entire race will die out," Russet answers, his voice dead serious.

"Oh." My gut twists at the thought of extinction. I wouldn't wish that on a people. "That's terrible."

Russet nods. "On a personal level, it is literally the worst thing that could ever happen to a Wingai. From birth to adulthood, Wingai spend their time preparing for their mate. Males are required to have a nest built before their eighteenth birthday. Females have chests they fill with belongings then present to their match to beautify their nest. They also usually come with a dowry since the males will have spent all their money building their home. So imagine, if you will, spending your entire life working for matched bliss only to find out you don't get it because there wasn't a Lead to recognize you. It's soul crushing."

I can't exactly relate, but I do understand working toward something only for it to fall apart. I tried so hard to keep things peaceful for Mom. After a few good days, it was always agonizing to see our progress slide.

Pushing those thoughts away, I focus on something else. "Does Cerulean have a nest?" I can't help but imagine twigs in a tree, though I'm sure that's not the case. Judging by his sports car and Wingai status, his nest is probably fancy like Russet's home.

"Yes, though I haven't seen it. Now, as Tipped, it is your duty to produce the next heir. Your first or even third child may not be Tipped. It is required that you have as many children as it takes until one arrives."

"Absolutely not!" I cry.

Russet's tone is final. "When you reach your hundredth birthday, you will lose your power to recognize. If you can't recognize, you cease to be Lead. It's nature's way of ensuring we don't have a tyrant ruling for centuries." He waves his hand. "A Tipped son or daughter of yours will need to take your place to ensure we don't have any matchless and our survival continues."

I glare. There's no way I'm equipped to be a mother. I'd be awful at it. Plus, I'd be passing on my mother's genes. The whole thing could be a future train wreck.

Russet clears his throat. "All Wingai have a match. A match is equivalent to a soul mate. On a male's eighteenth birthday, he gains the ability to find his match. Females can expect to be claimed starting from seventeen to nineteen. We keep meticulous records on births and often group the young ones together to give them an idea of who they could be paired with."

"You didn't have a record of me," I say.

Russet scowls. "No." A moment of silence passes. I get the impression Russet is angry for my existence being hidden. Me too. I wish I would have tried harder to demand answers from Mom. "Common Silver and Common Gold Wingai cannot be matches to each other. The exception are the Tipped." He raises a finger. "Bronze are a wild card. Color has no significance to our matches. Legend has it that there was once a shortage of Bronze, so they adapted to become matches with Gold or Silver."

"Do you think that could ever happen again with Gold and Silver?" I ask.

Russet shrugs. "If the legend is true, I suppose it could." He takes a breath. "When matched wings touch for the first time, they create a match design. It is a unique drawing that uses colors from each other's wings. Wingai who match with

Tipped always take on the gold, silver, or bronze for their match design. It sends a clear message to all that you're taken."

"Cerulean told me," I say. I'm still not very happy about it. I'm not sure I want it.

Russet's mouth twitches. "Did Ceril also tell you about the match kiss?"

"No." Curiosity and apprehension hold me in their grip.

Russet's expression and tone turn stern. "What I'm about to say will sound unbelievable, but take it as truth. I don't care to waste my time telling you falsehoods."

His gray eyes bore into me until I'm cowed. "Okay."

"Your first kiss with your match—done of mutual free will, not stolen—will unlock special abilities. You both gain access to your match's thoughts and emotions. This is done by touching your match with a wing. All females can project their feelings—not words—without the need for contact. For Common matches, females have to consciously express a desire for it to happen. For Tipped, if your emotion is strong, your mate will feel you whether you want them to or not."

I feel blood drain out of my face. My stomach drops, giving me the sensation I'm falling. The very idea of Cerulean touching me with his wing and gaining access to my mind makes me cringe. I rub the scars on my arms. I have memories I don't want anyone to see. Could he rifle through my brain and find them? I shudder. I'm not kissing him . . . no matter how appealing he is.

Russet watches me with something similar to regret, no doubt from what he sees on me. I don't care for it, considering his actions now. "Matches also have the ability to soothe hurts. With wing contact, we can eliminate the sensation of pain. We cannot heal instantly, but with constant touch, we can double the rate of our natural healing process."

"Painkillers would work too," I say quietly.

Russet shakes his head. "They are not as efficient. Males acquire a few more abilities to protect their match. They gain the power to camouflage and mimic sound, meaning they can hide in plain sight and use their voice to scare others off. Like those burrowing owls who sound like rattlesnakes. The power extends to whatever they touch with their wings."

Russet picks up a leather journal and extends a feather to touch it. I gasp as it morphs into its surroundings. Any doubt of Russet's talk of supernatural powers crumbles.

Russet grins. "If you look closely, you'll see a shimmer." I lean forward. Sure enough, the air ripples where he holds the book. "Only Wingai have the power to see through the illusion. Should a dangerous situation arise and a Wingai be found without a protector, he or she can look for the shimmer and may be able to find someone with the power to keep them safe."

Russet sets the book back on his desk. "The abilities you receive after your match kiss are strengthened by contact with your mate—specifically wing touch. If you spend little to no time together, your powers will lessen to the point you may lose them until you're in contact again. All powers gained with your match will be lost should he or she die. You don't even keep your match design."

That explains why Mom's wings were plain.

Fern flits into the room, her expression anxious. "I apologize for interrupting, but Lead Emerald and his son are here and wish to speak with you."

"As expected." Russet rises. "Fern, please take Azure to Pear for a good preening."

"Can't I see Cerulean?" I ask. I want to see a semifriendly face and call him out for selling me to Russet. I believe he's responsible since he's the only Wingai who knew my address.

Russet's gray eyes pin me down. "No. We're not finished with our lessons. You're not fit to see him." He strides out of the room without waiting for a response.

Not fit? I seethe at the verbal slap. He makes it sound like I'm a disgrace when I very well know I'm not.

Fern gives me her no-nonsense attitude. "Come along, Azure."

I follow her down the hall. "How old are you?"

"What an impertinent question." She huffs when I give her a pointed stare. "If you must know, I'm one hundred and forty-three."

"Such a very long time Wingai have to live," I say.

Stopping in front of a door, Fern knocks lightly. A woman bids us enter. We step inside an office. An auburn-haired woman with bronze stripes on pale green wings with a black match design shoots from her seat. "Feathers!" Her gray eyes are wide on mine. "Wow. It's like I'm seeing Auntie Amethyst again. The resemblance is uncanny."

I stiffen.

"Pear, Russet has asked that you give Azure a full preening," Fern says.

Pear brightens. "Of course."

With a nod of satisfaction, Fern leaves. Pear steps away from her desk and holds out her hand. We shake. "It's so nice to meet you, Azure. I'm Pear, Russet and Marigold's daughter." Her gray eyes take me in, head to toe. "You look so much like Auntie Amethyst—"

"I'm sorry, but are we related?" I ask.

Pear waves a hand. "Not in the blood sense, but we were very close. Amethyst was like a second mom to me growing up. She taught me all the girly things like braiding hair and makeup. We'd have movie nights with ice cream on the weekends. I like to think I get some of my vibrant personality from her." Her eyes take on a dreamy quality. "She lit up every room she walked into and always had a smile or a hug or something kind to say. You couldn't help but be enthralled by her presence. I keep a picture of her and me on my desk." Pear picks up a picture frame and hands it to me.

Pear had her arm slung around Mom's shoulder, pale green wings with a black design touching amethyst and silver. The other arm was held out in selfie fashion. Heads bent together, they smiled brightly with genuine affection. Mom had platinum-blonde hair a shade lighter than mine, purple eyes, and cream skin also lighter than mine. We shared a diamond-shaped face, an eyebrow curve, a small nose, and plush lips.

My heart seizes with black emotions long buried. The memory of our last moments together flashes in front of my eyes.

The sky darker than pitch, rain came down in torrents. The windshield wipers screeched across the glass, barely keeping up with the deluge. The forest closed in on us on all sides along the twisted turns of Baker Creek. I sat in the back seat holding a bag of groceries. My leg brushed against a cold gallon of milk. James Taylor crooned "Copperline" through the speakers.

"This rain is insane," Mom said, leaning over the steering wheel.

"Flood worthy," I agreed.

A buck jumped into the road. Mom slammed on the brakes. The deer hit the car and flew into the windshield. Antlers broke through the glass, impaling mom's throat. Blood and rain splattered across the front seats. I shut my eyes, a scream tearing out of my throat. Crunching metal grated my ears. It was so cold.

A soft hand touches my shoulder. I flinch, pulling myself out of the recollection. I haven't allowed myself to go back there in years.

"Azure, are you all right?" Pear asks gently, worry in her expression.

I clear my throat, forcing the choking emotion back. "I'm fine."

Pear takes the picture from me and puts it back on her desk. "It broke my heart when she left. I loved her so much. I cried this morning when Papa told me she died. Feathers, it was probably worse for you. I mean, I was just an honorary niece. You were her daughter. I bet she showered you with love."

"Yeah." I've never been prone to much jealousy—Josephina made me feel like I had the world in my hands—until now. Envy roars, drenching me like a crashing tidal wave. I hate Pear something fierce.

CHAPTER ELEVEN

AZURE

Turns out a full preening involves pampering my wings until they shine. Pear washes my feathers in an adjacent spa room. I wince when she scrubs vigorously at the gold markings. When they don't come off, she says, "Guess you really are matched to a Gold. How crazy is that?"

"Mmm." I'm afraid if I open my mouth, word lava will spew out. I resent Pear for having a good relationship with my mom when I didn't. Pear got an angel and I got the devil. It's not fair.

After the washing, she spritzes each feather with an orange blossom–scented spray. Then she smooths them. I make noncommittal answers while she chatters about her life. Her every sound grates me like nails on a chalkboard, but I listen anyway. Some twisted part of me wants to hear about her perfect life and begrudge it.

She's thirty-five. She has a brother named Burgundy two years younger. He has two children with his match, Pearl, and they are expecting a third. "His boys aren't Tipped, so he's still trying."

Pear is matched to Onyx from the Silver Guard. "He's gruff and muscle on the outside but a complete softy at heart. I just love him."

They've been trying for a family for the past two years and are really hopeful this year will be the one. "I want a little girl of my own to dress up. A boy would be good too; at this point I won't be picky. But I adore little girls in dresses with their tiny wings fluttering."

She works as an administrative assistant for Russet but dabbles in beautician work—thanks to my mother who apparently was a genius with makeup and hair. I never saw it. "Auntie Amethyst could turn a hairy beast into a beauty queen. She was the go-to person for match ceremonies. You probably remember her working her magic on you."

"Mmm," I say.

After what feels like centuries, Pear steps away. "All finished! And might I say, your wings are gorgeous. You'll turn all the heads in Mountain Hollow."

I stand in front of a floor-length mirror. My dark blue feathers gleam. The silver tips and gold arcs and swirls stand brighter. Every feather is even, not a single one ruffled. I've never had or spent this much attention on them before. I grudgingly admit to myself that Pear does good work. "Thank you."

She beams. "You're welcome."

"Feathers!" Fern gasps behind me. I swivel around to see her hand on her mouth, eyes wide as she takes in my wings.

Pear grins. "Beautiful, aren't they?"

Fern drops her hand, composing herself. "Quite."

I promptly retract my wings, ruining the effect. Pear's face falls, but I'm saved from her censure as I leave with Fern.

I return to Russet's office. He sits behind his desk, phone in hand. "Did you enjoy the preening?"

"It was lovely," I lie, taking my seat.

Russet sets his phone down. "What was your impression of Pear?"

"She's . . . nice." I never want to see her again.

"Yes." Russet smiles briefly, but his stare is too direct, like he can see straight through me. "Shall we resume our lessons?"

I nod.

Russet clears his throat. "I believe we're still on the subject of matches."

"The match kiss," I supply, hoping there aren't any more powers to worry about.

"Yes." Russet leans back in his leather chair and rests his elbows on the arms, fingertips coming together. "Your match kiss is also your wedding. Be prepared to say 'I do' with that first lip-lock." I blanch. Russet chuckles. "A little quick by human standards, isn't it?"

"The whole match thing is too much," I say.

Russet shrugs. "It's how Wingai have lived since the beginning. Our young are taught to look forward to it. Had you grown up here, you probably would have been excited for your match. It's a crowning glory moment after years of preparation."

Not for me.

"Did Amethyst tell you anything of your father, Fire?" he asks.

My hand moves to my cheek as the ghost of my mother's slap flares to life. My eyes sting. "My mother outlawed all questions. I know he died, and she fled."

"I do not care to speak on this subject, but Wingai will talk." Russet runs a hand through his hair, and his hard expression falters. "Nineteen years ago, Lead Emerald called Fire over to Soaring Heights for a meeting. Back then, relations between us were good. We often got together for match celebrations and holidays. No one thought twice about him going.

"When he got to the gate, he was informed that all Wingai were under lockdown. A crazed human had broken in and taken residence at the gas station with explosives strapped to his body. He filled the convenience store with hostages. The man believed Wingai were an abomination with demonic purposes.

"Fire hurried over and found Lead Emerald attempting negotiations. First he tried convincing the man we were angels and he would be killing pure innocence.

"The man said, 'All angels have white wings. Yours are colored. That means they're of the devil.'

"Lead Emerald then offered a substantial amount of money—two and a half million dollars. The man paused. He asked for double. Lead Emerald agreed, and it appeared the lure of greed had swayed him to stand down."

Russet's expression hardens. His hands, resting on the desk, shift into talons. "They were deceived. As Fire and Emerald approached, the man pressed the detonation button. The timer showed ten seconds before it went off."

Russet flexes his hands, and his nails recede. He clears his throat. "Emerald knew that Fire, as a Silver-Tipped, was the fastest Wingai alive. He turned to Fire and said, 'Please.' Fire rushed at the human, talons out. He took the man into the sky. They struggled." He shakes his head, pain showing on his face. "The explosives went off, killing them both instantly."

I inhale sharply. My chest tightens. My throat dries. My eyes burn with unshed tears. No wonder my mother wouldn't tell me. I read sympathy in Russet's face.

Russet scrubs his face with his hand. "Nearly all in Mountain Hollow believe that Emerald pushed your father into sacrificing himself. Soaring Heights does not account for it. Relations between us are . . . strenuous at best."

"What do you believe?" I ask quietly.

Russet sighs. "I don't think Emerald made any difference in your father's decision. If Fire had not reacted, everyone nearby—the hostages, Emerald, Fire, and the human—would have died, leaving both Soaring Heights and Mountain Hollow without Leads, without anyone to recognize our young. He knew Emerald's match was expecting their second, but he had no way of knowing whether their child would be Tipped. So he chose to sacrifice himself to ensure both communities would not become matchless."

How selfless. A surprisingly warm feeling lights in my chest. Why couldn't Mom have told me how brave and heroic my father had been? "But Mountain Hollow still blames Soaring Heights," I point out.

"It is easy to place the blame when they have been thriving for the past two decades and we have not," Russet says flatly. "To date, we have two hundred and thirty-seven matchless, and they have none."

"I see." It's like the jealousy issue I have with Pear. She had it good with Mom, and I didn't. Every day was exhausting trying to please her. She needed me close. "You're all I have." She needed me out of her sight. "I can't stand to look at you." She wanted my wings out. "Look at how the silver shines." She wanted them hidden. "It's too much, Azure. Get rid of them now."

My wings spring free from their confines as I get worked up over my memories. Rubbing the scars near my wrists, I'm half expecting Mom to come back from the dead and punish me for learning forbidden subjects. I struggle to catch my breath. "I need some air."

Russet surveys me, his eyes lingering on my flared wings. "All right." He picks up his phone and dials. "I need two SG to escort Azure about the garden."

Crimson and Onyx arrive a few moments later. One look at me and worry creases their faces. My chest aches something fierce as I follow them out. I'm desperate for an escape.

"You have our support if you need it." Crimson pats my shoulder. I shy away from his touch.

My mind bounces between Mom and my father's death. I know now, and there's nothing she can do about it. Replaying the story, I stumble as one part stands out. Onyx reaches out and steadies me. *Emerald knew that Fire, as Silver-Tipped, was the fastest Wingai alive.* Determination hits me. I have my out.

Crimson holds open a door. "The garden is quite lovely at this time of year."

"Pear loves it," Onyx agrees.

I step through, tilting my face toward the sun. I shut my eyes and take a deep breath, inhaling the heady aroma of roses. The tightness in my chest eases. I stretch my feathers, allowing the soft breeze to filter through. I turn around to face Onyx and Crimson. "Thank you." I flap my wings hard and shoot into the sky.

Crimson and Onyx lurch for me, but they're too late. They jump into the air, calling my name. Energy fuels into my wings. I pick up speed. I fly straight for the connecting forest and soar above the trees. I don't look behind me as I push my feathers to the extreme.

Onyx's and Crimson's voices fade until I'm sure I've lost them. I don't slow down, wary they might have something else planned.

Ahead, I see another town similar in size to Mountain Hollow nestled in the pines. I contemplate checking it out until I notice several Wingai gliding over it. Soaring Heights. I veer off. No way am I showing my face there. A paved road winds through the forest. I drop into the trees, keeping myself hidden, and fly alongside it. Eventually, I ease my pace.

I land and retract my wings when I spy the beginnings of civilization. This one better be human. Emerging from the foliage, I walk alongside the road. My hands ball into fists, and my neck is stiff. I can't help but look over my shoulder when I hear an approaching vehicle. I breathe a sigh of relief every time I don't see a blue Porsche. Cerulean found me once with his match finder ability—and sold me out to Russet. He can do it again.

A small red pickup slows down beside me. I'm about ready to flee back into the trees when I see the driver is an older woman, probably in her sixties, with a golden retriever sticking his head out the window, tongue wagging. "I don't usually see young girls walking alone on this road. Are you all right, dear?"

Her friendly demeanor reminds me of Josephina. My heart pangs, but my gut tells me this woman is nice. "Yes, I'm fine, thank you." I come up with a lie on the spot. "My Volkswagen beetle wouldn't start on me, so I'm walking to get a rental until Lady Bug is fixed."

"I used to own a bug. The dang thing always broke down on me too." She laughs. "I'm headed to the grocery store in Sandy. Would you like a ride?"

"Yes, please."

"Chester, in the back." She pushes her dog to the back seat.

I open the passenger door and get in. Once I'm buckled, she turns back onto the road.

"I'm Arabella, and this is Chester." The retriever pokes his head out and sniffs me. I hold out my hand, allowing him to get used to my smell, before I scratch around his ears.

"I'm Azure. It's a pleasure to meet you," I say.

Arabella nods. "That's a pretty name. So you're looking for a car rental place?"

We chat leisurely about the benefits and pitfalls of owning a Volkswagen. It's a conversation I easily get into. The ride into Sandy seems to take no time at all. Arabella drops me off at an Enterprise Rent-A-Car. I pull out some cash to pay her, but she waves it away. "Just take care of yourself."

I smile. "I will. Thank you so much."

A half hour later, I hop into a silver Toyota with the car GPS coordinates set for McMinnville. If I'm to avoid Cerulean, I'm gonna need some help.

CERIL

Dad sits at the dining room table surrounded by our immediate family and members of the Flock. I pace behind his chair. I'm too anxious to sit while ideas are thrown about. Quick jolts of Azure's emotions have been manifesting more frequently—all of them harsh and deep. I worry Russet's torturing her.

"Russet will expect us to retaliate," Dad says. "I believe he'll keep the Silver Guard stationed at his house until he deems Azure ready."

"Sky is a stickler for patrols," Cinnamon, commander of the Flock, says. "His team will be inside and outside at all hours in a randomized pattern. Whoever we send in will need to be an expert at dodging."

"And a master locksmith," I say. "Azure is being held against her will." Nothing I've felt from her says she wants to be there, and she fought the Silver Guard when they took her. "Russet should expect her to be looking for an escape."

"Slate can pick a lock in seconds." Cinnamon nods at his comrade.

I meet Slate's blue eyes. "Will you be fast enough to escape notice?"

Slate straightens. "I can handle it."

I don't read arrogance in his expression, just strong determination. I nod, giving my approval. It grates me to trust Azure to someone else, but I have no abilities until we seal the match. There's no way I'm going to be able to get in and out of Russet's house without being detected.

"It's settled," Cinnamon says. "Come nightfall, we'll send Slate to retrieve Azure."

"Then tomorrow we'll reveal her as Silver Lead to shift the power from Russet," Dad says. Eyeing the Flock, he adds, "I don't want a single word of this mission getting out. Keep it quiet, even from your matches."

Talk turns to preparing for Russet's response should our mission go as planned. I don't have the patience to listen. I turn and stare out the French doors past our expansive lawn and into the forest beyond.

Mom puts a hand on my shoulder. "You're not going to be any good to Azure if you're stressed to death. Loosen up some of that tension. We'll have her with us by tonight. I'm sure of it."

It's a little past noon. I have a good ten hours before our plan can be set into motion. "It's not soon enough," I growl.

Jade approaches. "Let's go take a flight. Maybe find a few punching bags to demolish too."

"That's a great idea." Mom opens the door and shoves me out onto the deck. "Jade, keep Ceril away from Mountain Hollow."

"On it." Jade waves at Mom. "Come on, bro." Jade hooks his hand around my upper arm. He pumps his green wings and lifts me off the ground with him. He lets go when I exercise mine. "Race you." He zooms into the trees.

I give him a few seconds head start before I dart after him. I'm a faster flier, courtesy of being Tipped, and he knows it. To make it harder, we're only ten feet off the ground. Half the battle of the race is dodging branches and trunks.

Some of the tension leaves as I push myself, zigzagging through the trees with Jade. We do five laps around the forest before we settle on our favorite rock outcropping overlooking Mount Hood. Both of us are breathing hard, our wings limp with exhaustion. I wipe the sweat beading on my brow and lean against the stone wall.

Jade swats at a bumblebee. "You think this'll come to war with Russet?"

"Probably," I answer.

"What if Azure doesn't want to be revealed to everyone as Lead?" Jade asks, his sea-green eyes meeting mine. "She might not want the job."

"She's the only Silver-Tipped out there. She doesn't have a choice," I say.

Jade crosses his arms. "You think this is going to be any better than what Russet's done? Twice stolen and then thrust into the spotlight as Silver Lead with the match of the century?"

I grimace. "You know I would ease her into it if I could."

Jade steps forward and pats me on the upper arm. "If you want this to go well, you better practice some match charm."

I kick a small rock over the ledge. "No kidding."

A snatch of Azure's emotions hits me. I inhale deeply, expecting to ride out another wave of anger and pain. My hands curl into fists as I experience aggressive determination. My heart pulses wildly with it.

Jade watches me curiously. "We need to go home," I tell him. "Azure's doing something." I jump off the precipice, stretching my wings as they catch an air current.

I fly over the fir trees, my shoes sometimes skimming the tops. Jade keeps his sight on me, his expression alert. He's probably working out a plan to stop me if I change direction to Mountain Hollow. I make a conscious effort not to leave him in the dust.

Jade casts a grateful and relieved glance my way as we land on the deck and head inside. Dad, Cinnamon, and Midnight are still sitting at the dining room table discussing plans. Mom and Scarlett stand at the kitchen island chopping bell peppers. The other members of the Flock have gone.

"Azure's up to something," I announce.

Mom and Scarlett put their knives down and come over by me.

"What are you feeling?" Dad asks.

Her aggressive determination hits me again. My wings twitch with energy. I clutch my chest as the homing beacon picks up speed. For a second I think she's on her way to Soaring

Heights until the spasms lessen. She's chosen a different direction, away from both Wingai communities. "She's not in Mountain Hollow anymore."

Dad's phone rings. He pulls it out of his pocket. "It's Russet." He swipes the answer button and puts it on speaker. "This is Emerald."

Russet exhales as if annoyed. "I'm sure your son's match tracking has informed you of Azure's . . . departure."

"Escape, you mean," I correct.

"Ah, Ceril," Russet sounds even more displeased to be broadcasted.

"Care to enlighten us on how that came to be?" Dad asks innocently.

"Azure took flight during a stroll in my gardens," Russet says with subtle ire. "As you know, Silver-Tipped speeds are unmatched."

"Indeed," Dad agrees. "What do you want from us?"

Russet speaks with the authority of Acting Lead. "Ceril, you're the only one who can track her. I request you bring her back."

"Absolutely not." I cross my arms. "You're torturing her over there."

"I have done nothing of the sort."

"The snatches of emotion I've felt from her say otherwise," I accuse.

"Azure's education is full of hard truths," Russet snaps. "I have been blunt with her about the power of matches, being a Silver Lead—her father's death."

Feathers.

Dad grimaces. "She knows everything, then."

"Better it's said so she can come to terms with it all at once," Russet says decisively. "Now, since Ceril *will* be going after Azure, perhaps we can come to a mutual arrangement."

I scoff. "Not likely."

"Bring Azure back, and I'll let you remain in her company while I finish training her to become Lead," Russet says.

"And if I don't?" I ask.

"I'll tell all of Mountain Hollow that you're holding our Lead captive." Russet's tone turns innocuous. "It's no less than what you were already plotting."

"You should have allowed me to stay with her in the first place," I say. "As her match, I could've helped her with these revelations about her life."

Russet muses. "Perhaps, but what's done is done. Now, do we have a deal or not?"

I rub the back of my neck. "I can't promise anything. Azure's not easily persuaded."

Russet speaks with certainty. "No woman is immune to your good looks and charm. Even in Mountain Hollow they gossip about your appeal."

Mom and Scarlett nod vigorously. I roll my eyes. "Azure isn't a typical woman." My one day with her proved that.

"Tell me, how bad is your pain level?" Russet asks.

I scowl. "I'm handling it."

"It will only get worse the longer you wait to seal your match." Russet sounds gleeful at the prospect of my misery. "Desperation will have you pulling out all the stops to get Azure to kiss you. Once she's enamored, you shouldn't have a problem convincing her to come home."

I let out a frustrated breath. As angry as Russet makes me, he's right. "I will not lure Azure into a prison. I need assurances to give her."

"She will be Lead. That should be all the assurance you need," Russet answers.

I'm two seconds from throwing Dad's phone across the room. I run a hand through my hair, resisting the urge. Mountain Hollow is desperate for a real Lead. If they think we're withholding her, their talons will slash us to ribbons. Yet, agreeing to Russet means I run the risk of irreparable damage with my match. Still, the needs of many outweigh the needs of one. For the sake of Soaring Heights, I have to do it. "All right. I'll bring Azure back."

"In a timely manner, Ceril. No more than three days." Russet's unspoken threat is clear.

"Fine," I growl.

Russet's tone turns cheery, as if speaking to a friend. "Excellent. I'll see you soon." The call ends. Dad slips his cell back into his pocket.

"Feathers!" I curse, stepping away from the others.

"Ceril." Dad's bright green eyes find mine. I see respect shining in them. "Thank you."

Jaw clenched, I nod.

CHAPTER TWELVE

AZURE

I knock on Bree's door, hoping she's home. I drove straight here, making only one stop at a Fred Meyer store to buy a new shirt.

Mr. Ashlander opens the door. "Azure, how nice to see you." He gives me a big smile.

I fidget with the car keys in my hand. "Is Bree home?"

"She's watching a movie with Ben in the basement. Come on in." Mr. Ashlander peers over my head at the rental car. "Something happen to your bug?"

"I have to take it to the shop." I keep up my lie as I step inside. The house smells like an ad for Glade. Mrs. Ashlander is a fanatic for plug-in scents.

Mr. Ashlander chuckles. "The perils of owning a Volkswagen."

I laugh with him. "Indeed." *I really hope I have enough time to outwit Cerulean.* I jog down the stairs, calling out for Bree. I'm not interested in catching her making out with Ben.

Sure enough, she is sitting on his lap, both appearing very cozy. *Avengers* plays on the flat-screen. "Azure! Why aren't you with Porsche guy? I texted you a couple of times, but you never answered. You missed some epic grad night scandals. Jack caught Mrs. Garrett kissing Mr. Piper in a utility closet. Can you believe it? They've been having an affair—"

I cut her off. "You can tell me about that later. Right now, I need your help."

Bree snaps her mouth shut. Her eyes take me in as if she's noticing me for the first time. Even Ben raises an eyebrow at me. I realize I may have sounded harsh without intending to. I rub my face, tension oozing out of me.

Bree gets off Ben's lap. She comes over to me and puts a hand on my arm. "What's up?"

"Let's go get ice cream and I'll tell you about it." I don't want her parents to overhear.

"Is this girl talk, or can Ben come?" Bree asks, looking at Ben over her shoulder.

"Ben is welcome. We should invite Jack too." He'd kill me if I left him out. "Can you text him? I don't have my phone anymore."

Ben pulls out his cell. "I'll give him a call." He dials and holds the phone up to his ear. "Hey, something's come up with Azure. We're going to get ice cream and talk about it. Are you free?" He looks at me. "He's free, er, I mean, will be."

I'm grateful Jack is canceling whatever obligations he had to come. "Good. Let's pick him up," I say.

"We'll pick you up," Ben relays. "Yeah, see you soon." He slips his cell back into his pocket and stands.

I follow Bree up the stairs as she shouts to her father. "Dad, we're going out for ice cream. I'll be back later."

Mr. Ashlander calls from the kitchen. "Have fun, stay safe."

Stepping onto the porch, Bree stops short. I dig my feet into my shoes to stop from plowing into her. I step to the side. Bree's eyes zero in on the rental. "Where is Lady Bug?"

"At home," I answer, striding to the Toyota.

"Is it broken?" Ben asks.

"No." I open the driver's side door. "Get in, and I promise I'll explain."

Bree takes the passenger seat, and Ben hops in the back. I start the car and head to Jack's.

"What happened with Porsche guy?" Bree asks. "I thought you were hanging out with him to get some answers." Bree gasps loudly, causing me to jump. "He didn't turn out to be a serial killer, did he? Just because he's Wingai doesn't mean you should've trusted him right off the bat. I'm sure your race has bad guys too."

Ben speaks from the back. "Bree, you've been watching too much CSI. Don't jump to conclusions. Azure will tell us when we get there."

Bree flushes, caught in the act. "All right."

Jack is leaning against a large maple tree in his front yard when I pull up to his house. He eyes the Toyota with a confused expression.

Bree rolls down her window. "Get in."

He slides into the back seat. "Did Lady Bug break down?"

"Lady Bug is fine." I pull onto the street.

"Which ice cream shop are we going to?" Bree asks.

"Dairy Queen." I say the first one that comes to mind, probably because we frequent it often.

At the drive-through I toss out everyone's orders, then pay before anyone else has a chance to pull out their wallet. I hand Bree the tray. She passes the cups out. I place my Oreo Blizzard in the cupholder.

The sun is just setting as I park behind Josephina's house at the base of the hill, out of view from the road that leads to mine. I bank on the chance whoever Russet sends will try my place before Josephina's. I get out, clutching my ice cream. I walk a little way into the trees to the gazebo with a firepit Josephina's husband made. She faithfully maintained it for years. My friends follow.

"Have a seat." I gesture to the benches.

Jack and Ben take seats.

Bree sets her ice cream down and crosses her arms, facing me. "Spill. What happened with Porsche guy?"

"First he claimed we were matches, then he sold me out to other Wingai who came and took me right after graduation.

That's why I don't have Lady Bug or my phone. I've just escaped," I say.

"He did what?" Bree's tone rises.

"Supposedly I'm the only Silver-Tipped Wingai in existence and I'm super important. The Wingai couldn't wait to get their hands on me," I explain. "I learned a ton about my race, then hightailed out when the opportunity arose because it's too much."

"Azure."

My heart plummets. A cold dread steals the warmth of summer off my skin. I slowly turn around. Cerulean stands a few paces away from the gazebo, concern etched in his face. Probably fake.

"Fantastic," I mutter, kicking myself for not staying on the move. I cross my arms, looking around for the other Wingai. "Where is Sky?"

He meets my eyes. "I'm alone. Can we please talk?"

"What's the point? I can't trust you," I say. My friends huddle around me.

Pain flashes across his face like I've physically wounded him. My insides twinge. I don't like to be the cause of hurt, even if he deserves it. "Azure, please. I'm so sorry. I didn't want to give your address out, but I had no choice. Russet has been out for Soaring Heights ever since your father died. Keeping you a secret from him would have meant war. I won't risk my people, even if it costs me."

He paces, and his hands dig into his hair. Dropping them, he says, "I had no idea Russet was going to take you. I expected a delegation of some sort, but snatching you the way they did was completely out of line." He rubs at the dirt with the tip of his shoe. "Feathers, you have no idea how sorry I am for not being able to protect you. I have been worried sick over you, and I'm kicking myself for being a failure as a match."

I've never seen somebody look as contrite as he does. Not Josephina, not my friends, especially not my mom. She was always sorry after a breakdown, but not like this. I'd never heard as much meaning in her apologies as I just did from Cerulean. I feel inclined to forgive him. Would it be a mistake if I did?

CERIL

Though Azure hasn't spoken, the hardness in her expression has softened. I push on, silently praying she won't shut me out for good. "Please, you're the most important person in my life. The last thing I want to do is mess us up."

Bree asks Azure, "Why is he talking like you're together?"

"What is a match?" Jack asks.

"Sounds like a boyfriend or something to me," Ben supplies. He turns his gaze from me to Azure. "Did you agree to date him before he got you kidnapped?"

"Wingai don't date like humans do," Azure explains. "They have mates, commonly referred to as matches. When a male turns eighteen, he gains a tracking ability to find his. Cerulean is mine. If I kiss him, we'll be considered married."

Bree's eyes pop. "Are you serious?"

"Man, that's insane!" Jack says.

Ben shrugs. "It's not that far out of the realm of normal, if you think about it. Lots of birds have a mate for life. Penguins, eagles, barn owls." Hope flares in my chest for him trying to rationalize it.

"Azure isn't a barn owl!" Bree exclaims.

Ben rolls his eyes. "I know that, but she's part bird, isn't she? She's got wings, talons, and killer eyesight." He waves his hand flippantly. Bree gives him a pointed stare. "I'm just saying we can't call it crazy because it doesn't fit our human norms." He gestures to me and Azure. "They're not human. Different species will do what's best for them."

Yes! Thank you. Jumping on his train of thought, I plead with her. "Azure, you're what's best for me, and I want to be what's best for you. Will you please give me another chance to prove myself?"

She closes the distance between us. My wings press against my back, eager to reconnect. "You seem really sincere, but this whole thing . . ." She shakes her head. "It's too much. I don't think I can go through with being your match. I definitely don't want to be Lead."

Feathers. This isn't what I want to hear. "Our match is so strong. We haven't even sealed it, but already I can sense your emotions. I've felt your anger, your fear, your hurt. You've been through hell." Azure's eyes widen with alarm. I plunge on, silently appealing to any power above that I'll get through to her. "I don't want to add to it. If you're not ready for a match, that's fine. I won't press myself on you in that way when I'm not wanted. I beg you, though, to please take the time to think things through before you completely shut me down."

Azure sighs, indecision written on her face. "Who says you won't take me back to Russet and force me to be Lead?"

"Why would I? I want a relationship with you. Taking you to Russet is a surefire way to ensure that never happens," I say adamantly.

"Watch out. He's playing to win," Jack calls from the gazebo.

"I can see that," Azure says over her shoulder. Her dark blue eyes find mine. "I like you, Cerulean. Minus selling me out, you've been nothing but nice since we met." My stomach drops as I wait for the but. Her hands move to rub her scars. "I just can't get behind those match abilities. I don't want you to have access to my mind. There's stuff there nobody should ever see."

I hold my hands up. "Then I won't use it. We can have as human of a relationship as you want." Azure's lips quirk, but I still read the indecision in her eyes. I conclude that nothing I say right now will convince her.

I change tactics. "You know, a lot has happened to you in the last few days. How about I give you some space to think things over."

Azure raises her eyebrows. "You would do that?"

"It's the least I can do, considering." I rub my chest. My heart pulses painfully. My wings push against their confines. "I've got to be honest, though. This pain is getting unreal."

Concern flickers in Azure's eyes, along with confusion. "What pain?"

"The pain of not sealing our match," I say. Azure raises an eyebrow. Now it's my turn to be puzzled. "Russet said he explained everything to you."

She shakes her head. "He never said anything about pain."

I curse. A scowl forms on my face. "Of course he didn't, arrogant prick." I tap my heart. "It's a male thing. That same homing beacon that helps me find you also screams at me to seal the match. It's like a volume button on the TV. It turns up the pulse the longer we wait because it thinks I can't hear it. Except I do hear it, and it hurts like a beast."

"Oh. I didn't know. I'm sorry," Azure says with sympathy.

"It's all right." I shrug like it's no big deal to put her at ease. "Is it okay if we meet up in a day or two when things have calmed down?"

"What about Russet?" Azure asks.

"He's not going to snatch you like that again, I promise," I say, making it clear I've got it handled. I think she'd reject me for good if she knew I came out here with his blessing.

Azure nods. "Okay." I'm not sure she believes me, but I get the feeling she wants to. I hope that will eventually translate into sealing our match.

"I'll see you later. Again, I'm really sorry about everything. Take care of yourself." I give her a little wave, hop in my Porsche, and take off. Fire encases my heart as distance separates us. I scream, punching the steering wheel. The horn blares, scaring a flock of crows out of the trees. My eyes sting. I blink rapidly to see the winding road.

I don't choose a destination as I drive. Left, right, straight—it doesn't matter. I need to give Azure as much time as I can physically handle, and there's no way I'm going back home right now. The sun fully sets. I flip on the lights and keep going, passing small towns, stretches of open field, forests. When the gas light flashes empty, I pull into a rest area. I lean my head back and shut my burning eyes.

I wake to the sound of my phone ringing. The sun has crested over the horizon. Its rays permeate my windows, heating the inside. I roll down my window for some air, then reach for my phone.

"Dad" flashes across the screen. I swipe to answer. "Hello." I rub my forehead, blinking rapidly to wake up.

"Have you found Azure yet?" Dad asks.

The events of yesterday come flashing back along with the fiery pulse in my heart. "I found her."

"And?" Dad says.

"I left her."

"Ceril!"

I sigh. "She told me she doesn't want the match, nor does she want to be Lead. I'm giving her some time to calm down and think things through before I try again. She needs it after what Russet did."

Dad doesn't sound pleased. "How much time are you giving her? Wingai don't survive well without their match, Tipped matches especially because they're so strong."

"I know, but Azure needs space right now. It's the only way I think I might get through to her. If I show I respect her and her needs, I think she'll be more willing to accept me," I answer. "Go tell that to Russet if he's asking for an update. Under no circumstances let him send Sky or someone else out." He might enlist another shifter. Cat shifters, for example, track with scents that give them a vision of their prey. They would have no problem catching her smell from Russet's that would give them an image of her location. "It will ruin everything."

"All right." Dad's tone turns stern. "Don't kill yourself with human nonsense trying to be Azure's hero." He mutters under his breath, "Space is the last thing Wingai need."

"Got it. I'll talk with you later." I hang up and throw my phone onto the passenger seat. I start the car, refuel at the closest gas station, and drive out of the area. Sometime later, I end up in Pacific City, a tourist town on the Oregon Coast. I park in a lot by a huge sand dune. Already the place teems with people, some carrying surfboards, others picnic baskets and blankets, children in tow.

I debate on getting out. A bevy of people ogles my car as they walk toward the waves. I decide to leave and find a quieter place. I'm not interested in the attention. I continue up the road into a forest. Mossy trees and large ferns line each side of the pavement. A large brown sign reading "Cape Lookout" sticks out. I pull into a parking lot and park among a few other vehicles. An older couple with hiking gear loads up a yellow SUV. A walk sounds good.

Climbing out, I breathe in the salty ocean air. The strong breeze calls to my wings. I stiffen as they try to break out. Shoving my hands in my pockets, I take the trail. The dirt is muddy under my shoes. Roots and rocks litter the narrow path. The bright green foliage glistens under the sunrays breaking through the tree canopy. It's nice. I wish I had the heart to appreciate it more.

The few hikers I pass on the trail nod or say hello, prompting me to do the same. Occasionally I stop to allow a bigger group past. I press against a tree to allow two young women to go by. Both openly check me out. The brunette with chocolate brown eyes brazenly says, "Hey, handsome."

I smirk. At least I'm appreciated somewhere.

I reach the end of the trail and stare at the vast expanse of sea. An eagle swoops around the cliffs, and I resist the urge to jump and join him. Several hikers arrive, marvel at the view, and go. I rest my hand on the rickety iron fence, trying not to think or feel. Azure needs this space, but feathers, it is killing me.

A large family of hikers arrives. I step to the side, allowing them more space at the fence. I cast my eyes back to the eagle now swooping to perch on a large fir tree. A young woman sidles up to me. A black baseball cap shades most of her face, which is tilted down. I turn to leave, not interested in her advances.

She speaks, her tone low but playful. "What's a lovebird doing out of his nest?"

I inhale subtly, catching her musky scent. *Cat shifter.* I turn to face her. She tilts her face up, showing off tawny golden eyes and a wide pink smile.

Recognition flares. I relax. "Kiana." She's flirty and sassy and takes no crap from anyone. I see her every three months at the North American Shifter Summit. Her father, Danyon, rules their Pride. They're incredibly powerful beings.

We hug. "Long time no see, Ceril," she says when we break apart.

"What are you doing here?" I ask.

"Staying at our summer house. I've been running this trail every day for a week," she explains. "Still looking for your match?"

I shake my head. "No, I found her."

"That's great!" She makes a show of looking around. "But she's not with you. Trouble in paradise already?"

I laugh bitterly. "You could say that."

"Uh-oh. This sounds like a story I want to hear." She tilts her head in the direction of the trail. "Ready to head back?"

I nod. While dodging muddy puddles and hopping over tree roots and rocks, I explain my match troubles. It feels good to get it out to a friend.

"You matched to a Silver-Tipped?" Kiana is dutifully shocked. "Oh my goodness. I thought they died out."

"So did we," I say.

When I talk about Azure's kidnapping, Kiana flexes her hands. "Bet they wouldn't have tried that with me around."

No one in their right mind would willingly go against a cat shifter. "Too bad you weren't there." I finish the story by the time we make it to my car.

Kiana's tawny eyes meet mine. "That's some serious crap for a lovebird." Most shifters call us by that nickname. We have more bite than that, but since we're obsessed with matches, it's stuck.

I chuckle humorlessly.

Kiana nudges my arm. "Come to the house. Mom would be upset if you didn't say hello."

"I'm sure she would," I agree with a smile.

Every time we meet at the shifter summit, Tiana laments that I'm not a cat shifter. "You and Kiana get along famously. You'd make beautiful babies with your fair looks. It really is a shame you're a lovebird."

"So, you coming?" Kiana asks.

I nod. I've got nothing better to do.

I follow Kiana's Jeep and arrive at a large white house with a wraparound porch surrounded by a copse of trees. Kiana's parents sit on matching rocking chairs outside. Matching their daughter, both are tall and sinewy with heavily tanned skin. Cat shifters have a thing for sunbathing.

Kiana loops her arm through mine as we walk up the front steps. "I caught us a bird for dinner!"

"Very funny." I laugh sarcastically.

"I knew I raised a hunter. Let's roast him on the barbecue with the steaks." Danyon grins at me.

Tiana stands and holds her arms out. "Ceril!" I step into her hug. She squeezes me tight, then lets go. "What's a lovebird doing out of his nest? Still looking for your match?"

I open my mouth to say no when Kiana takes over. "He matched to a Silver-Tipped. Can you believe it?"

Two sets of eyebrows raise.

"Go ahead," I tell Kiana, knowing how much she likes to hold the reins.

I lean against the porch railing and settle in while Kiana rehashes my match troubles with her parents. I stiffen as Azure's regret races across my heart. She's been awfully quiet until now. The pain kicks up a notch. I rub my chest. I hope it doesn't send me into cardiac arrest before I can convince Azure to be my match.

Danyon cocks his head to the side as if listening to something when Kiana finishes the tale. He eyes me with glowing golden eyes. "Your match is too strong for rejection. Your heart will burst if you cannot convince her to seal it."

"Well then, I hope this space thing works." Otherwise I will have doomed the future of Soaring Heights to become matchless like Mountain Hollow.

"It is too bad you are not a cat shifter." Tiana pats my cheek. "Why don't you stay with us for a day or two? Kiana and the twins will enjoy your company."

I nod, knowing it would be foolhardy to reject a cat shifter's hospitality. They don't usually give it. "Thank you."

Another Jeep pulls into the drive and parks beside my Porsche. Kiana's twin younger brothers, Jandon and Jakai, jump out. Jakai carries a string of rainbow trout. He holds it up for his father to see.

"Good catch, boys." Danyon turns to me. "Looks like we won't need to roast you after all." He winks.

Two days pass. I run with Danyon on the beach in the early mornings, fish with the twins, hike with Kiana, and cook with Tiana. I send a text to Dad to let him know where I'm at and who I'm with. I ignore his attempts at further communication. I don't want him to tell me how to handle Azure. I want to give her as much time as I can.

The pain builds. When I roll out of bed on day three, I'm gasping, hand on chest. I manage to dress and step outside, hoping the cool morning air will help. I lean against the porch railing, taking measured breaths to combat the fire. I've got to go back to Azure. I can't wait any longer.

Danyon quietly slips outside and joins me. His golden eyes survey me, lips turned down. "It's time."

"Yes." Abruptly my pain peaks. I clutch my chest with a startled gasp. Blackness creeps into my vision. I fall.

CHAPTER THIRTEEN

AZURE

B ree invites me to stay with her to get away from it all. To
her parents, she cites Josephina's passing and needing girl
time. They accept it with no questions. Jack and Ben stay
for a late movie. We take over the basement living room
with tubs of ice cream and chips. While a Marvel film plays in
the background, I bring them up to speed on everything I
learned about the Wingai.

When I finish, Bree says, "I don't blame you for running.
A match and Lead, plus all those extra abilities—it's a lot to
handle at once."

"Exactly," I say, pleased someone agrees with me.

"That hiding in plain sight sounds cool," Ben says. "That's
only a male thing though, right?"

"That and the mimicking to distract or deter a potential
threat," I say, dipping my spoon back into my chocolate chip
cookie dough ice cream.

"So what are you thinking?" Bree asks. "Cerulean's going to come back and want an answer. He seems crazy determined to have a relationship with you."

"Wouldn't you, if you spent your whole life preparing for a mate?" I ask, dropping my spoon into the container. "Russet told me getting a match is like a crowning glory moment for them. It's the most anticipated moment of their lives. Just think of all those match abilities they get. They all grow up excited for it. Then Cerulean gets me, and I keep shutting him down." I scoff at the irony.

"Is that what you really want? To shut him out?" Jack asks, his blue eyes meeting mine.

I shrug. "I don't know. My life hasn't been all roses and fairy tales. I mean, I think I do a good enough job of seeming put together, but I'm not." I gesture to my arms. "These scars aren't from a car crash, like I've told everybody." My friends know my mom was psychotic, though perhaps not to this extent. Their eyes roam over me with new horror. "Accepting the match means Cerulean will see deeper than maybe I want him to."

Jack puts the lid back on his mint chocolate chip ice cream. "If those mind powers work both ways, then Cerulean could be making himself just as vulnerable. He seems willing to risk himself for a shot at love."

"I highly doubt his childhood messed him up like mine," I counter. "What does he have to expose?"

"Just because he's hot and probably rich doesn't mean he doesn't have his own demons to face," Bree says.

I concede. "True."

"I saw an energy between you two when you were talking," Jack says. "Guys have never affected you, but he does. You may not want all the powers and responsibility, but I think you want him."

"Jack's right. I saw the same thing." Bree smiles ruefully, like she didn't want to admit it. but now that Jack's said something, she could too.

"There's a spark there, like what I have with Bree." Ben places a kiss on Bree's cheek.

I don't deny it. Cerulean offers a chance at romance. Of course I have some interest. However, I've structured my life to accept a relationship of that nature wouldn't be happening. What's to lose when I never thought I would have love to begin with?

Our conversation shifts to my father's death and becoming Lead. "Mountain Hollow blames Soaring Heights for killing him, but I think the blame is misplaced. I don't think Lead Emerald persuaded my father to sacrifice himself." How many times had I heard Mom shout "How could you?" acting like she was seeing someone in front of her. I think she knew my father made the choice, and she hated him for it because it took him away from her. "Also, because of that one bad human, Mountain Hollow speaks like you're all trash. They'll make me Lead, then hate me for not having the same prejudice."

"If that's really their mindset, I wouldn't want to lead them either," Bree says. "You can't judge a society as a whole just because of one bad guy."

"Exactly." It feels good to have friends who can see my point of view. I hope Russet doesn't try to rip me away from them. We finish the movie. Ben and Jack go home, and Bree and I fall asleep.

I spend the following day finishing what errands I can for Josephina's passing. I borrow Bree's laptop to close out Josephina's social media accounts. I visit the bank, insurance company, and a few other businesses Josephina frequented. I buy a new phone.

While I'm running around town, Ben and Bree go to my house to retrieve Lady Bug and some clothes. I expressed concern that if Russet had sent someone, they could be used against me, but they were willing to take the chance.

"Someone's got to take the plunge. You can't hide out forever," Bree said.

Later, we meet up at a fast-food restaurant. Jack joins us after helping his parents out at their shop.

"This was on your door." Bree hands me a small piece of paper.

It reads, "We received a suspicious call from this area. If you have any information, please call the McMinnville Police Department." A number and officer's name accompany it.

"Are you going to call?" Jack asks.

"I better if I don't want them to show up again." I dial the number and leave a message with my contact information, explaining that I've been with friends the whole weekend celebrating our graduation, so I haven't seen anything out of the ordinary. I also give them Jack's, Ben's, and Bree's numbers in case they want to corroborate. I hope that's enough.

"We didn't see any evidence of someone around, but that's not saying much since matched guys can camouflage," Ben says.

I nod. "Thanks for checking."

The following morning, Jack, Ben, and Bree help me shop for a security system. Afterward, I go to the mortuary to pick up Josephina's urn. Tears escape as I hold it carefully against my chest. I miss her so much.

I return to my house with my friends. I'm ready to check things out. Jack drives Lady Bug for me, due to my emotional state. He parks, and I half expect to see someone from Mountain Hollow jump out of the bushes or drop in from the sky. I keep my eyes peeled for ripples in the air, but I catch only the breeze ruffling leaves.

I gesture to the urn in my hands with a tilt of my head. "I'm going to take care of this real quick. Feel free to make yourselves at home." Gently, I set it on the passenger seat of Lady Bug so I can take off my shirt, leaving on my tank top and bra. I pick it back up and release my wings. They unfurl with a blast of energy. I stumble, on the verge of losing my footing. "Whoa."

Something's wrong. I've gone months without freeing my wings. A couple of days shouldn't have accumulated this much power.

"You okay?" Jack asks me.

I don't want to worry him. "Yeah, my wings are just overexcited. See you in a bit."

Flapping hard, I jump into the air, taking Josephina's urn with me. I fly over our property and distribute Josephina's ashes like she wanted. I blink through tears. My heart aches, but it's a good kind of pain. A letting-go kind. As the last of the ashes disperse into the trees, I put the lid back on the urn. It's done. She's at peace now.

Once inside my house, I set the urn on the mantel over the fireplace. When I feel up to it, I think I'll donate it to Goodwill or something. I don't want to hold on to it forever. Josephina is where she wants to be, among nature. The urn was just a transportation device. I get hugs from my friends. Their support buoys me up.

Ben points to a row of cameras on the coffee table. "These are ready to be installed."

"Thank you." They won't tell me if a camouflaged Wingai flies in, but at least I'll know about cars driving up the hill. I figure it's better than nothing.

I meet resistance as I try to tuck my wings in. A sharp pain shoots from the feather tips into my back and straight to my heart. "Ouch!" The pain causes my hands to shift into talons.

My heart pulses wildly. My feathers rustle and twitch, as if telling me off for trying to hide them.

"What's wrong?" Bree asks, her brown eyes concerned.

"I don't know." I try retracting them again. The pain, throbbing heart, and shuddering feathers kick up a notch. "Oh!" I gasp, eyes wide. Fear churns my stomach. "I can't hide my wings. They won't go back."

"What about your talons?" Jack asks, eyeing the long curved nails with some trepidation.

"I'll try." Flexing my hands, I manage to make them disappear. Relief melts the concern on my friends' faces. "I won't be able to help with the security camera at the bottom of the hill. Someone could see me."

"No problem," Ben says. "Jack and I can do it."

Jack smiles. "We've got you covered."

I help my friends wherever I can with the camera installation. As long as my wings are out, they don't give me many problems, though they continue to pulse and twitch with an unusual amount of energy. I suspect this may have something to do with Cerulean. I brace myself for the fact that I may have to seal the match if I want my wings to return to normal. I'm not exactly thrilled at the recourse. What if Cerulean ends up being a complete jerk after sealing the match?

We celebrate our hard work with a small bonfire party. We roast hot dogs and marshmallows and go through a case of Pepsi. They fill me in on what I missed at the grad night party, who broke up or hooked up with who. I get the whole story of Mr. Piper and Mrs. Garrett's affair.

"Dad gave them a formal reprimand. If school weren't out, I think they'd be suspended," Bree says of our former teachers.

"Mr. Piper deserves it. He is the worst." Jack makes a face. "I can't believe he offered me money to keep my mouth shut. Ten dollars wasn't going to cover it."

We all shake our heads at this.

Around 1:00 a.m. we crash. Jack takes a couch. Ben and Bree share a guest room. Falling asleep with my feathers wrapped around me, safe in my own bed, my last thought is of Cerulean. I wonder if he's having as many problems as I am and whether he's okay.

By the next morning, my wings give me more trouble than ever. The little twitches have increased to nearly full-on flapping. My hands keep unexpectedly shifting into talons. My senses switch to Wingai mode and back. When Bree says good morning as I walk into the kitchen, I cringe at the shout.

Jack hands me a glass of orange juice. "You look terrible. I think you should consider getting Cerulean back."

"I think so too." My talons make an appearance, causing me to drop the cup. It hits the floor and breaks, splattering juice all over our feet.

Ben is there in a second with a rag. "I've got it."

"Why don't you just sit down." Bree puts a hand on my arm and leads me to a chair.

I grimace. "I think my body is making my decision for me. Seal the match or be left in this miserable state." Fear twists my insides at the prospect of tying myself to Cerulean. I shove it down. I have to do it. I can't live like this.

"Look at the bright side. Cerulean is really easy on the eyes." Bree waggles her eyebrows.

I laugh. "That's definitely the deciding factor."

Bree chuckles. "It sure is a bonus, and you never know. He might turn out to be a sweetheart."

"Or not," I say.

Bree lightly slaps my arm. "Don't be so pessimistic. You might have a better chance if you go into this with a good attitude."

"You think he's having the same problems you are?" Jack places a new cup of orange juice in front of me. I murmur a thanks.

Ben asks, "If he can't hide his wings like you, how is he going to get here undetected?"

"He said something about his tracking ability causing him pain. Maybe it's different for him?" I shrug.

Adrenaline jolts into my feathers. I hop out of the chair as my wings go crazy. My friends step back to avoid getting swatted. My phone blares with the security alarm. Gritting my teeth, I force my nails to retract. I pull my phone out of my pocket. A red Jeep, followed by Cerulean's Porsche, is coming up the drive.

"Cerulean's here, but someone's with him," I say. Worry snakes around my stomach. Could it be Russet? I'm willing to seal the match, but I refuse to be Lead. The last thing I want is that much responsibility.

"What do you want to do?" Jack asks.

"I guess we'll go meet them." I hope they don't try any funny business.

To be on the safe side since I can't hide my wings, I peek from behind the curtains to be sure it really is Cerulean before I step out. Bree, Ben, and Jack stand on the porch. A dark-haired girl jumps out of the driver's side of Cerulean's car. An older woman with the same coloring climbs out of the passenger side. Where is Cerulean?

They hurry to the Jeep, where a thirties-something man and identical young male twins get out. The father reaches into the back seat and pulls out a body. I gasp as I recognize Cerulean.

My heart leaps into my throat as I throw open the door and race down the steps to reach him. His eyes are closed, face pale, body limp. Terror slinks through me when I think he might be dead. "What happened? Is he . . . ?"

"He's not dead . . . yet," the man holding him growls. I notice his eyes glow bright gold. I inhale a deep musky scent and stiffen. He's not human or Wingai. Another shifter? I take a step back, gulping at the anger I see in his face. "Seal the match or watch him die. Your choice."

I don't hesitate. I've made my decision. "Bring him into the house."

"Nobody said anything about death with these matches, did they?" Bree asks me as I dart back up the stairs.

"No," I answer, throwing the door open.

I direct the man to lay Cerulean on the couch. My feathers stretch for him, and I narrowly avoid falling on top of him.

Cerulean stirs at my touch. "Azure," he murmurs, eyes fluttering. His wings release and mesh with mine. My heart pulses with the contact, sending energy through my wings and into Cerulean.

"I'm here," I say.

"Let's give them some space," the dark-haired woman says.

Everyone shuffles out of the room.

His sea-green eyes pop open. He stares at me with glassy pain filling eyes. "Don't kiss me," he whispers.

I'm taken aback. "What?"

"Don't kiss me out of pity," he repeats, his voice getting stronger.

"It wouldn't be pity. I made my decision to seal the match before you showed up," I tell him.

Cerulean sits up, seeming to get stronger with my presence. He eyes me skeptically. "You did?"

"I can't retract my wings. My hands keep shifting, and my senses are haywire. I think I'm being punished for holding out," I explain.

"So you'll kiss me just to get back to normal," Cerulean surmises, now standing. He clutches his chest, shoulders hunched as he steps away, tucking his wings in to avoid my touch.

"No, I'm interested in a relationship if some ground rules are set up," I answer.

Cerulean pauses. "Like what?"

"I don't want you using your powers on me. No looking inside my head, or feeling me out." I shudder at the thought of him prying. My secrets are mine to keep. "And . . ." I hesitate.

"What?" His eyes will me to continue.

"No intimacy. Not now. I still don't know you well enough for that." I look away. My body yearns to get close. My wings burn to wrap around him. But my mind says it's too soon.

Cerulean shakes his head. "I seek a match, not platonic friendship."

My insides quiver. Is he seriously wanting the full liberties of a husband?

Cerulean softens a smidge as his eyes dart over my face. "I'm not going to share a bed with you yet. You're right, we don't know each other well enough for that. But I need you to see me as husband material—that we'll eventually be in a place to love one another. You can't friendzone me—that's not what matches are."

"I know that." A vision of my mother's soulless eyes swims in front of me. I flinch. Cold fear steals the warmth out of my bones. I'm convinced Mom's losing her match unexpectedly is what broke her. If I fall in love with Cerulean and something tragic happens to him, I could break too, and I've spent my whole life avoiding anything that could make me turn into her.

However, underneath the waves of anxiety, I feel interest in seeing where we could go. I hope I can make that curiosity strong enough to see us through. "You might have to go slow with me. I haven't had as much time to prepare as you have."

Cerulean dips his head in acknowledgment. His lips curve into a smile. "I can do that." He closes the distance between us. Our wings collide. His hands find my waist. Mine grip his upper arms. It reminds me of the way Jack and I danced at prom except I never felt nervous with him.

Cerulean searches my face, his sea-green eyes bright, aware. Gently his hands move up to cup my cheeks. I shiver with nerves. He lowers his head. "Last chance," he whispers. I tilt my face to meet him, hating and loving the anticipation.

I slide my eyes shut as our lips touch, hesitantly at first. I find his mouth soft and pliable against mine. When I don't pull away, he deepens the kiss, perusing my lips with conviction. The butterflies turn into warmth as I give in, craving more, craving *him*. His hands roam to my lower back, pressing me flush against him. Adrenaline propels through my pulsing heart and barrels into my wings like an electric charge. Our grip on each other tightens. The match is sealed.

Cerulean rests his forehead against mine as we catch our breath. "Thank you," he whispers.

"You're welcome." The earlier warmth dissipates, leaving cool anxiety in its place as I grapple with what I've done. I step out of his grasp, trying to find my legs in the process. He turned me into jelly. My lips still tingle. I work hard not to touch them. "Feel better?" I ask, needing a distraction.

He rubs his chest. "The pounding has stopped. What about you?"

My wings slide into my back with no issue. I'm relieved. "Better. Thanks."

Cerulean watches me, giving me the impression he's trying to figure me out. I admit to myself the kiss we shared was probably more heated than he or I expected. I flush with the remembrance of it. Air. I need air. I stride to the front door. Cerulean follows.

I breathe in a lungful of sunshine, earth, and pine as I step onto my porch. Questioning eyes from seemingly all directions descend upon us. I stiffen from the attention.

Cerulean shoves his hands into his pockets as he stands beside me. "We sealed the match." His voice betrays no emotion.

"Hallelujah!" the shifter girl shouts with obvious relief.

Bree gives me a mischievous grin while she leans into Ben. "Welcome to the married life."

I frown at her, causing my friends to chuckle. Yet her words ring in my head. By Wingai standards, I'm officially married. It's certainly how Cerulean is going to see it. I make a conscious effort not to shudder.

CHAPTER FOURTEEN

CERIL

My mind is stuck on repeat with the kiss I shared with Azure. Feathers, she lit me up in flames. I can still feel her body pressed against mine, her hands massaging into me while I explored her mouth. She tasted like heaven. Sweet, soft, angelic. It was better than I could have imagined . . . and it isn't going to happen again anytime soon.

Azure's walls have slammed back into place. I can tell from her stiff movements. She's strung tight like a guitar string. One more turn and she'll snap. Our match isn't a love story. It's a tragedy.

I thank Danyon and his family for bringing me here. I'm glad they were able to catch Azure's scent off me and follow their visions to get me here.

"Her scars share a tale of great suffering, but I sense she has spirit and is strong of mind, like her father." Danyon grins at me. "I wish you well in your efforts to keep up with her."

He casts his golden eyes on Azure and her friends. "Humans are a liability."

"From what I've seen, they care for Azure too much to harm us," I answer.

"I gathered that much as well. It is why they're still standing," Danyon says, his tone casual. Cat shifters don't stand for threats to their survival. If they thought Azure's friends were a problem, they'd be dead before they could scream. "You must bring them to the next summit to be approved."

"I plan on it," I agree.

Jakai lightly punches me in the arm. "Show me your new match powers!"

"Yeah, give us the disappearing act," Jandon encourages.

I shut my eyes, using my mind to search for the magic within my wings. *Whoa.* Intense energy vibrates through each feather. I feel it travel into my heart, then up to my brain, where it lies in my subconscious as a slow beating pulse waiting for a command. I'm enthralled. This is feather-freaking fantastic!

Focusing on the raw power, I bring it to the forefront of my mind. I express a desire to blend in, using emotion and thought. My wings tingle and twitch. I open my eyes and see that my body has blurred, like water thrown on paint. Feathers, this is amazing!

Jakai jokingly makes binocular eyes with his hands. "Hey, where'd you go?"

Jandon scratches his head, wearing a wry grin. "Some friend. He up and vanished on us!"

Laughter bursts out of my mouth as I make myself seen by releasing my hold on the magic. It slinks back to rest under the surface. I receive another round of congratulations from Danyon and his family, then we say our goodbyes.

Tiana embraces me with a kiss on my cheek. "Take care. Your match is lovely."

Kiana hugs me. "I'm glad to see your match isn't a prissy like Magenta. You've done well."

I laugh. "I'm glad you approve."

Jakai winks. "Your match is hot for a lovebird."

Jandon nods. "You lucked out."

"Yeah," I agree.

I wave them off as they get in their Jeep and drive away. I walk over to Azure, who's speaking to her friends. "I promise I'll call in case I need rescuing, but I think I'll be fine. I'll just be busy figuring things out."

My phone buzzes in my pocket. I pull it out. "Dad" flashes across the screen. I answer it. "Hey." I stroll to my car and lean against it. Azure follows me with her eyes, her brows puckering. She's probably worried I'm talking to Russet.

"Ceril." Dad exhales with relief. "I've been so worried about you."

"I'm fine. I'm with Azure. We sealed the match," I tell him.

"You what? How?" Dad's voice rings with excitement.

"Don't get excited. She may technically be my wife now, but we're not solid yet. She's really skittish about everything." I watch Azure say goodbye to her friends as they load up in a blue Honda.

"How did you get her to seal the match?" Dad asks.

"I passed out this morning. Danyon and his family brought me back to Azure. She was having problems too, with her wings, talons, and stuff. She said she thought her body was punishing her for holding out," I explain. "She agreed to try for a relationship as long as we took it slow."

"You're both Tipped. The strength of a match like that is unparalleled," Dad says. "I'm glad you weren't alone."

"Yeah." Azure walks over to me, arms folded. I pull the phone away from my mouth. "My father."

She nods, her lips pressed tight.

"When will we get to meet her?" Dad asks.

"I don't know. I'll have to see what Azure wants," I say.

Her eyes flash upon hearing me say this. "I'm not going back there," she says loud enough for him to hear.

Dad curses. "Let me talk to her."

I put him on speaker and hold the phone between us. "Go ahead."

"Azure, congratulations on sealing the match." Dad inflects enthusiasm. "Welcome to the Hatch family. We are thrilled to have you."

"Thank you." She looks at me. "Is it traditional for Wingai to take on their husband's last name, or is it different?"

I shrug. "It can go either way. I take on your name, or you take mine. Wingai go to the county courthouse after sealing the match and get a civil ceremony to blend in with the humans. We'll need to do that. If you want, we could see whether there any openings today. It would be nice to have everything said and done."

"All right," she agrees, but I sense no enthusiasm for it.

Dad speaks. "I would really like to meet you, Azure, and speak to you face-to-face. Would you please reconsider coming to Soaring Heights?"

"No," she says, jaw set.

Her abhorrence washes over me.

"I'm not sure you realize how important you are to us," Dad says. "Russet is leaving in fifteen minutes to get you—as you know, he's not afraid to take you forcibly."

I curse. I'm out of time.

Azure shakes her head, her blue eyes glinting with determination. "He won't get me."

Dad sighs, his patience is running out. "Russet will lay waste to Soaring Heights if you refuse him."

Azure stiffens. Dad's finally got her attention. "What do you mean?"

Dad explains. "Mountain Hollow is desperate. They've been without a Lead for nineteen years. Their rising generation is currently matchless. For Wingai, there is nothing worse. If you don't come, Russet will reveal your existence and tell them we are holding you hostage here in Soaring

Heights. They will rip us apart looking for you. Many innocents will be hurt or possibly killed."

Azure's eyes widen. "You can't be serious."

"Dead serious," Dad says, his tone stern. "Russet is done giving Ceril a chance to bring you back."

"You've been in this with him the whole time?" she asks, her expression accusing.

Feathers. "Russet thought I could charm you into going back home, but I couldn't do it," I say.

Azure doesn't miss a beat. "Couldn't or wouldn't?"

"Both," I say with an apologetic smile.

"Unbelievable!" Azure hisses, throwing her hands up. I wince as the full force of her anger barrels into me. "This is exactly why I don't want to come. You birds are crazy." She takes a breath, seeming to think things over. "Fine. I'll come, but only to tell you all to freaking leave me alone! No amount of force or scare tactics will get me to lead a lunatic society."

"You got that?" I ask Dad.

"Yeah, I heard." Dad sounds thoroughly insulted. "I'll let Russet know."

"Thanks. See you tonight." I end the call. "To the courthouse?" I ask Azure.

Azure talks to me over her shoulder as she trots up the stairs. "Let me change first."

"You might want to pack an overnight bag," I say. "I don't want you falling asleep at the wheel coming home."

Azure holds up a finger. "One night only."

I find my bag in the Porsche. In the downstairs bathroom, I switch out my gray T-shirt to a short-sleeved black button-up shirt. It's not a tux, but it's better than a T-shirt. Once refreshed, I sit in the living room and wait for Azure.

A few minutes later, she descends carrying a small black duffel bag. She wears a short-sleeved knee-length navy-blue dress with a black lace overlay. Her blonde hair falls in waves behind her back. She's applied a smidge of makeup, eyeliner, mascara, and shiny lip gloss. My breath catches in my throat. Feathers, she's beautiful, and she's mine.

I reach for her bag. "Let me take that for you."

Azure insists on driving her own getaway car, so I park mine in her garage, and we take Lady Bug.

Her nerves make me jittery as we fill out the paperwork for a marriage license. My wings push against my back, responding to the low hum of anxiousness. "What last name do you want?"

Her expression turns thoughtful. I feel her emotions darken, then abruptly cut off. "I'll take yours."

"Are you sure?" I ask, trying to understand what I sense from her.

She nods. "Positive."

Warmth blooms in my chest. A satisfied grin slowly forms on my face.

We hand the paper back to the middle-aged lady manning the desk. I pay the extra money to waive the three-day waiting period.

Judge Harrison is a paunchy older man with short gray hair, critical brown eyes, and a hard, thin mouth. "So, you want to get married today, huh?"

I take Azure's hand in mine. "Yes, sir, we do."

Judge Harrison addresses Azure while jerking his thumb at me. "You think he'll be a good husband?"

My heart leaps in my throat as Azure casts her dark blue eyes on me. "He is my perfect match, made just for me."

Feathers, she's doing a good job of making me fall in love with her, whether she wants it or not. I squeeze her hand. "I'll always be yours. Forever." I mean it.

Judge Harrison smiles briefly, seeming satisfied. "Let us proceed."

The ceremony itself goes rather smoothly, much to my surprise. Azure and I both say I do at the right parts. We then exchange the set of white-gold diamond rings I've been holding on to since I turned eighteen. When Judge Harrison pronounces us husband and wife, I capture Azure's lips with mine, tasting strawberry lip gloss. I keep it short but sensual, knowing I probably won't get another opportunity for some time. A soft blush stains her cheeks when I pull back. My chest constricts. She's perfect.

AZURE

I hop in Lady Bug and start the car to go to Soaring Heights. Hands on the steering wheel, I notice how the sun glints off the heart-shaped diamond ring on my left ring finger. So much for first dates. I'm equal parts mortified and mystified by the turn of events. The beaming smile Cerulean gave me throughout the ceremony rattled my need for distance. His kiss flipped on all the switches in the desire department. I start to contemplate a real marriage with all the bells and whistles until images of my scars pop into my mind. I'm not exactly prime material. What if he becomes disgusted when he sees every mark? What if his desire for a match has been outweighing his repulsion this whole time? Better to stay cautious until I know him better.

Halfway through the drive, we stop to get gas. I allow him to test-drive Lady Bug the rest of the way. We reach the gates of Soaring Heights a little after 5:00 p.m. A heavily muscled man steps out of a small security post, recognizes Cerulean, and waves us through.

I keep my eyes glued to the glovebox, not wanting to familiarize myself with a town I want nothing to do with.

Barely three blocks in and I'm anxious to leave already. I can't help but think Cerulean is leading me to a trap. I'll get to his house, and Russet will be waiting there with manacles. I shudder.

Cerulean parks in front of a lodge-style mansion with warm homey tones. It's the complete opposite of Russet's house. "How do Wingai afford such nice places?" I ask.

Cerulean laughs. "We love investing in anything marketable. We're big on the internet. For lots of new products and ventures you'll see online, don't be surprised to hear a Wingai's dipped their feathers in them. The stock market is an obsession, and everybody's grandma carries a stack of savings bonds bought fifty years ago."

"Oh." I wonder if they'd get involved in get-rich-quick schemes too.

Cerulean gets out of the car and trots over to my side. He opens my door. I press my back against the seat, not eager to get out. "Relax. No one is going to hold you hostage here."

I hate that he can sense my emotions. I don't want him getting too close yet. He holds out his hand. I take it, allowing him to help me out. "Thank you," I murmur, pulling my hand free the second I'm stable. He hands me my keys, and I drop them in my purse.

Cerulean reaches in the back and grabs my bag. I follow him up the front steps and onto the porch. The door opens as he reaches for it. A woman with pale-pink wings with a gold match coloring and Cerulean's dark-brown hair snatches him into a hug, forcing him to drop my bag. I reach down to pick it up. "Oh, Ceril, thank heavens."

Startled, he freezes for a moment before hugging the woman back. "Hey, Mom."

His mom pulls back. Grasping his arms, she gives him a hard glare. "You worried me to death. Don't you dare do that to me again."

Cerulean has the decency to appear bashful. "I'm sorry."

"You better be." She caresses his cheek. "I love you."

"Love you too," he replies easily.

My fingers dig into the straps of my bag. My heart reels with unexpected jealousy. Cerulean's gaze snaps to mine. I quickly avert my eyes, trying to tame the beast inside me. Deep breaths.

"Come into the house and let me meet your match." She ushers us inside, her expression full of excitement.

The rest of his family stands in the entry hall. Cerulean wears the biggest grin I've ever seen as he introduces us. "Everyone, this is Azure." He gestures to his mom, now tucked beside a man with dark brown hair, green eyes, and deep-green wings with a reddish-pink match design and gold tips. "Azure, this is my mom, Rose, and my dad, Emerald."

Emerald smiles. "It's a pleasure to meet you in person, Azure."

I force a small smile and nod, not trusting myself to speak.

"My older sister, Scarlett, and her match, Midnight," Cerulean says, gesturing to a fair woman with sea-green eyes and scarlet-and-black wings. Her hands rest on her protruding stomach. Midnight lives up to his name with coal-black hair, ice-blue eyes, and black-and-scarlet wings. I receive friendly smiles from both of them.

"And last is my younger brother, Jade."

I see similarities between Jade and Cerulean with their facial structure and hair, although Jade's eyes are a darker green like his father's, and his build is slightly stockier and a little more muscular. I suspect he works out more. His green wings are simple and unadorned.

"Welcome to the family." Jade winks at me, then says to Cerulean, "Way to make me jealous, bro. She puts Magenta to shame."

Is that his potential match? At least he's not comparing me to my mom.

"Don't be thinking thoughts about my match." Cerulean puts his hands on my shoulders, holding me to him.

Emerald, Rose, Scarlett, and Midnight laugh as Jade exclaims, "I can't help it! You've got a hotter-than-sin match, and I'm probably going to get stuck with Peony. The girl eats worms for breakfast."

"That was a dare," Cerulean exclaims.

"But she said she liked it." Jade shudders, his face wrinkled in disgust.

Cerulean reaches down and takes my bag from me. "Come on, I'll show you to a room. You probably want to change into something to release your wings. I know mine are getting pretty stifled."

I did want to get out of this dress, but I wasn't comfortable enough yet to release my wings.

He shows me to a beach-themed room on the second floor. "This okay?"

"It's fine," I say. I take a breath. The house smells like gingerbread, perhaps keeping with the woodland theme of the main parts of the home.

Cerulean rubs the back of his neck. "My room is directly across from yours, if you need anything. I probably should have taken you to my nest, but I thought this would be easier since we're conducting business here. Plus, my fridge isn't stocked."

"This is fine, Cerulean," I repeat. We're definitely going to need to talk about living arrangements soon. I'm not prepared to give up my home to live permanently at his place.

"All right." He steps out, closing the door behind him.

I set my purse on the bed, and then I change into a pair of dark jeans and a pale-blue T-shirt. I pull my hair back into a ponytail. Feeling more like myself, I step out. Cerulean leans against his door, thumbs hooked in the pockets of his jeans. He's switched out his black button-up for a white T-shirt. His blue wings rest openly on his back.

His casual smile turns into a frown as he peruses me. "You don't have to hide here, Azure. Your wings are gorgeous. They should be displayed."

"Thanks, but I'd prefer them contained for now," I say.

Cerulean sighs. He peels off the wall and stands face-to-face with me, the tips of his shoes touching mine. His hands move to rest on my shoulders, his thumbs rubbing the exposed skin on my collarbones. "What do I have to do for you to let me in? We're married now. I want to be a support and confidant to my wife."

His eyes plead with mine. I part my lips, tempted to throw caution to the wind. His gaze dips to my mouth. The air supercharges. Warmth pools all over as I remember our earlier kisses. He lowers his head.

Somebody sneezes. I spring apart, embarrassment dousing my desire like water thrown on flames. What the heck am I doing? I can't let his kisses persuade me to open up, not until I can trust him more. I look over and see Jade standing at the top of the stairs, his expression apologetic. I take another step back, making my stance clear.

"Feathers," Cerulean curses.

I turn on my heel, heading downstairs. He follows, anger radiating like sunrays upon my back. I pass Jade and hear Cerulean stop. "This close to making a connection," I hear him say, frustration lacing his tone. I imagine him using his fingers to show how close we were.

"So sorry, bro." Jade sounds genuinely remorseful.

Emerald stands by the door. "Russet should be here any minute."

"Good." Let's get this over and done with. I'm not cut out to be their Lead. The sooner he realizes this, the better.

CHAPTER FIFTEEN

CERIL

I stand beside Azure, cursing my luck. I almost had her. Feathers, she wanted me. I could see it in her eyes, feel it through our match connection. It was going to be epic, life changing. Our first kiss not born out of duty . . . gone with a feather-freaking sneeze.

Dad opens the door for Russet. "Welcome."

Azure puts on a mask of indifference, but I read the tension lying under her skin. She's gearing herself up for battle.

Russet smiles at Azure and me. "I hear congratulations are in order."

Azure says nothing.

"Thank you," I say.

"Come on in to the living room and we'll talk." Dad leads the way.

Midnight, Scarlett, Jade, and Mom are already situated. I pull Azure to sit with me on a couch while Russet and Dad take their seats. A tray of drinks and cookies rests on the coffee table.

"Is there to be a celebration for the new couple?" Russet asks, draping one leg over the other. "It's customary, is it not?"

"It is," Dad agrees.

Azure stiffens. "I'm not staying here any longer than necessary."

"I'll take that as a no," I say, trying not to let it bother me.

"You belong with your people, not among the humans," Russet says to her. "Why must you insist on staying in their realm when they can do nothing for you?"

"I have my reasons," she says stiffly.

"Name them," Russet orders.

Azure's hackles raise. "I don't answer to you."

Russet's eyes flash. "Until you agree to be Lead, yes you do."

My chest burns with Azure's anger. I want to grab her hand, comfort her in some way, but I suspect she will push me away.

"I am not your property," Azure says. "I've lived my whole life without this." She waves her hands at all of us. "I'm here only to tell you to leave me alone."

Russet drops his leg and leans forward, his hands gripping the arms of his leather chair. "That is impossible. You are the only Silver-Tipped Wingai in existence. Mountain Hollow needs you. Our entire rising generation is matchless. Without you, our entire race will die."

Azure purses her lips, her eyes critical as she thinks. "I'll fix it, then go."

"This isn't a onetime fix," Russet counters. "New Wingai will be born and require recognition."

Azure doesn't bat an eye. "So I make a monthly visit."

Scarlett raises her eyebrow, silently communicating, "Is she serious?"

I subtly nod, giving her a "tell me about it" expression back.

Russet gestures to me. "What of your match? Ceril is Gold-Tipped. He will eventually take on the role of his father and become Lead for the Golds. He will need to stay here to do so. Are you to abandon him?"

Azure says nothing. She rubs her temples as if fighting off a headache. The tension I feel in her has got to be killing her. It's starting to get to me. I extend a wing to soothe her. She stiffens and leans away.

The whole room stares at me with pity as I retract my wings. "Russet makes a good point. It would be hard to conduct business from McMinnville."

"Business over the only home I have ever known. Over my mother's and Josephina's ashes scattered around the trees. I have worked very hard these last three years to make my property a place of healing and respect. Please don't take that away from me. It's all I have." Azure rises. Her pain punches me in the gut. "Excuse me. I need to catch my breath." She flees the room. The front door opens and closes.

I run a hand through my hair, a curse escaping my lips. Something's got to give: my desire to save Soaring Heights and Mountain Hollow or my need to have a relationship with Azure. Right now, I'm of a mind to let the Wingai world crash and burn if it means I get to keep her.

I refocus on the conversation. Mom has her brows furrowed as she speaks. "I remember Amethyst as warm and loving. She couldn't hurt a fly."

"Amethyst was an utter wreck after losing Fire," Russet says flatly. "I agreed to let her leave Mountain Hollow because I worried that if she had to see another happy match, she was going to commit suicide. I knew she and Fire had been trying for a child, but she assured me nothing had come to fruition. I wouldn't have given her a pet rock to watch over in her condition. Then to have a child with Fire's markings? The damage is written all over Azure. I shudder to imagine how she must have lived."

My stomach twists sickeningly as I put Russet's admission to Azure's scarred arms, her darkness, and her jealousy at my mother's affection. "I'm pretty sure it was hell." I stand. "I'm going after her."

Russet's gray eyes meet mine. "Don't let her fly away. We still need her."

"I make no promises," I call over my shoulder.

AZURE

I lean against Lady Bug, taking large gulps of summer evening air to combat the tightness in my chest. Betrayal burns through me. Of course Cerulean's in league with Russet. They'll team up together and force me to stay here. I'm married to the enemy.

A sleek black BMW with pink accents pulls up. A girl with long black hot-iron-curled hair, dark pink wings, bronze strips, and no match design steps out. She wears hot pink heels and a tight open-backed black dress that ends just above her knees. She has the beauty of an Instagram model with smoky eyes and plum lips. She probably makes tutorials for other Wingai.

She tugs her dress down with a shimmy, then closes her door. Her vibrant green eyes lock on mine. "Who are you?" She has a rasp in her voice, one I know Bree would die for.

"Guys go crazy for that sultry voice," Bree told me once. "I sound like a chain-smoker when I try it."

"Azure," I say. "You?"

"Magenta." Ah. The woman Jade mentioned earlier. Her eyes peruse me with a critical gaze. "Something wrong with your wings?"

I take offense at the judgment in her tone. "They're perfect, thank you."

"You must be from Mountain Hollow. What are you doing here?" She acts like she owns the place.

Great. A prima donna cheerleader. So not my type. "Business."

"With your match?" she asks.

"He's inside." I wave casually in the direction of the house.

The door opens, and Cerulean steps out, his wings still retracted from my rebuff. He trots down the stairs.

Magenta's focus shifts. Her wings flutter with excitement. She launches herself at him. "Ceril!" She plants a kiss on his cheek, leaving a plum lip stain. "You didn't text me at all. I missed you, baby." She pouts, batting her long eyelashes. Extensions probably.

"Magenta." Cerulean's eyes lock with mine over her head. I read blatant fear.

She fists his shirt, her eyes rolling. "Please tell me you'll stop going on these foolish match quests and stay here with me."

"Magenta." His voice hardens. He tries to pull her off, but she burrows closer like a tick.

"What? Ceril, it's insulting." She speaks with forceful condescension. "I'm basically your girlfriend. You love me."

I give the two of them an assessing stare, earning a glare from Magenta and terror from Cerulean. "Girlfriend, huh?" I kick off Lady Bug and stroll to the house.

Cerulean curses and tries to get Magenta off him, but she won't budge. Simultaneously, Magenta asks, "What's it to you?"

I stop at the bottom of the stairs and turn around to face her. I force a smile. "Absolutely nothing. Have a nice life with the jerk."

Magenta rounds on him. "Ceril, what did you do? Why is she calling you names?"

I stride up the stairs and into the house to get my keys, ignoring Cerulean shouting my name. I don't want to leave without Lady Bug. This whole thing has been nothing but a mistake. I run into Emerald and Russet at the bottom of the stairs on my way out, stuff in hand.

"I'm done," I tell them, my tone harsh. "I'll fix the matchless problem, then I'm out of here. If Cerulean's on death's door again, send him my way. Other than that or the recognition thing, don't contact me again."

They follow me as I walk toward the front door.

"Azure, you're meant to be here," Russet argues. "You can't ignore destiny."

"Watch me." I throw open the door.

Magenta shrieks unintelligibly at Cerulean while he shoves her into her car. I head to mine.

Cerulean sprints over to me, blocking my path to Lady Bug. "Azure, it's not what you think, I swear."

"Oh really?" I arch a brow, noting the purple smears on his face. "Then why are there more lipstick kisses on your face? You two deserve each other."

Russet snorts. "Leave it to the Golds to mess everything up. So typical."

I try to sidestep Cerulean, but Russet grabs hold of my arm. I drop my bag. "We're not finished."

"Ceril, what is the meaning of this?" Emerald demands, clearly outraged.

"Magenta attacked me!" he cries. "I came out to talk to Azure, and Magenta threw herself at me, whining about match quests and calling herself my girlfriend. That's when Azure went inside."

I don't want to listen anymore. I try to pull free from Russet, but he tightens his grip.

"I pushed Magenta off and told her to stop, but she wouldn't take no for answer. When I finally got through to her, she slapped me." He reaches up to touch his reddened cheek.

"Serves him right," I mutter, causing Russet to chuckle.

Cerulean also hears me. "Azure, I swear nothing is going on between us. She was trying to take the bull by the horns and force something that would never happen. Your wings choose your match for you, not your head or your heart. Even if I liked Magenta romantically, which I don't, I couldn't make her mine."

"She said you love her," I accuse. Loving is a far cry beyond liking.

Cerulean runs a hand through his hair. "I won't lie. There was a time when I enjoyed Magenta's attention, but I never acted on those feelings. I never sought to hold her hand or kiss her or anything. I stopped considering her the second I stood in front of her with my newly activated tracking sense and felt absolutely nothing. My wings didn't want her. I told her to give up on me—multiple times—but she keeps coming back. I promise I'm not encouraging her." He turns to his father. "Dad, you've got to do something about this. Magenta's gone too far this time."

Emerald nods, a hard glint in his eye. "Magenta knows the rules. I'll be speaking to her and her father." He pulls a handkerchief out of his pocket and hands it to Cerulean.

With a muttered thanks, he rubs it furiously over his face, wiping off the makeup.

"There now. It's all a misunderstanding." Russet smiles at me.

I don't trust him. This story is another ploy against me.

Cerulean reads as much in me. He shoves the handkerchief into his pocket. "Azure, please, I would never jeopardize my match."

"I can't take your word for it. I barely know you," I say.

Emerald speaks to me. "It's against the rules for young Wingai to date. We don't want them falling in love with someone who isn't their match. Those who break this law are swiftly punished." He puts his hand on Cerulean. "Ceril is Tipped and therefore considered a hot commodity. Every girl close to his age has wished to be his, Magenta more than most. This does not mean Ceril returns that affection. You can't blame him for the actions of someone else."

"No, I can't," I agree. Of course Cerulean would garner interest. He's attractive and set to be a leader. My eyes dart to him. "But you have consistently tricked me. You tell me how much you want a relationship while leading me to the lion's den."

He grips his forehead, his fingers digging into his hair. "You're right. I'm sorry. But it's only about the Lead stuff. Not Magenta. My feathers are getting pulled in two different directions trying to save the fate of all Wingai and have a relationship with you. I thought I could do both, but it's becoming clear I can't." He takes a step forward, his sea-green eyes earnest on mine. "My loyalty should always be to you first. It's how matches work. But Tipped don't have that luxury. Our entire world rests on our wings. It's not an easy burden to give up or bear."

"Don't you think that's why I keep saying no?" I say. "I know burden and stress. I've spent my whole life dealing with crap nobody should have to. The last thing I want to do is add a truckload of it back on by being Lead. I've got enough anxiety over this match business as it is."

Cerulean doesn't skip a beat. "Then show me how to alleviate that. Show me how to be your support—how to love you the way you need."

I rear my head back, caught off guard. "Love the way I need?"

Cerulean smiles. "Yeah."

No one's ever asked me that before. Mom treated affection like the plague. The only times she ever hugged me was for show in front of someone else or when she was having one of her episodes and thought I was going to leave her. Even then, her hugs were always too tight—possessive. Josephina treated me with the warmth and care ingrained in her. She never asked whether I wanted it; she just gave it. My friends show their devotion through actions, like Bree letting me stay over and making sure she's stored my favorite ice cream in the freezer, or like Jack and Ben helping with the security system. Over time, I grew to appreciate and reciprocate the affection Josephina and my friends provided, but it didn't come easy. Mom didn't raise me to love or be loved by others. Staring at Cerulean, I'm at a loss on how to answer.

My inability to respond seems to speak volumes. Emerald rubs his forehead, his expression grieved. Russet drops his grip on me and steps back. His wings flare, and his hands shift into talons.

Cerulean takes my hands in his. "When you figure it out, let me know. I want things to be easy between us." He squeezes lightly, then lets go.

187

"Me too." His consideration touches me and sends my emotions spiraling into uncharted territory. I feel this desperation to know my needs and this anger that I was so deprived of love that I struggle to connect to it. How are we going to work if I can't even make sense of what love is to me?

CHAPTER SIXTEEN

CERIL

My wings release at the conflict I feel from Azure. It takes constant mental effort not to wrap them around her. Asking how to love her stopped me cold when she reacted to my question like love was a foreign subject. It kills me to suspect she hasn't had enough of it.

Russet flexes his talons as if ready to slash something or someone to ribbons. Dad has a faraway look in his eyes, distress heavy in his stance. I rub my chest at the swirl of emotions Azure emanates. I don't think anybody is in the right mind frame to continue this conversation.

"Why don't we take a break?" I suggest. "It's been a long day for me." I look at Azure. "Probably for you too."

"Yes," she says.

"Then let's continue our discussion after we've rested," I say.

"That's a good idea," Dad agrees. His wings drop as if relieved.

Russet retracts his talons. "Fine. Take the night, but that's it. Mountain Hollow can't afford to waste any more time without a Lead."

Azure's attention snaps to him. "I don't want to be Lead."

Russet sweeps his arm out. "Then go tell every Wingai in Mountain Hollow that you'd rather they continue to face extinction."

She glares. "They won't go extinct. I said I'd fix the matchless problem."

"Then you'll take off into the human realm, where you could get into all kinds of trouble, thus returning us to the same fate," Russet counters. "We need you here where it's safer."

She crosses her arms. "I'm not your property. I'm fully capable of protecting myself."

Russet raises an eyebrow. "Those talon slashes you carry suggest otherwise. I think your mother won far more often than you."

I stifle a gasp as Azure's raw pain barrels through my chest. She flinches as though Russet slapped her.

Feathers. Lifting my hands, I step between them. "I think enough's been said for the night. Azure, would you like to go to my nest? I'd love to show you around."

She smiles, but I can tell it's forced based on what I'm feeling from her. "That sounds nice."

"Awesome." I pick up her bag, then reach for her hand. I tip my head at Russet and Dad. "Good night."

"Night," Dad says.

Russet calls out to us on our way to her bug. "If you think about flying out of here in the night, I'll tell everyone in Mountain Hollow that Soaring Heights is holding our Lead captive. It will be war."

Dad curses, stress and panic on his face. Azure's anger mixes with my annoyance. I look over my shoulder. Russet stands with his feathers taut, fierce determination etched in every fiber of his being.

"We'll see you tomorrow," I say.

I help Azure into the passenger seat, then hop into the driver's. "Keys?"

She digs in her purse and hands them over. I start the bug and take off. My house is on the other side of Soaring Heights. I'm grateful for the distance.

"Thanks for getting me out of there," Azure says a few minutes into the drive.

"No problem." I look over and smile. She stares ahead, expression pinched, rubbing her wrists over her scars. It breaks my heart. "Do they hurt?"

"Huh? Oh." She looks down at her hands. "Not so much anymore. I guess it's turned into a habit." She shrugs.

It's a good thing I know Soaring Heights so well, because I'm paying more attention to her than I am to where we're going. "I'm glad they're not causing you pain."

Azure smiles bitterly. "No, not in the physical sense." She takes a breath. A nervous energy swirls around her. "I think you know well enough now that there are dark parts of me—my history. I've worked really hard to put the past behind me, but I still struggle with some things. Josephina—" she stops abruptly. My heart sears with her grief. She clears her throat. My chest eases as she pushes the emotion back. "Josephina helped a lot."

"I'm glad you had her," I say, parking in front of my house. The sun has nearly set, casting everything in a twilight glow. "Welcome to my nest."

Azure throws a hand over her mouth, stifling a gasp at my mansion of gray stone, dark-blue siding, and white trim. "It's . . . wow." The front boasts a green lawn, manicured flower beds bursting with dahlias, and a stone fountain depicting birds shooting water out of their mouths into a birdbath.

I unbuckle. "Come on, I'll take you for a tour." I grab her bag and lead her to the wraparound porch. We stop in front of the white double doors while I fiddle with my keys. I shove the right one into the lock, then push the door open. "I'm a huge fan of open concept, so this first level is super exposed."

The house is cool with a lingering new-paint smell. I need to buy some air fresheners. The kitchen, dining, and living areas reside in one big space, separated by furniture expertly placed by Scarlett. Huge windows take up the back wall, allowing a view into the backyard from the front door. I decorated everything in shades of blue, wood, and white.

"It's gorgeous," Azure whispers. "Like something you'd see in a magazine."

"Thank Scarlett. She's got an eye for design." I set her bag on a couch and take her farther into the house. I stop at a glass door. "This is my office. It's basically a big glass case. Jade calls it a fishbowl because you can see everything inside. I don't like feeling closed off. I want to be able to see my family while I'm working." I've always craved a deep connection with my match. Not being able to see her while I worked would kill me.

"It's nice," Azure says good-naturedly.

"Upstairs or down next?" I ask.

"Down," she says.

I have one main staircase with stairs leading up and down. Downstairs houses a few bedrooms and bathrooms, a laundry room, a game room, a small kitchen, a movie theater, and a gym.

After we explore everything, I take her upstairs. "A few more bedrooms and bathrooms. Down at the end of the hall is a small library and homework station. I put lots of windows in there so it doesn't feel stuffy."

"It's very airy. I like it." Azure smiles.

"I have two laundry rooms, one in the basement and one up here. And last is the master." I stop in front of the white double doors. "This is my favorite room in the whole house."

Azure takes the initiative and turns the knob. A king-size bed takes up the back wall with two nightstands. A large skylight above the bed allows a person to watch the sky. The left of the room leads to a small nursery, two walk-in closets, and a bathroom with a shower, a Roman jetted tub, double sinks, and lots of cabinetry. The right wall is almost entirely made up of windows. A glass door leads to a balcony with a spiral staircase giving access to the backyard. Near the front of the room, two comfy blue chairs reside near a fireplace, and above the fireplace rests a flat-screen TV.

"You like it?" I ask.

Azure bobs her head. I can feel her pleasure. "It's wonderful." *Yes!* I grin. "This house must have cost you millions to build."

I shrug. "My Dad's consulting company has treated us well. He's a bit of a genius solving business problems. Also, as the next Lead, I require the space and the statement this house provides. Jade's and Scarlett's nests aren't nearly as big."

"A Lead has to look the part," she murmurs.

"Exactly," I agree. Moving closer, I reach for her hands. She lets me take them. I look down into her dark-blue eyes. "Azure, I want this room to be ours. I won't stay in here until you're comfortable enough to sleep in the same bed with me." She stiffens. I clarify. "Just sleep. We're not going any further until our feelings for each other are more solid. Call me sentimental, but I want this room to mean something."

I feel her relax. "All right."

I close up the house and take her to the backyard, where there is a stone patio, a built-in grill and sink, and a firepit to roast marshmallows. I fenced in a large grassy area and left it empty. "To play games." I smile.

Hand in hand, we walk on a small garden path through the evergreen trees to a bubbling creek with a small gazebo beside it. My heart soars that she's letting me thread my fingers through hers. "A place to think," I say.

Azure smiles at me. "It's nice."

"I'm so glad you think so." I take a breath, surveying the land for any changes and thankfully not seeing any. "That's everything, unless you want to see the garage. I bet I could find a perfect spot for Lady Bug." I wink at her.

She laughs. "I bet you could."

I take her back inside. "You hungry? I could order a pizza. We could watch a movie or something." I try to think of something innocuous that'll help her relax. The last thing I want to do is set her off.

Azure tucks a stray hair behind her ear. "That sounds good."

"What kind do you like?" I ask, pulling out my phone.

"Pepperoni's fine," she says while she runs her fingers over the marble countertops.

I call the pizza place on Main and put in an order. While we wait, I take Azure's bag up to a room of her choosing. All of the bedrooms are set up identically with queen-size beds, white or blue covers, and white furniture: a desk, nightstands, and a dresser. The walls are bare. I always figured my match could add the finishing touches.

I set her bag on the bed, then reach for Azure. I gently place my hands on her upper arms. She tilts her face up to meet my eyes, thankfully not pulling away. "It's just us here."

"I'm aware," she says, the corners of her lips curving up.

"Will you let your wings out?" I plead. "They're so gorgeous. I miss them terribly."

Azure chuckles. "All right." She steps back and pulls her hair down, letting it fall down her back. Then she takes off her shirt, revealing a white tank top underneath.

My breath catches in my throat as she reveals her cobalt-blue wings. "Feathers." Our wings reach out to each other. Stuck under their pull, I grab Azure's waist as we collide. Her hands grip my arms. Energy shoots into my wings straight to my pulsing heart.

Feeling bold, I pull her flush against me. I wrap my arms around her waist. She rests her head on my chest. She fits perfectly. I'm grateful she's allowing me this chance to hold her when I suspect it isn't easy for her. Feeling her pain today made me want nothing more than to soothe her. I want to be that person she can lean on. Tentatively, I reach out, wanting her to know my thoughts and feelings.

Azure tenses with fear as a link opens between us. She wants to pull away. *"Please, I just want you to listen. I'm not asking for anything in return,"* I tell her through our connection.

Azure relents. I sense some curiosity for what I have to express.

I start with my gratitude that we sealed the match and my excitement. *"I'm looking forward to creating a connection with you."* I share my desire to prove myself worthy to deserve her. *"For the longest time, I felt like I wasn't good enough—that somehow in my preparations, fate decided I was unworthy to have a match."* I let her feel my rising confidence since finding her, but I express my frustration that I keep messing things up. *"I'm trying to be my own man, but it's hard with Russet and Dad yanking on my feathers."* Last, I let her feel my respect. *"I admire your strength. You carry yourself so well. You have support in me, a friend, and I hope eventually a lover."*

The doorbell rings. I tuck my wings closer to my back, breaking the connection. "That's our pizza." I wait until I know Azure is steady on her feet before I let go and head downstairs and open the door.

Sugar holds a box, her white wings fluttering in the breeze. "Hey, Ceril."

"Hi, Sugar." I hand her a twenty. "Keep the change."

She takes it and gives me the box. "Word's flying around that you found your match. Is it true?"

I smile brightly. "Yes. I've just sealed it today. Now if you'll excuse me, I don't want to serve her cold pizza."

"Of course, yes!" Sugar exclaims. "I'm so happy for you, Ceril. Can't wait for the official announcement." She jumps into the sky and zooms off.

I grab two bottles of water from the fridge and take the pizza down to the movie room with Azure. I haven't stocked the shelves with movies yet, so we rent one from the internet. Azure picks an action movie, jam-packed with blazing guns and karate. With her temperament, I'm not surprised.

I feel like the richest man in the world when Azure allows me to wrap my arms and wings around her during the second half of the movie. My gamble of expressing some of my thoughts and feelings has paid off. I appreciate the effort she's putting in to be less resistant. It makes me want to work harder to keep earning her trust and make sure she knows this chance she's taking on me isn't misplaced.

By the time the credits roll, Azure has fallen asleep on me. I watch her for a moment, seeing no worry lines in her expression. At peace, she's breathtaking. My gaze falls upon her parted mouth. Feathers, I want to kiss her again. Tamping down the urge, my own tiredness sets in. I fall asleep breathing in the scent of her coconut shampoo.

AZURE

I wake lying half on top of Cerulean on the couch. My head rests on his chest over his heart, my arm wrapped around his torso, snuggling him like a teddy bear. His arms and wings hold me against him. Warmth spreads from head to toe. I've never felt this comfortable with someone ever, especially a man. I wonder if it's the power of our match making me feel this way or if it's truly me. Whatever the case, I'm loath to leave.

Cerulean tightens his grip. "Then don't," he whispers.

Without conscious thought, my senses delve into him. His heart beats fast under my cheek. Adrenaline heats his body. He's wide awake and . . .

"You're high," I say. It's the only explanation I can come up with for how deliriously happy he is.

Cerulean laughs. "On you, yes."

I think his joy is misplaced. I've been fighting him left and right, resisting him and the Wingai culture. I still don't want to be Lead. Falling asleep on him and cuddling doesn't erase my overall objection of this place. I'd still rather be home.

"This is your home now too," Cerulean says.

Shivering from the lack of privacy, I climb off him and sit up. "No peeking inside my head." I retract my wings.

"Sorry. You were thinking so loud, I think it just kind of turned on. I didn't deliberately do it," he says.

Oh. "I guess I better watch myself better, then."

"If that will make you feel better," he answers. "Just know I believe you're allowed to think what you want and be your own person. I'm not trying to judge you, just get to know you."

"Thanks." Unexpected warmth touches my heart. He's doing a good job of catching me off guard.

I glance at my phone. It's almost noon. We slept the morning away. I help Cerulean clean up the remnants of our movie night. Then I find my room and take a shower, wanting to get the old pizza smell off me. When I come back downstairs, I find him leaning on the kitchen island, his eyes glued to his phone.

He smiles at me as I join him. He's showered too and is wearing a formfitting gray T-shirt and dark jeans. I breathe in the strong scent of his mint soap. He extends a feather to mesh with mine. "I'm so glad you left these out."

I chuckle. "You just want me for my wings."

He laughs with me. "You caught me." The doorbell rings. "That'll be Dad. He's bringing some groceries." Cerulean moves to answer the door.

I follow. "Is this in an effort to keep me here?"

"Probably," Cerulean says.

MATCHING FEATHERS

"It won't work," I answer. "As soon as I help the matchless and get Russet to give up on my being Lead, I'm going home."

Cerulean turns to look me in the eyes, his hand resting on the doorknob. "Azure, I've never seen Russet more determined in his life. I don't think he'll ever give up on trying to make you Lead."

I lift my chin, showing my own resolve. "We'll see about that."

Cerulean opens the door. "Hey, Dad. Come on in."

"Thank you." Emerald walks in carrying two bags. Cerulean takes them and sets them on the kitchen island. I help him unload, putting the cold stuff in the fridge. Cerulean puts the rest in a closet pantry.

Emerald's eyes rest on my openly displayed wings. I'm tempted to retract them, but Cerulean wraps an arm around me. "Gorgeous, aren't they?" he says with pride.

"Yes," Emerald agrees with enthusiasm. "The gold and silver complement the dark blue nicely. You two make an attractive match."

"Thank you," we say.

Emerald nods. "Russet has asked that we meet him again"—he glances at the clock—"in about ten minutes. I wondered if you both would be up for a drive?"

Cerulean and Emerald look to me for a response. "I'll go, but my answers won't change," I say, seeing this as an opportunity to shut Russet down again—hopefully for good.

Emerald's eyes narrow in displeasure, but he puts on a reassuring smile. "All right. Shall we go?" He gestures to the door.

Cerulean hands me a granola bar. "Breakfast, since we missed it."

We get in the back of Emerald's truck. A minute into the drive, Cerulean asks, "Where are we meeting Russet?"

"Here, in Soaring Heights," Emerald says.

Emerald turns right onto a bumpy dirt road, forest lining both sides. A mile or so in, the trees thin, and we stop as the path ends at a grassy field. I see hundreds of Wingai, men, women, and children, standing in two groups and poised for battle. An imaginary trench separates them. Russet stands in the middle of the two groups with his arms crossed, wings taut. He looks triumphant.

"Dad, what is this?" Cerulean cries, gesturing to the field.

Emerald turns around in his seat. "Your match announcement."

"Are you kidding me?" Anger coats every word coming out of Cerulean's mouth.

"No. Ceril, they deserve to know. Now come on." Emerald opens his door and steps out.

"If he thinks I'm going out there, he's got another thing coming," I tell Cerulean.

"What choice do we have?" Cerulean asks. "One word from Russet and we'll have a bloodbath right here. Look at the Wingai from Mountain Hollow. They're ready to fight."

"So is Soaring Heights," I say, gesturing to his side with a tilt of my head.

Cerulean curses. "You're right."

"You know what, this is fine," I say, gathering courage. "This gives me the perfect opportunity to tell them all to screw themselves." Cerulean's eyes widen. I unbuckle my seat belt, open the door, and jump out.

"Azure, wait!" Cerulean scrambles after me.

I leave my wings out as I march to Russet and Emerald. I want a better chance of escape when I'm through. Cerulean catches up with me and takes my hand in his. Gasps and chatter erupt on both sides.

"Silver-Tipped!"

"Look at their match design!"

"It's Amethyst reincarnated."

"Gold and Silver together? This is impossible!"

Russet grins like a hawk rising from the ground with prey. Turning to the people of Mountain Hollow, he lifts his hands and says, "Mountain Hollow will have a Lead once more in Azure, daughter of Fire and Amethyst."

Emerald addresses the Wingai of Soaring Heights. He sweeps his hand out, gesturing to Cerulean and me. "Ceril has found his match in Azure, soon to be Lead of Mountain Hollow. I would like to formally congratulate them on the sealing of their match, performed yesterday."

"To a Silver!" a man from the Soaring Heights side shouts. The Wingai beside him grumble along, eyeing me with distaste. Their hate fuels my fire to leave.

"Where has she been all this time?" a woman from Mountain Hollow asks. "Where is Amethyst?"

"Amethyst died in a car crash," Russet says bluntly. "She lied about her pregnancy and hid Azure from us in the human realm." A collective "oh" sounds from their side. "We are blessed to have discovered her."

"But she's matched to a Gold!" a man from Mountain Hollow points out.

A slew of grousing starts on both sides. "I don't want a Gold influencing Mountain Hollow!"

"We don't want a Silver dirtying Soaring Heights!"

"The match is wrong!" both sides wail.

"That's it." I can't stand another minute of this. Pulling my hand free from Cerulean, I flap my wings and rise. Eyes from both sides rest on me as I hover just above their heads. Silence reigns. Apparently I'm interesting enough to be heard. "It's been made clear to me that matches can't be chosen, so quit crying about what can't be changed. This animosity you have toward each other is stupid—"

"Stupid?" a woman from Mountain Hollow screeches. "The Gold killed our Lead! It's their fault we've lived in despair with matchless children for almost twenty years!"

"We did not!" practically the entire host of Soaring Heights yells.

I raise my hands as another shouting match ensues. "Hey! I wasn't finished!" Again the people quiet down. I clear my throat. "I understand my father's death and my mother's actions created a matchless problem in Mountain Hollow. However, you have me now to fix it, so the resentment for being matchless can stop." I take a breath. "Also, for blaming Soaring Heights for killing my father. As his daughter, I believe I have more of a right to speak on this matter than you, and I think you have it wrong." I turn slightly to face the Soaring Heights people. "I don't hold Soaring Heights accountable. They didn't invite the human in, or make the explosives."

Another Mountain Hollow resident starts in. "But Lead Emerald—"

I hold up a hand. "No. I'm stopping you right there. Lead Emerald took on the crazed human first, and my father stepped in to help. They were working *together* when the situation changed. Once that detonation button had been pressed, I don't think Emerald's 'please' changed anything for my father." I speak as clearly as I can. "*Fire* decided that the needs of many outweighed himself. He *chose* to sacrifice his life. You can't put that on anybody else."

I read relief in some of the Soaring Heights faces. Emerald smiles at me with obvious gratitude. Even Russet is staring at me with something akin to respect. I continue. "This hostility you've built up over the last nineteen years for my father's choice disgusts me. How dare you use his life to start petty wars among yourselves. You've insulted me and my father's legacy to the highest degree." I add salt to the injury. "I see self-serving bigots squabbling like children."

I ignore the harsh gasps coming from both sides. For the moment, they've combined their anger and shine it on me. "One last thing." I raise a finger. "I'm not staying in Soaring Heights or Mountain Hollow any longer than necessary. I will fix your matchless problem, then perhaps make monthly visits for new children. I refuse to be Lead."

I drop to the ground. Cerulean pulls my back into his chest, and his hands rest on my waist. Russet's hands are balled into fists. His glare could cut through steel. Emerald's thankful smile has turned into a pinched frown. They were wrong if they thought gathering the Wingai together would change my mind.

Mountain Hollow goes up in arms, shouting at each other, Russet, me, Ceril, Emerald, Soaring Heights. The field is a cacophony of flapping wings, raised voices, and confused wailing children. Blame is thrown all over the place.

"She can't abandon us!"

"Our new Lead is damaged!"

"Her Gold match is brainwashing our Lead. They want to take over Mountain Hollow!"

"What about our future children? We need her here!"

It takes about a second before Soaring Heights starts shouting as well.

"The Silver Lead will take Ceril from us. We will become matchless like Mountain Hollow!"

"She's bewitching Ceril into thinking matches don't matter! Soaring Heights will be ruined!"

Magenta steps forward and faces Soaring Heights. Her voice carries to both sides. "Ceril won't go anywhere. He's in love with me."

"Cheater!" rings across the field.

Cerulean curses. Letting go of me, he strides over to Magenta. He speaks harshly. "I don't love you, Magenta. I have not nor will I ever be yours. Quit trying to ruin my match with lies."

A man who I assume is Magenta's father based on the similar hair and facial structure grabs her by the arm. I take note of his white wings, purple match design, and bronze tips. Soaring Heights Second. No wonder Magenta thought she had claim on Cerulean. She probably grew up right alongside him as their fathers worked together. "You're embarrassing us. This is not acceptable behavior."

Magenta insists. "But it's true. I know Ceril loves me. I should be his match, not a dirty Silver."

"Magenta!" her father hisses.

"We were friends, Magenta. Not lovers," Cerulean says forcefully. "I would never betray my match."

The damage has been done, despite Cerulean's dispute. I see questions and distrust forming on faces. They've probably come to the same conclusion I did. Just how much time had Cerulean spent with Magenta while their fathers conferred?

CHAPTER SEVENTEEN

CERIL

I block out the chatter and insults being thrown across the field from Mountain Hollow and Soaring Heights. Anger radiates from the top of my head, down to my toes, and to the tips of my feathers. How many feather-freaking times do I have to tell Magenta we are nothing? Now she's made me out to be a cheater in front of Soaring Heights and Mountain Hollow. I am so done with her. Thank feathers she didn't inherit her dad's bronze tips.

Diamond tries to pull Magenta away, but she resists. "Your match doesn't love you. Look at her. She hates Wingai." Magenta gestures to Azure, who stares at us with a cool mask, her arms folded across her chest. Her suspicion and unhappiness pulses through my heart. "Leave her in Mountain Hollow with the rest of the dirty Silvers. Your heart is mine already. Love me as your match."

Diamond's eyes widen in surprise and fury at the words spewing out of his daughter's mouth.

I shut her down. "Azure is my perfect match, and I will love and cherish her regardless of what she gives me in return. I don't appreciate your telling people we're an item when we're not, nor has it ever been true." Magenta starts to retort, but I cut her off. "One more lie out of your mouth about us, Magenta, and I will have you thrown out of Soaring Heights for good."

Diamond rounds on his daughter. "I want the truth, Magenta. Has Ceril made any advancements to you? Has he tried to kiss you?"

Magenta's lower lip sticks out. I read the anger and hurt in her bottle-green eyes. I sense she wants to lash out at me for rejecting her. I tense, expecting another lie.

"Magenta," Diamond's voice is glacier ice, his grip on her upper arm tight.

She glances at her father with a flash of guilt. "No."

I let out a breath of relief.

"But he belongs with me," Magenta insists. "We've been planning it for years."

Diamond clenches his jaw. "Have I taught you nothing? You don't choose your match with your head or your heart. Your wings make that decision."

"But Mom—" Magenta starts.

Diamond interrupts. "Enough, Magenta. We will speak about this at home." He turns to me. "I'm sorry, Ceril." He drags his daughter back into the crowd.

Russet is chewing Azure out when I return to her side. "Are you happy with yourself? Look at the sheer panic you've caused. Why can't you take your place as you're meant to?"

Azure's dark-blue eyes flash. "You forced my hand by gathering everyone. I've told you a thousand times, I won't involve myself here any more than necessary."

"You can't run from this," Russet counters. "Mountain Hollow will not be your downfall. We're here to support you." He tilts his head in my direction. "Your match is who you need to watch out for. He has the power to turn you into your mother."

I jump in, not wanting to see where this is headed. "Because we're all gathered together, how about Azure start fixing the matchless problem? I think that will go a long way in restoring relations between our people. We'll be equal again."

Dad latches on. "That's a great idea."

Azure nods. "Fine."

Russet jumps into the sky, facing the Mountain Hollow people. He holds out his hands. "Calm yourselves," he tells the wailing, grumbling Wingai.

Dad motions for Soaring Heights to be silent. It takes a few moments, but eventually both sides quiet.

Russet speaks. "Do not fret so much over Azure's refusal to be Lead. She has been abandoned in the human realm for far too long. Our ways are new and scary to her. She thinks refusing us is protecting herself, and that's simply not true. I am doing everything in my power to help her become one of us, but I'm going to need your assistance as well. Be kind. Make her feel welcome among us. Show her there's nothing to fear."

A change of understanding and resolve comes over most of the people of Mountain Hollow as they digest Russet's words. I'm slightly amazed at the trust they hold for him.

Dad says to Soaring Heights, "The same goes for us. We must support Ceril as he helps his match adjust. This is not the time to be high-winged."

Azure's eyebrows furrow. Her hands rub her scars, and her wings are tucked in close. I get the sense she's not sure how to fight Russet's new tactic. I reach over and take her hand in mine. My wings brush against hers as I offer her my comfort. Surprisingly, she takes it. Excitement blooms in my chest. Azure gives me a brief smile. One day I'll get through to her and lay claim to her heart.

"Since we're gathered, Azure would like to start recognizing the matchless. I think it would be prudent if we go from oldest to youngest." Russet drops to the ground.

Mountain Hollow pushes their children forward. Azure joins Russet.

Dad puts his hand on my shoulder. "Recognizing takes a lot of power out of our wings. Azure will not be able to do as many without you. She may be sick afterward. Keep your touch on her."

I'd recognized a few Wingai over the last year as part of my training to be Lead. Though it was rather quick, it sapped my energy. "Of course."

"Good." Dad pats my shoulder. "I'm going to send our people home."

AZURE

Cerulean takes my hand while Russet explains the recognizing process. I'm grateful for the contact because I'm starting to feel nervous. "Your wings will sense what needs to be done as soon as they touch another. You'll feel an adrenaline high as your energy transfers into them. As soon as they gain their recognition, their wings will automatically pull away from yours. From there, you move on to the next person."

"So all I have to do is touch their wings with mine?" I ask.

Russet nods. "No conscious thought involved. Your wings will automatically start the process. It's simple but extremely tiring. Ceril's touch will help, but we're going to have to do this in stages to get through everyone."

I don't like the sound of that. I want to get this done and fly out of here. "Am I going to be able to recognize everyone today if I rest in between?"

Russet shakes his head. "With Ceril's help, you might make it to twenty-five before you pass out."

My shoulders drop. Lovely. "How many matchless does Mountain Hollow have?"

"Two hundred and thirty-eight now," Russet replies. "A baby girl was born three days ago."

Great, he'll get to push his agenda longer. Guess there's nothing to be done about it. I promised I'd do this. "Okay. Let's do it." I shake out my feathers, gearing myself up.

Cerulean meshes his wing with mine. A low hum of adrenaline warms me.

Russet says to him, "It's possible your soothing will quit with how much energy you're going to need to give her to get through the first batch."

He nods. Russet motions for the first Wingai to step forward.

A blonde guy with bright-blue wings approaches. The crowd behind him claps and cheers. Grinning ear to ear, he turns and waves. Coming to a stop before me, his pale-blue eyes openly peruse me. "I'm Aqua. I'm excited to meet you. How hard is it to live in the human world?"

I shrug. "It's easy if you have good control of your wings and talons."

"What's your record?" he asks.

"For longest contained?"

He smiles. "We host a yearly competition to see who can go the longest. My record is one month six days. Last year's winner made it three months before she couldn't stand it anymore. It was really impressive. So what about you?"

"I'd tell you, but you'll think I'm boasting," I say. Especially if they have a competition for it.

Aqua holds his hands up. "I won't, I swear. You lived among humans. You had to have kept them hidden a lot."

I lived with a mother who couldn't stand the sight of them most of the time. I allow a memory to resurface.

I sat at the kitchen table, circling fruit names in the word search book Josephina brought me for my fourteenth birthday. Mom walked in carrying medical gauze and tape. "Did you hurt yourself?" I asked her.

"No, this is for you," she said, setting her supplies on the table. "Your wings are hurting me. You're going to get them out of my sight, and I'm going to tape up the ridges so they can't escape."

Quick as lightning, I retracted my wings. Fear curled low in my belly. "You don't need to. I can keep them contained."

"I don't want any accidents." Her hands shifted into talons. "Remove your shirt."

I blink away the images, forcing myself back to the present. Aqua stares at me intently. It takes me a second to realize he's waiting on an answer. "Six months."

He jerks in surprise. "Six months?"

I read subtle horror on Russet, Emerald, and Cerulean.

Mom would take off the bindings for me to shower, then put them back on. As the months continued, my discomfort had slowly risen to unimaginable pain. I had too much energy built up with nowhere to go. The night after my fifteenth birthday, I snuck out of the house. First, I waited for mom to go into her room to sleep. When she did, I sat outside of her door for what felt like hours, listening for her breath to even out. After, I ran as far as my legs could take me into the woods. Reaching behind my back, I pulled off as many of the bandages as I could. I screamed in agony when my wings shot out of their confines. The next morning when Mom saw they were out, she chided me for having limp, crushed feathers. Her focus had finally shifted to be hurt about something else, and I was allowed to have them out again.

"It wasn't my first choice. I don't recommend it." Eager to get away from this topic, I focus on the task at hand. "You ready to try out this recognizing thing?"

Aqua's face lights up. "Absolutely."

We extend our wings to meet. I tense as energy, like an adrenaline high, propels out of me and into him. About thirty seconds later, the power flow stops, and he disengages. Fatigue sets in immediately. I lean on Cerulean, taking a moment to catch my breath. Russet wasn't kidding about the exhaustion thing.

Grinning with pride, Russet claps Aqua on the shoulder in a congratulatory manner. "Do you feel anything yet?" Aqua shakes his head. "Then your match must be a Silver also. You should be able to find her as soon as she's recognized."

Aqua beams, his blue eyes shining with desire. It's clear this means the world to him. "Can't wait. Thank you, Azure."

I smile. "Of course." One down, two hundred and thirty-seven to go.

CHAPTER EIGHTEEN

AZURE

I reach twenty-three when my legs buckle. Cerulean catches me as I falter. "Easy there," he murmurs. I take a breath, trying to calm my churning stomach and pounding head. My body and wings quiver. Sweat perspires on my brow. I have to force my eyes to stay open.

"There are only three people left who could match today," Russet tells me. "Can you make it through?"

"Yeah." If these people want it, they shouldn't have to wait on me.

Since the Soaring Heights Wingai returned to their homes, the field has turned into a party for Mountain Hollow as those I recognize find their matches. For the last hour, it's been nothing but dancing, hugs, and cheers. Emotions are high. I've lost count of the number of people I've seen with tears in their eyes. I'm now looked at like a savior. Maybe I am, I concede, as I watch a newly discovered couple, a boy with velvet-purple wings and a girl with sunflower-yellow, twirl together in the sky, their lips meeting to seal their match. I'm awestruck at the pureness of their immediate love.

I get through the next person. At this point Cerulean physically holds me up. My wing touching his is limp, and I struggle to extend the other to connect with the next person.

"You're almost done, Azure." Cerulean presses his lips to my temple. I feel his pride and concern for me through our link. He's sending me every bit of energy he has, but I know he's wearing down too.

Last person. A girl with dark red feathers. My wings won't extend anymore. I hold my shaking arm out, clutching onto a fistful of feathers to connect. I feel a surge of adrenaline as the last of my energy transfers into her.

"Thank you, Azure," she says with heartfelt emotion.

"You're welcome." I collapse against Cerulean.

He stumbles as he takes the brunt of my weight. Then his grip around me tightens. "I've got you, gorgeous."

"Ruby!" Aqua sprints to the girl I last recognized. "You're it! We're matches!"

"You're sure?" she asks, her wings fluttering with excitement.

"Yes! My heart just went crazy for you." He laughs as they embrace.

Russet takes my hand and squeezes with gratitude. "You've changed many lives this day. Thank you." I manage a nod. Russet flies into the sky to be seen by all and shouts, "All Silver Wingai who could match today have been recognized."

The field erupts into stadium-sized cheers. I cringe as the cheering adds injury to my raging headache. Mountain Hollow will be celebrating tonight for sure.

Cerulean turns to his father standing quietly with us. "I've got to take Azure home."

"Do you need help getting her to the truck?" Emerald asks.

Cerulean gently lifts me into his arms. "I've got her."

My eyes slide shut. I wake briefly as Cerulean lays me down on the soft bed in the master bedroom and takes off my shoes. He kicks his own off, then joins me. I roll onto my side, and he wraps his wings and arms around me. "Sleep," he whispers, and I do.

I come to snuggled against Cerulean with my cheek on his chest, my palm over his heart, his hand over mine. One of my legs is draped over his. Short of lying completely on top of him, I can't get any closer—a fact I soon realize Cerulean is absolutely thrilled about. Of course he's awake, propped up against some pillows and enjoying every second of this.

I untangle myself and sit up, scrubbing my face with my hands to hide my heated cheeks as I fully wake up. I feel pretty rested, and I don't detect any aches and pains. I know it's because of him—a thought I'm not quite sure how to handle.

I drop my hands. Cerulean grins at me. "Hey."

Unable to help myself, I smile back. "Hey."

"Sleep well?" he asks, grinning.

"I did, thank you." I lift my hands in a stretch, my back arching, wings flaring.

His eyes darken with desire as he takes me in. He pushes himself off the pillows. "Can I kiss you?"

I hesitate for a fraction of a second as my fears try to make themselves known. Swallowing, I shove my insecurities back down. Recognizing all those Wingai and seeing the pure joy and love on their faces changed me. I don't want to be Lead, but I do want him. I want to see whether I'm capable of experiencing the kind of joy and love he offers. "Yes."

Cerulean puts his hand on the back of my neck, tilts his head, and presses his lips to mine. His mouth gently glides over mine. It's not enough. I deepen it. "Feathers," Cerulean mutters against my lips. His hands roam to pull me against him. Warmth dances with the butterflies in my stomach.

Cerulean's phone rings. I break the kiss. "Your phone."

"Voice mail." He goes in for another kiss. I don't resist. His phone dings with the missed call notification before lighting up again. With a groan, Cerulean drags his mouth from mine. He reaches over, snatches his cell from the nightstand, and swipes to answer it. "Russet." His sea-green eyes, bright with mirth, find mine. Russet speaks low enough in the phone that I can't hear what he says to Cerulean. "Yeah, she's awake." He pauses. "She's fine. Nothing sleep couldn't cure." Another pause. "Well, I was in the process of convincing her when you called." He winks at me.

I roll my eyes at him, but heat pools. My resistance around him is starting to crash and burn. The back of my mind registers terror. Could I really be falling for him that quick?

"Hang on, I'll see." Cerulean turns his phone away from his mouth. "Russet wants us to come over. You up for that?"

"As long as he doesn't lock me up," I answer.

"I won't let that happen," Cerulean promises. To Russet he says, "We'll be over in a few." He hangs up.

I climb off the bed. "How long was I out?"

Cerulean glances at the light streaming in through the window. "About a day. It takes a lot of power to recognize so many."

It took only twenty-six people to wipe me out. "And I still have over two hundred to do." I make a mental note to text Bree that I'll see her in the afterlife. This is going to take weeks. I bet Russet loves having me cornered.

"We'll get through it together," he says good-naturedly. "So, my wings have eaten all of my energy. I'm starving." He rubs his stomach. "Are you up for breakfast?"

I laugh. "I'm starving too."

His face lights up. "How about pancakes and bacon?"

"Let's do it."

CERIL

Fern answers the door to Russet's house with a beaming smile. I'm taken aback. Azure arches her eyebrow at me, surprised too. "Come in." She ushers us inside. She flits down the hall and returns a moment later with Russet. He beckons us into his office.

"How are you feeling?" Russet eyes Azure over as he moves to sit behind his desk.

She shrugs as we take our seats. "Fine."

Russet smiles. "Good. I thought we should discuss a schedule for further recognizing."

"I'd like to finish it as fast as possible, please," she says.

"Everyone else you recognize is not of age to find their match. Therefore, I'd like to slow it down to make sure you keep your health up." He rubs his chin. "I was thinking fifteen Wingai every other day."

She shakes her head. "Make it twenty." She glances at me. "With his help I can do it."

I agree. "Yeah, you held up well enough until then."

Russet leans back in his chair. "Fine, but if I see signs of exhaustion after you've rested, we're slowing it down." He pins me with his stare. "Keep a close eye on her. Don't let her tell you she's fine when she isn't."

I meet his stare with one of my own. "I won't. Her health and safety mean everything to me."

Russet smiles approvingly. "Good. We'll start with the next group tomorrow." He casts his full attention on Azure. "Before Ceril discovered you, what did you see yourself doing? You recently graduated from high school. I assume you have a plan in place for the next few years of your life. College? A job?"

She flushes. "To be honest, I planned on traveling to find the Wingai community Mom fled from—this place I guess." She's quick to add, "I wasn't necessarily interested in aligning myself with the community once I found it, but since Mom kept almost everything about our race a secret, I wanted to know what she refused to tell me, so I could take care of myself better."

Feathers. I hate that she was out there on her own, trying to figure things out without help. She's got me now. I'm going to make sure she has everything she needs.

"What did you plan to do after your little quest?" Russet asks, dropping his hands to rest on the desk.

She shrugs. "Stay home, out of sight. I have enough money squirreled away that if I manage it right, I won't need a job. At least for a human life span," she amends.

"That's it?" Russet asks, seeming surprised. "No other ambitions or goals?"

"Protecting my survival has been my first priority for as long as I've been alive. I haven't given much thought to anything else," Azure answers.

Darkness emanating from her rolls across my heart like a creeping fog. I mesh my wings with hers to soothe her anger and mine.

"Understandable considering your previous circumstances," Russet says smoothly, but I can see his hands are clenched, relaying his displeasure at Azure's childhood too. "However, your life has changed. You are, without doubt, *the most* important person to Mountain Hollow—"

"To me and Soaring Heights too," I cut in.

"Yes." Russet nods. "Your safety and well-being are paramount to us. Mountain Hollow and Soaring Heights are well protected. Even more so after what happened to Fire. Now, I know your home in McMinnville means a lot to you. I won't ask you to give it up, but I'd like you to consider making Ceril's nest your primary residence. It would go a long way in helping Mountain Hollow feel safe if we saw you more often. If you need to return to McMinnville for a couple of days or so every month, feel free to do so—no questions asked."

Azure eyes him dubiously. "Really?"

I'm surprised and suspicious too. Russet has been hell-bent on keeping her under his watchful eye. Switching tactics must be costing him.

"Really," he insists. "Just tell me beforehand so I can account for your absence, and call me to let me know you've arrived safely, there and back."

Azure bites her lower lip as she thinks. "I reserve the right to go home whenever I want. I don't want a schedule of which days I can go."

"That's fine as long as you stay here primarily—at least three weeks out of every month," he says. "Is that agreeable?"

Azure sighs. "Yes." She doesn't seem very thrilled about it. I hope with time I can change that. I want her to love Soaring Heights as much as I do.

I press a chaste kiss to her temple. "Thank you. I'll make it fun for you here, promise."

She smiles briefly. "You better."

Russet leans back in his chair, a big smile on his face. "Excellent. Now about being Lead . . ."

"Azure should be eased into it," I tell him with confidence. "I suggest she take some time to get used to Mountain Hollow and Soaring Heights, explore what we have to offer. She should feel like one of us before she takes over. I'm sure you can keep things going while she gets settled and makes some friends."

Azure makes a face, distaste written all over. I get the sense she's thinking of ways to get out of this. I wonder how crafty she can get.

"I suppose I can allow a month of settling in," Russet agrees slowly. She rolls her eyes. He leans back in his leather office chair, his eyes darting between Azure and me. "One last thing. You should start trying for children within the year."

Azure jumps to her feet. "Don't you dare push children onto me too." I cringe as the blast of her outrage hits me. "*If* I want them, I'll do it in my own time."

"Mountain Hollow's and Soaring Height's futures depend on this," he maintains. "We can't afford 'if.'"

She crosses her arms. "I can't think about being a mother. I barely know what a good one looks like."

Russet's gray eyes bore into her. "Your mother's deficiencies don't have to define you in the parent you become. Amethyst was weak, easily consumed by emotion and carelessness. How she became matched to a Lead is beyond me." His expression morphs into disbelief. "Fire balanced her. After his death, she spiraled out of control, and clearly you suffered for it." He leans forward, meeting Azure's angry stare. "You may carry much of your mother's appearance, but your personality, your strength, is all Lead, like Fire. That force will make you a good mother, not anything Amethyst gave you."

Azure steps away from the desk and paces. "What if you're wrong? What if something catastrophic happens that changes me and I end up becoming unstable just like her?" Her voice chokes a bit at the end.

Feathers. I stand and move to join her. My hands flutter as I gauge whether Azure will receive me or not.

"I would stake my life on being right." Russet tilts his head to meet Azure's gaze. "If it would make you feel better, we can put a plan together should something unforeseen happen. There have been some occasions in Mountain Hollow when another Wingai has had to take in children due to an unbalanced parent. We have also been improving our resources to help those who suffer mentally—our matchless issues have given rise to many problems with mental health."

"That's true," I tell Azure. "Dad has sent a few of our struggling people over here to receive services. Currently, I think Mountain Hollow is better equipped in this area than we are."

"Mmm." She purses her lips, and her brows pull low as she considers.

Russet emphasizes, "I *don't* think you should allow Amethyst's bad parenting to be the basis of your refusal."

Azure's eyes flash. "A bad parent gives kids ice cream for breakfast and forgets to remind them to brush their teeth. My mother wasn't a bad parent. She was a psychotic abusive monster." She grabs a fistful of her wing. "When I was six, she tied me to a chair and plucked every feather because she couldn't stand the sight of my silver tips. It took a full year before they grew back. She told Josephina—who had just learned about us—I had gotten sick and they mysteriously fell out."

Feathers. My stomach drops. Russet and I both cringe. I imagine what Azure must have felt: a sharp sting, like ripping hangnails out, sometimes tearing the skin underneath, over and over again. Anger builds in my chest. My hands shift into talons. To inflict that on a child!

Russet stands and walks around his desk to stand toe to toe with Azure. "I understand your reluctance. I've been kicking myself for taking Amethyst at her word ever since I learned of you. I would have taken you from her in a heartbeat and raised you with Marigold as our own. You wouldn't have known any suffering. Unfortunately, I can't change the past." He places his hands on Azure's shoulders. "I am sorry for it."

Azure stiffens with surprise, then quietly says, "Thank you."

Russet steps back. "Even if you don't feel ready to have a family right away, I want you to at least be thinking about it. You're the only Silver-Tipped in existence, and you're matched to a Gold-Tipped." He nods his head in my direction before turning his powerful gaze back on Azure. "Each of us is nothing without our match. If you don't have children, you'll condemn all Wingai to a slow hell of extinction. Do you want that?"

"No," Azure says.

"Then find the Lead in you and plan for it," he says.

Azure shudders with fear. Taking the plunge, I wrap my arms around her. She stiffens at first, but as my wings mesh with hers and I express my need to calm her, she relaxes. I turn my head to face Russet. "I think you might be pushing this on us too fast. I think we need to focus on us before we go down this path."

"It took well over a decade of actively trying for Amethyst to become with child. Unlike the Golds, Silver females have difficulty with conception. Not even in vitro fertilization as proven to be successful. There are high chances it will take years." Russet shrugs.

"But Azure and I are an unconventional pair. It could be much quicker since I'm a Gold without issues," I counter. Azure goes rigid in my arms. Her displeasure at this topic screams at me. "We're going to take this one step at a time. Children are definitely out of the question for now."

"Thank you," Azure murmurs, her relief keenly felt.

"I'll leave it alone for now, but I can't promise anyone else will. Wingai will be looking to you both for their future," Russet says with frankness. Great, we're going to get bombarded with other Wingai asking.

"So is that everything?" Azure steps out of my grasp, making it clear she's done here. Me too.

"For now," Russet drawls, his expression pensive.

As we're walking out, he pulls me aside. "I'm leaving it up to you to use everything in your arsenal to get Azure in line. Romance her until she's intoxicated and agreeable."

"I make no promises. Azure's smart enough to see through any crap."

"Yes." His eyes dart to Azure standing by the door receiving a basket of sweets from Marigold. "She has everything she needs to be a great Lead once she's over her inhibitions and the damage her mother inflicted."

I follow his gaze. "Definitely."

Azure silently stews on the drive home. I can feel her irritation with Russet and his demands. "Whatever happens with us will be on our schedule, not anybody else's. Don't let Russet's requests stress you out. We're not in that much of a hurry." I reach over, squeeze her hand, then let go.

"Time means nothing, Cerulean. Ten, twenty, thirty years—it doesn't make a difference." Azure waves flippantly. "Mountain Hollow and Soaring Heights are going to end up screwed because I don't think I can be a mother."

I park in front of the garage and turn to meet her eyes. "You seriously think you'd be that bad at it?"

"I don't have a nurturing bone in my body," she says flatly.

I decide to speak honestly and hope it doesn't backfire. "That's not true. You care for people: your friends, Josephina, me. I've felt it. You care enough about Mountain Hollow to recognize the matchless—"

Azure interrupts. "No, I'm recognizing them because I want Russet to leave me alone and let me live in peace, and because their ability to find a match should not be up to me. They should have the power to make their own choices."

"That's caring," I point out. Azure gives me one quick look of disbelief, then shrugs. "You have heart, Azure, but you fear getting close. You think getting close means pain, but it doesn't." Her narrowed gaze and past experience belie my words. "I mean, it can, if things go south, but no one here, especially me, has any desire to hurt you."

Azure fires question after question at me. "Do you think my father knew about the pregnancy when he chose to sacrifice himself? Do you think he banked on the chance that I would be Tipped to take over his role? Do you think he knew this would destroy my mother? Did he feel regret? Did he hope a new baby would heal her? A piece of him to be remembered by?"

My chest aches from Azure's hurt. Feathers. I sigh, running a hand through my hair. "You know I can't answer those."

Azure nods. Her dark-blue eyes glisten. "I know." She resituates in her seat, turning to face me more. "Cerulean, if I fell in love with you, if I loved you with everything that I had, became Lead, had children—the whole picture—and something happened to you, do you believe the same as Russet? That I wouldn't become my mother?"

I don't hesitate. "I do."

"Why?"

A soft smile creeps around the corners of my lips. "You're stronger than you think. You're so focused on not becoming her. It's a little damaging, because you're not allowing yourself the freedom to embrace what's in front of you." I gesture to us while I ramble my thoughts out. "But it's also good because your resolve is so powerful. I think you would be extra conscious of your actions and how they may affect others. I think you would do everything in your power to make sure your family stayed safe, even giving your children to someone you trusted if you felt yourself slipping. You'd probably also have a backup person to take control in case you couldn't see that you're spiraling."

"You really think so?" Azure asks, appearing doubtful.

I put as much confidence and conviction as I can in my voice. "I know so."

"Hmm." Azure purses her lips.

I put my hand on hers. "I think Russet is pushing a family on us too fast, and probably my dad will too. For me personally, continuing the line of Leads has been a huge tension point between Soaring Heights and me. These past couple of months searching for you, I've been accosted with an insane amount of disappointment, worry—fear." My expression hardens. "I thought, and I'm sure everybody else did too, that I'd be the one to deliver Soaring Heights to their doom. We'd turn out like Mountain Hollow, and that'd be the end of us all."

I take a breath. "Since we've matched, those worries for me have lessened immensely. I trust that everything will happen in its own due time as we continue to work on a bond together. And if Russet and Dad and whoever else get mad we're not doing things as quickly as they want, well, they can go take a flight. They're not the ones doing it. We are."

"Exactly," she says with obvious relief. "Thank you for recognizing that our needs should come first right now."

My lips quirk into a smile. "Of course."

CHAPTER NINETEEN

AZURE

I hop out of Emerald's truck the second Cerulean shifts it into park in front of my garage. I inhale a large breath of fresh pine air while unfurling my wings. Though I've been away from my house only a few days, I feel like it's been centuries. I'm tempted to fly around my property and hug every tree in sight. Too bad we're returning to Soaring Heights early tomorrow morning for more recognizing.

Jade chuckles good-naturedly at me. "Somebody missed home."

Cerulean laughs with his brother.

I turn, tilting my face to meet Cerulean's eyes. I gesture to my house and land. "Remind me again why I'm basically giving this up to stay with you?"

His eyes are bright with warmth. "Because you care."

"Hmm . . ."

Cerulean snatches onto my waist and pulls me flush against him. My breath catches in my throat. My heart pounds.

He smiles, fully aware of my reaction to him. "Because you think I'm the most awesome match ever, and you can't wait to fall madly in love with me."

His mouth stretches into a wide grin. I laugh at him to dispel the fluttery feeling in my chest. "That's definitely it."

Cerulean chuckles with me, but his tone holds a promise. "It will be, just you wait."

I believe him. I step out of his grasp before I do something crazy like kiss him. "Come on into the house."

I hear Jade slap his brother on the shoulder as they follow me inside. "Keep your feathers up. You'll get through to her."

"I'm not worried," Cerulean responds lightly.

While Cerulean calls Russet to let him know we're safe, I check my messages to see Bree, Ben, and Jack are on their way here, then I get to work. I grab boxes from the garage and put them in the living room.

Jade deposits himself on the couch with his phone. "Let me know when you need me."

"Thanks, Jade." I scan the room, noting the couches, recliners, TV. Josephina and I never got around to hanging pictures on the wall. I don't see anything worth taking. Cerulean's place is already furnished with pristine rich pieces. My stuff would be ugly there.

Cerulean speaks. "Take whatever you want. I want you to be comfortable in our nest."

"I'm not going to ruin your place with my old and worn-out things." I move on to the office with a box.

Cerulean clenches his jaw. Anger peeks through his eyes.

"We're married, Azure. It's *our* place, and I seriously have no problem with mixing our things."

"Well, I do." I turn my back on him and open the filing cabinet. I place the important documents in my box. They should be where I'm going to stay most of the time. "Your house is a multimillion-dollar home with immaculate handcrafted materials. Josephina and I enjoyed bargain finds at garage sales. We don't mix."

Cerulean grabs my shoulders and spins me around to face him. His wings mesh with mine, and I feel his frustration at my solitary thinking. "We mix just fine." His eyes drop to my lips. I read his desire to prove it as his mouth lands on mine.

Rational thinking vanishes with one taste. Molding myself to him, I kiss him back. His tongue sweeps across my lower lip, seeking more. I part my mouth, allowing him better access. Heat settles in my lower belly and travels outward. Holy heavens, he's intoxicating.

Whistles and slow claps break us apart. Bree, Ben, Jack, and Jade stand just inside the office. Jade's eyes are wide and alarmed at the presence of my friends. I belatedly realize I never told him about them. Oops.

"Well, well, well, I'd say married life agrees with Azure. What do you boys think?" Bree tilts her head at Ben and Jack while wearing a large conspiratorial smile.

Jack laughs softly. "She's into him, all right."

Ben grins. "For sure."

I shrug. No point in denying it, since they all had a front-row seat. "He's a good kisser."

"Bet he's good at other things too." Bree winks suggestively at me.

I give them the flat truth with another shrug. "I haven't gone there yet."

"Does that mean you're interested?" Cerulean asks me point-blank. A soft smile tugs at the corners of his lips. His eyes are bright with energy and mirth.

My insides heat and shiver at the prospect written all over him. I tamp it down, not ready to face my feelings and desire. "Don't push your luck." I lightly press on his chest, feeling the muscles underneath, then step away. Laughter permeates the room.

Jade hooks his thumb in the direction of my friends, his eyes on Cerulean. "Do Dad and Russet know?"

Cerulean shakes his head. "No."

"You need to tell them," Jade urges, his expression serious. "They have to be presented. It's the law."

"I know, Jade. Calm down," Cerulean says, his tone soothing. "I was going to mention it."

Jade crosses his arms. "The Summer Summit is this Thursday."

Cerulean pulls out his phone. "Feathers, you're right." He slips his phone back in his pocket. "The date snuck up on me."

I stand in front of my friends. My eyes dart between the brothers. "What law are you talking about? What Summit?"

"Why don't we go sit in the living room and I'll explain," Cerulean suggests, gesturing to the door.

"We brought pizza and drinks," Bree offers.

I hurry to the kitchen and grab plates and napkins. I stack them on the coffee table as Bree and Ben open the three boxes of pizza. The smell of pepperoni blasts me in the face. Once I'm assured everyone is settled, I turn to Cerulean. "Spill."

He untwists the cap on his bottle of Coke. "We take great care to hide from the humans. Experience has shown us most can't be trusted."

Jade adds. "You also outnumber us by a landslide. Our survival depends on our secrecy."

"So what are the repercussions for Azure's telling us?" Jack asks, grabbing a second slice of pepperoni.

Cerulean takes a bite of pizza, chews quickly, and swallows. "First you have to be presented to our Lead. If you gain favor, you're allowed within the community. Our people will be told you're trustworthy."

"If we don't gain favor?" Bree asks.

Cerulean coughs. I read uneasiness in his eyes. I raise an eyebrow at him and lift my chin, demanding an answer. "We don't like to kill, but our safety is paramount. Sometimes we inject the person with a concoction that scrambles the memory section of their brain. They'll be 'confused' for a long time. In a high-threat situation, they're quietly taken out."

"Lovely," Bree deadpans.

"No kidding." Ben grimaces. Jack mirrors him.

"That's not gonna happen to you guys, I swear it." I inject steel into my voice, promising with my tone. "Now what's this Summit?"

Cerulean rubs his face. "It's a meeting with other shifters to discuss what's going on with each of our races and to help us all stay safe. You guys will have to be presented to the Shifter Council—"

"Shifter Council?" Ben repeats. "Just what exactly makes up the council?"

Jade wipes his hands on a napkin. "There's us, the cats, the bears, the wolves, and the foxes."

Cerulean clears his throat. "Presented humans are recommended by an advocate, generally the leader of the group they're associated with. Then the humans are given a chance to speak and plead their case. If they're approved, then they're fully welcomed among all shifters. If it's decided they're a risk, they're executed on the spot."

"No repeals?" Ben asks.

Cerulean and Jade shake their heads.

"And this meeting is this Thursday?" I ask.

Cerulean nods. "They are held every three months, with the beginning of the new season."

"Four days?" Bree squeaks.

I glance at my friends, seeing the concern on their expressions. Guilt snakes through my gut. I brought them into this. "Where is it held?" I ask.

Cerulean rubs the back of his neck. "It rotates between groups. The wolves are hosting this year's summer meeting at their lodge. Their land borders ours. It's about a twenty-minute drive."

"What's the likelihood of being rejected?" Jack asks.

"And killed." Bree shivers. Ben drops his pizza back in the box and wraps his arms around her.

"Honestly, I think you guys will be fine." Cerulean shows a bit of confidence. "The cats that brought me here to seal the match thought you were harmless, and they're really hard to win over. They're a "shoot first, then ask questions" type. You're lucky to be alive after your encounter with them in shifter business."

Jade chuckles and says in a gruff, comical voice, "Cats don't take prisoners."

Cerulean laughs quietly alongside his brother in what is obviously an inside joke.

Bree gives them a death glare. She dusts off her hands and rises, moving out of Ben's hold. "I think I've heard enough." She smiles brightly at me, but I know her well enough to see it's only for my benefit. "Azure, it's been fun, but I'm not interested in going to any meeting where I greet the possibility of death."

"Me neither," Ben says, getting up.

"Yeah, it's a no from me too," Jack agrees.

"I don't blame you," I answer. "I'm sorry for bringing you into this. I wouldn't have had I known."

Cerulean jumps to his feet, his hands out to stop my friends from leaving. "You have to go. I already promised the cats that you'd be there. If you don't show up, they'll view you as a threat and take you out. Their tracking skills are unparalleled. You've already been seen and memorized. Trust me when I say you won't be able to hide."

Stress escalates on my friends' faces like gasoline thrown on a campfire. I stand and move in front of Cerulean to face my friends. "Look, guys, nothing will happen to you if you go, I promise." Remorse coats my features. "I dragged you into this when I shouldn't have. This is not your fault; it's mine." I fan my wings, and determination fuels my voice. "I'm the only Silver-Tipped alive. I'm matched to a Gold-Tipped. The entire future of my kind rests in my hands. I am not disposable. If anyone decides against you, I will threaten them with my life. If you don't get to live, then neither do I."

Cerulean and Jade inhale sharply.

"You would do that?" Bree asks, her mouth parting in surprise.

I don't hesitate. "In a heartbeat."

Bree tugs me to her and Ben, then grabs Jack, cramming us into a group hug. "Besties for life."

"For life," Jack, Ben, and I repeat. Then we break apart.

"Does that mean you'll go?" Cerulean asks, anxiousness written on his features.

"We'll go," Ben says, glancing at Jack and Bree for confirming nods.

"Thank feathers." Cerulean's shoulders drop with relief.

Jade claps his brother on the shoulder. "You better go make a phone call to Dad and Russet. They'll need to be accepted there first."

"Yeah." Cerulean grabs his phone out of his pocket. He puts his hand on my arm. "So, we'll plan on your friends' coming home and spending the week with us?"

"Yes. We'll figure out something to tell their parents." I hope it won't be too hard.

Cerulean presses a quick kiss on my cheek. His feathers brush against mine as he steps out to make a call. Jade follows.

CERIL

I lean against the truck, my cell against my ear as I wait for Dad to pick up.

It nearly goes to voice mail before he answers. "I didn't expect a call from you. Everything okay?"

"We're fine. I . . . it's just, I forgot to tell you something important." I absentmindedly kick at the dirt with the toe of my shoe.

"Tell him," Jade hisses.

"What is it?" Dad's tone sharpens into his Lead voice.

I speak in a rush. "Azure has some friends who are aware she's Wingai. Over their winter break, they had some sort of miscommunication, and they caught her with her wings out. She's been turning to them for help since I showed up. She went to them after Russet took her, and they were here when we sealed the match. They know everything."

Dad curses. I pull my phone away from my ear as he shouts, "Of all the things, Ceril!"

I cringe, expecting a tongue-lashing that would top any of the ones I'd gotten over the stupid stuff I'd done as a child—including the time I took a corner too fast and crashed my

Dad's prized 1967 Mustang into a fence line, catching the engine on fire.

"I know, I should've said something earlier, but it slipped my mind," I apologize. Jade grimaces with me. He stands close enough to hear Dad. "You know how hard I have it with Azure. I've spent every waking second trying to secure her to me. Her friends' knowing seemed inconsequential in the scope of things."

"All right." He sighs, relenting. "How many 'friends' are we talking about?"

I take a breath, grateful for his reprieve. "Three. Bree, Ben, and Jack. They're Azure's closest friends and fiercely protective of her. I trust them, plus they made it through an encounter with Danyon when he brought me here."

"That's no easy feat," Dad murmurs with interest.

"I know. Azure and I are going to bring them with us to Soaring Heights and to the Shifter Summit this week to be accepted as required," I say.

"Good."

"Could you tell Russet for me?" I ask. "They'll have to be approved in Mountain Hollow too."

"Sure, but I can't speak for him," Dad says. "There's no telling what he will do."

"I know. Just tell him we're bringing three human guests with us tomorrow. Azure and I will handle the rest." I have no doubt Russet will try to twist this to his advantage. I make a mental note to warn Azure.

 right else you might have 'forgotten' to tell

"Is there anything else you might have 'forgotten' to tell me?" Dad asks.

"Nope, that's it. See you tomorrow." I end the call, anxious to get the weight of Dad's displeasure off me. I hate disappointing him. I shake out my wings, inhale deeply, and exhale slowly. Jade claps me on the shoulder with silent brotherly support, and we head inside.

Azure's laugh envelops the living room. Her eyes are rimmed with tears, her face red. I enjoy seeing the easy camaraderie she has with her friends. From the few things she's told me of her past, she definitely deserves good friendships and fun.

My heart leaps when she smiles and invites me to sit with her on the couch. "Everything all right?" she asks.

I grin, buoyed by her lightheartedness. "We're good." My phone rings. Russet's name flashes across the screen. That didn't take long. I swipe to answer it. "Hey, Russet." Azure's eyes sharpen on me.

In clipped tones, Russet says, "Put Azure on the line."

AZURE

Cerulean hands me his cell. I stand. "Hello."

"You should have told me you made yourself known to three humans," Russet practically shouts into the phone. "This is the worst sort of liability. They're not to be trusted."

My wings flare at the anger I hear in his voice, prompting ire of my own. "I don't regret what happened. I trust them a whole lot more than I trust you." I pace, garnering a host of trained eyes.

"Then let's make a deal," he says smoothly. "You agree to be Lead, and I'll give my support for your friends' approval."

I still, widening my eyes in fury and resignation. Of course he'd turn this into becoming Lead. Out of the corner of my eye, I see Cerulean rubbing his chest, cursing. Bree, Ben, Jack, and Jade glance between me and him with concern. "Why am I not surprised?"

"You may be important to us, Azure, but your character is still widely unknown. Without my endorsement, you will not succeed among the Wingai or at the Shifter Summit." Russet digs his talons in deeper. "I hear the cats have your friends on their radar. They do not take any threats to their survival. They may end up wanting to pay them a visit."

A trickle of fear runs down my spine at the thought. I hate that Russet is using my friends' lives against me, but if it weren't this, it'd be something else. The man can't fail. He is too crazy determined. I just hope I can handle the responsibility. "Fine. We have a deal."

"I want to hear you say it."

My hand shifts into talons. "Seriously?"

"Say it or no support," he insists.

"All right, all right," I say hastily. "I agree to be Lead."

"Excellent," Russet says with pleasure. "I look forward to presenting you to Mountain Hollow and the Shifter Council."

I roll my eyes. "Of course you do." We say our goodbyes. I lightly toss Cerulean's phone at him.

"What was that about?" Bree asks me.

I rub my forehead. "Just another concession." I tack on a smile because I don't want them to worry. "It's fine."

"It most definitely isn't," Bree insists. "What's the deal?"

I resume my seat beside Cerulean. He releases his wings and wraps them around me. He takes my hand in his and squeezes lightly, conveying support.

"Russet refused to give his support unless I agreed to be Lead," I sigh with resignation. "We can't attend the Summit without him, so I said yes."

Gratitude shines in Bree's expression. "Wow, you really meant it when you said you'd sacrifice yourself for us."

"Yeah, you've been pretty vocal against the job," Jack says, mirroring Bree's appreciation.

I shrug, a smile on my lips. "I'm not thrilled, but I can deal. It was going to happen sooner or later anyway."

I receive sympathetic stares in response.

As the sun fully sets, Bree, Ben, and Jack head home to prepare for their visit to Soaring Heights. We told their parents I got an amazing deal on a house rental in the Cascade mountains for a week of luxury camping. A last hurrah before the real world starts, before moving out and heading to college.

I finish going through the house and packing what I want to bring. It isn't much: a few boxes of important documents, clothes, toiletries, my favorite kitchen spoon, and other odds and ends. Jade and Cerulean load it all into the truck, and then we call it a night.

Settling into bed, Cerulean pulls me against him, my wings to his chest, his arm tucked around my stomach. I'm surprisingly comfortable.

He whispers, "I'm sorry about Russet forcing you to be Lead. It's a low blow to use your friends against you."

I shrug. What's done is done. "He's a traditionalist, and he's desperate."

"Very." He takes a breath. "For what it's worth, I think you're going to be great at it, even though it's not what you want."

"Thanks for the vote of confidence," I say quietly, awed at his faith in me. He smooths my hair back and presses a kiss to my temple. "Always."

CHAPTER TWENTY

AZURE

Bree, Ben, and Jack arrive in Jack's blue Honda at half past nine in the morning. Jack pulls a couple of fishing poles and a tackle box out of the trunk. "I had to take this stuff with me. My dad insists it isn't camping without fishing. Can I leave these in your garage?"

"Sure." I press the garage opener on my key chain.

"He's totally right, though. Fishing *is* the best part of camping." Ben wraps his arm around Bree.

"I think it's s'mores," Bree says with a wink at Ben.

"I love you s'more." Ben places a kiss on her lips, making her giggle.

Cerulean holds out a fifty-dollar bill to Jack. "For gas."

Jack eyes the money hesitantly. "I can pay—"

"Just take it, please," Cerulean insists.

"Thanks." Jack takes the cash. He slings his arm around my shoulder. "Is it all right if Azure becomes my navigator?" He leans forward and says in a lower tone. "Being the third wheel sucks."

Our gazes dart to Bree and Ben kissing each other as though starved for air. "You've got me, Jack," I promise.

He grins with relief. "Awesome."

We fill the drive with radio tunes and an epic game of slug bug. When we turn onto Soaring Heights Road, I tell my friends, "It's just a few miles inland."

Cerulean slows to a stop less than a mile in. I poke my head out the window to see a plain black delivery truck parked on the side of the road. Pieces of shredded tire and a metal rim are scattered beside it.

A hulking young man with ash-blonde hair and nondescript black clothes holds onto a tire iron. I get the stark impression he flagged Cerulean down.

"Looks like a guy needs help," I murmur.

Cerulean and Jade hop out of the truck. They exchange words I can't hear. Abruptly the man swings the tire iron, striking Cerulean over the head in one fell swoop. I gasp sharply. He crumples to the ground like a marionette whose strings have been cut.

My sweaty fingers slip on the car door's handle as I yank at it. A frustrated yell escapes my lips as I kick and shove the door open. I jump out of the car.

"Azure, wait!" Jack shouts at me.

My heart thuds in an adrenaline-induced panic. I can't lose him, not this soon, not ever. With no conscious thought to my well-being, I sprint to Cerulean.

Talons out, Jade grapples with the guy. The man throws Jade into the side of the van. Cursing, Jade shakes his head, recollecting himself. He lunges as the man snatches the tire iron off the ground. The man knocks Jade over the head, sending him careening back into the van. Jade falls to the ground, unmoving.

I'm nearly to Cerulean when the hulking monster blocks my path. His eyes glow bright gold. I recognize the look from Cerulean's friends. *Cat shifter.* "Not so fast, Birdie." He grabs me round the middle and hoists me against him. I choke on the cloud of spicy musk enveloping him.

"Let go!" Shifting my hands into talons, I dig them into his arms. I tear through the black fabric only to discover he's wearing thick leather underneath his clothes. I can't get my talons through. A growl of frustration escapes my throat. I flail, kicking my feet, raking the leather for a weak spot. The man is like a boulder.

A deep chuckle rumbles out of his chest at my useless attempts to break free.

"Hey! Get your hands off her!" Jack yells, running to me with Ben and Bree on his heels.

The man sniffs, then wrinkles his nose. "It's beginning already." He tosses me over his shoulder in a firefighter's hold. "Sorry, Birdie, it's for the good of all."

"What? No!" I protest as he darts into the trees.

CERIL

My head. Feathers. It hurts.

Someone shakes me. I blink, catching a glimpse of Bree before I black out.

I wake again to the sound of shouting. "We need help!"

"Emergency at the gate. I need extra security and a medic now!"

I struggle to open my eyes. Oh. It hurts.

"Don't shoot!"

I slip under.

AZURE

The forest is a blur of browns and greens as the man runs with me over his shoulder. My stomach sloshes sickeningly with the constant bobbing. We're moving faster than humanly possible and the man's not even remotely out of breath.

I've given up scratching him. "Where are you taking me?" He doesn't answer. I huff. "Why are you doing this? I haven't done anything to you!"

Again, he doesn't respond. Frustrated and close to throwing up, I release my wings. They rip through my shirt. Cool air hits my back. Flapping my feathers, I push at the man. "Let me go!"

A growl rumbles out of his throat. He snatches my left wing and squeezes. I hear a snap. White-hot electric pain shoots through me. I scream. Tears prick my eyes. My wing falls loosely against my back as he lets go. I can't move it.

He grounds his feet to a stop and tosses me onto a bed of ferns. I cry out as his actions jostle my broken wing. I glance around me, noting the acres of trees in all directions. We're close to a stream. A mossy fallen log makes a bridge over the water. I shake off a mosquito that's landed on my hand.

The man glares at me with golden eyes. I see no remorse. He reaches into his pocket and pulls out a cell phone. He fiddles with it for a second before putting it up to his ear. "I've got her. Now, where are you?"

His face morphs into anger. A red hue creeps up his neck and into his cheeks. His golden eyes burn brighter. "What do you mean you can't come? You said we would do this together!" He growls into the phone, raking a hand through his ash locks. He turns his back to me as he listens. He lowers his voice, making it impossible for me to hear.

While he's engrossed in his argument, I take the chance to escape. I cautiously get to my feet and walk backward, careful to make as little sound as possible. Every movement sends excruciating pain into my wing. I bite the inside of my cheek. Silence is key. Whoever I'm dealing with means business.

A small branch snaps under my shoes. He swivels around to face me. I freeze. His lips curl in amusement. He ends the call and slips his phone back into his pocket. I swallow down the fear gliding up my throat. With nothing to lose, I turn tail and run.

I breathe heavily through my nose and out my mouth. Blood rushes in my ears. My heart thunders. Sweat trickles down my forehead and into my hair and down my cheeks. I sprint through the foliage, dodging trees, huckleberry bushes, fallen logs, mossy rocks. The air around me reverberates with a shrieking yowl. My stomach flips with terror. Adrenaline surges into my limbs. I don't dare waste time looking back.

I hear a metallic click. White blinding pain shoots up my leg. I open my mouth in a high-pitched scream. I fall awkwardly, my hands claw into the dirt, one knee bounces, and the rest of me sprawls out. I come inches from smashing my face into a wild rosebush. I scramble to turn myself over until I'm sitting on my butt. A mud-coated animal trap is clamped over my lower calf. Blood blossoms onto my jeans.

Low growls fill my ears over my quiet sobs. I look up into the golden eyes of the shifter. He crouches in front of me. His mouth opens wide. Saliva drips down his canines. I shut my eyes and wait for his killing bite.

CERIL

My head throbs something fierce as I come to. I squeeze my still-closed eyes, willing the pounding to stop. I breathe in the smell of antiseptic and Clorox. Something squeezes my upper arm. I force my eyes open. Dr. Sage hovers over me, his light-green eyes probing, lips pursed. There's a blood pressure cuff over my arm and an oxygen reader on my finger. I touch my head and feel a bandage.

A series of quick images flash through my mind. Driving Dad's truck home. The van with the shredded tire. Jex, seeking help for it. Some screaming, and then . . . nothing. What happened? And why am I in so much pain?

My gaze darts around the room for Azure. Dad stands off to the side, hands digging into his hair, his wings hunched. Worry coats every facet of his face. Other than him and Dr. Sage, the small white room is empty. This isn't right. Where is Azure?

"Ceril?" Dr. Sage asks gently. He shines a light in my eyes, then nods to himself. "How are you feeling? Any dizziness?"

It takes a second for me to unglue my tongue from the roof of my mouth. "Azure." Panic thrums. I push myself to sit up. The room spins. I grip my head. "Where's Azure?"

Dr. Sage hands me a couple of pills and a glass of water. "Drink this."

I quickly swallow the medicine, then repeat with some frustration, "Where is Azure?" My heart pounds. Something is terribly wrong.

Dr. Sage steps back, giving my Dad the go-ahead to speak to me. "Who did you stop for with the shredded tire?"

"Jex." A cat shifter near my age, slated to become the next Danyon in terms of strength. I considered him a friend. "What does it . . ." I start to ask until I see the surprise and fury and flat-out fear on Dad's face. My brow furrows as I try to put the pieces together. Van, shredded tire, Jex needing help. He held a tire iron. My eyes widen. Feathers! Why would he—?

Unexpected electric pain slices through my heart. I cry out. My hand flies to my chest. I fall forward, off the bed. Dad throws his hands out to catch me. My wings spring free, tearing through my navy T-shirt. Cold terror drenches me head to toe. I can barely move. "Azure!"

I throw Dad off me and run for the door. I blink rapidly as the world spins before righting itself. Dr. Sage presses against the sink to get out of my way. In the hall, Bree and Ben sit on a green bench. Jack paces beside them, his tennis shoes squeaking on the glossy floor. Their heads whip around to stare at me. I notice Bree's brown eyes are red and rimmed with tears. My stomach drops.

"Get her back!" Bree shouts as I race by.

I push at the automatic doors when they don't open fast enough. Dad catches up with me. I pump my wings hard, jumping into the sky. Dad keeps pace with me on my right. Pure instinct drives me out of Soaring Heights.

The wind whips through my hair and stings my eyes as I fly at breakneck speed. My chest is on fire. A dread-filled hole gnaws its way through my stomach. I struggle to breathe through the fear squeezing my throat.

Passing the gates of Soaring Heights, I dive into the forest, dodging Douglas firs and pine. The thumping of my heart intensifies. She's in here, but where? I have thousands of acres to go through. I veer left with a prayer I'm not steered wrong.

"Ceril, wait! There's Russet with the wolves. Let them get her scent off you." Dad points below us.

I cast my eyes down to see Russet, Sky, and Onyx speaking with Axel, Alpha of the Cascade pack, and his Beta, Brexton. They shift into their wolf forms as we descend. My heart spasms right as my feet hit the ground. Pain. So much pain. An agonized yell escapes my lips. "Azure!" I falter. Russet and Sky catch me. They hold me out to Axel and Brexton, who sniff at my clothes. Axel barks, and they take off, darting through the undergrowth.

I try to take off, but my wings won't flap hard enough. I curse at the sudden weakness taking over. Dad and Russet grab hold of my arms. Together they lift me into the air. Sky and Onyx fly just below me, ready to be a support.

Hang on, Azure. I'll find you.

AZURE

Claws dig into my flesh. One paw rests on my thigh, the other on my shoulder as my kidnapper pushes me down. His hot, heavy breath tickles my face and neck as he hovers over me. I reach for his throat with my talons. There's no leather in cat form. He rears his head away. My nails graze. He comes at me again, his mouth open for a slaying bite. I swing my hand out. He yowls as my nails connect and sink into his fur.

Something big slams into the cat shifter. He shrieks, claws slashing my skin as he tumbles off me. Two exceptionally large wolves, one pure white, the other black with gray feet, face the puma, their hackles raised. A cacophony of growls, barks, and hissing fills my ears. I turn my head slightly, unable to do anything but watch.

The white wolf snaps at the cat shifter. He darts out of the way and swipes, clearly telling them to back off. Tail flicking angrily, he turns as if ready to run off. More snarling wolves emerge out of the trees and box him in. The cat emits a low yowl while slinking around in a circle, searching for an exit. A few of the wolves snap at his heels to keep him in place.

Exhaustion seeps into my bones, but I can't seem to shut my eyes. A gray wolf holding a bundle of clothes in its mouth tosses them at the white wolf. His white body blurs, then transforms into a naked male, his back turned. I avert my gaze. The man crouches beside me. His electric-blue eyes pierce mine.

Above him, I catch snatches of color peeking through the dark-green foliage. A group of Wingai land.

"Azure!" Cerulean drops to his knees beside me, his sea-green eyes liquid with unshed tears and fear. A white bandage covers his temple. He stretches his wings taut to connect with mine.

"Oh!" I gasp as he soothes the waves of excruciating pain.

Cerulean lays beside me, careful to keep his touch on me. "I've got you," he murmurs. "You're going to be okay."

I'm dimly aware of others working over me to remove the trap, but I focus on Cerulean. "You're all right?" I whisper.

He touches his bandaged temple. "Just a bump."

"And Jade?" I ask. The pressure on my leg eases. The trap is off. Thank heavens.

Cerulean frowns. "Did something happen to him?"

"He went down too," I tell him.

"Oh." Cerulean's brow puckers with the information. "As soon as I woke up, I ran out to find you."

I manage a weak smile. "I'm glad you did." Feeling nothing but a gentle warmth, my eyes slide shut into oblivion.

CERIL

Russet takes Azure into his arms. I stand as he does, careful to keep my touch on her. I don't have enough energy to hold her and keep her pain at bay. We climb onto a small trailer hooked up to an ATV one of the wolves brought. I'm grateful for their quick pack telepathy.

Through a gap in the circle of wolves, I see Jex has shifted back into his human form. He sits on the ground, a gray wool blanket thrown over him for modesty. What in the world possessed him to commit this senseless act? We've been nothing but friendly with each other. I've always been careful to cultivate good relationships with cat shifters. I'm hurt and confused.

His senses alert him of my stare, and he tilts his head, golden eyes finding mine. With a hard scowl, I shift closer to Azure. He will pay for this—with my hands around his throat. Jex dips his chin in a subtle nod, accepting the broken friendship between us.

Onyx hops in the driver's seat, revs the engine, and takes off. Dirt flies in our wake. Russet holds Azure tight against him to soften the worst of the bumps on the drive. He grimaces for

Azure's sake at every significant jostle. His investment in her matches mine. He's not going to let her go easily.

His gray eyes are cold and hard when he looks at me. There's no question he won't trust me with her again. I don't blame him. I failed Azure epically. Feathers, how could this day go from good to hell? "Do you have any enemies, Ceril? Anyone who would wish you harm?"

I can't think of a single person. As a future Lead, I've made it my goal to be nice to everyone. Sure, I don't always succeed, but I don't think I've done enough damage for someone to want to kill my match. "I don't know why Jex would do this. We were friends."

"You really have no idea?" Russet presses.

"None." There's a bite to my tone as I emphasize my innocence.

"All right." Russet eases up on me.

Onyx makes it to the main road and cranks the speed up. Azure's eyes flutter. I get the sense she's fighting a losing battle. How much blood has she lost? My heart lurches. "Hang in there. We're almost there," I tell her.

We race through the gates and speed through town, dodging cars here and there, not following a single traffic law. The few Wingai strolling on the streets stare at us with mouths open. The whole town and Mountain Hollow will be buzzing about this.

Onyx parks right in front of the automatic doors of the Soaring Heights Medical Center. He sprints inside to get help while Russet and I gingerly get off the back of the trailer and carry her in.

Nurse Tulip and Dr. Sage jog toward us pushing a bed. I lose contact with Azure for a second while Russet lays her on it. Her eyes snap open, a cry on her lips. I climb into the bed with her. Jolts of energy flow through my wings and into her as our link reestablishes. Her expression clears, and she falls unconscious again.

We're pushed down the hall and into a room. On the way Russet gives Dr. Sage the details of Azure's condition.

"Feathers," Tulip and Sage say.

They mask, gown, and glove up, then go straight to work. They snip off Azure's clothes, leaving her in a dark-blue bra and underwear. I freeze at the talon scars I see underneath her wings on her back and shoulders. An IV line is put in, then she's put through the wringer of ultrasounds and X-rays to get a complete picture of her injuries.

"Prognosis?" Russet asks.

Sage holds up an X-ray image of Azure's leg. "There are a few indents where the metal trap touched the bone, but overall her leg's intact." He grabs another picture, this one of her wing. "This bone has been snapped in half."

My hold on Azure tightens. Russet pales. The unspoken possibility travels around the room. Azure could never fly again. That's as good as a death sentence. Feathers! I want to scream, pummel Jex into the ground with my bare hands.

Russet digs his fingers into his hair, his wings twitching. "Just do what you can to save her."

"We are," Sage says, though he and Tulip are grim as they return to patching Azure up.

Russet's phone trills. "Emerald." He moves to the corner of the room. The ensuing conversation is too quiet for me to hear over Sage and Tulip working over Azure. Russet remains there for the next hour, making phone calls. He walks over just as Sage snips the thread to the stitches in Azure's shoulder. Tulip rubs a cream into the bruises showing up. Then Sage and Tulip slip a gown onto Azure.

Sage's gaze darts between Russet and me. "We've done all we can. Now we have to wait. Ceril, I suggest you rest with Azure. You're expending a lot of energy keeping her pain at bay. Sleep will help."

I nod, noting the exhaustion settling into every fiber of my being. Russet refuses to let Azure out of his sight, so a recliner is brought in for him.

Before I drift off, I ask him, "Any word on Jex?"

Russet scowls. "The wolves are holding him in one of their cells. He refuses to explain his motives, and he appears to be under the impression that the shifter community is doomed. The wolves are contacting Danyon. Hopefully he'll be able to get answers out of Jex. Now go to sleep," he orders. "I need Azure well."

I do too. "Stay with me, Azure." I kiss her forehead, then shut my eyes.

AZURE

I wake to an incessant beeping. Blinking slowly, I wrinkle my nose at the smell of Clorox. I lie in a darkened room on a bed with Cerulean curled beside me. His wings wrap around me in a feathery embrace. His chest rises and falls softly as he sleeps. I lift his wing and peek under my hospital gown to see I've been mummified. I account for all of my limbs with relief. An IV and other wires dominate my right hand. I feel no pain.

My lips part in surprise. I spy Russet resting in a green recliner in a corner of the room by a window, shades drawn closed. I read the worry in the pull of his brows as he sleeps, his wings tucked around him like a blanket.

A nurse with pale-pinkish-orange feathers opens the door and tiptoes in. She speaks in a quiet voice to avoid waking the others. "You're awake." She fiddles with the IV machine by the bed, and the beeping stops. "I'm the night nurse, Peach." She takes my vitals, then hands me a cup of water with a straw. After I take a few sips, she puts it on an adjacent table. "Is there anything I can get you?"

I shake my head.

"Press this button if you need anything." She points to a remote beside the bed. As Peach leaves, I see Crimson standing by the doorway. Guarding me? Am I a prisoner again?

Too tired to care, I turn my head to watch Cerulean. He sleeps with his mouth slightly parted, his eyebrows faintly furrowed, though he doesn't look as troubled as Russet does in his sleep. For a man, Cerulean has exceptionally long dark eyelashes. I reach over and brush a lock of his hair away from his eyes. His expression clears. I bend my head to touch his and slip back into slumber.

I wake to an argument. A doctor with mint-green wings, Russet, and Emerald stand by the end of the bed. Frustration shows on all their faces. Next to me, Cerulean watches with rapt attention.

"This is a medical facility, not to a place to hold vigils!" the doctor exclaims. "The parking lot is filled. We need the room for other emergencies."

"I can't ask them to leave," Russet insists. "Azure is our Lead. Mountain Hollow is nothing without her."

"Then at least tell them to stop harassing my people," Emerald says. "Soaring Heights is tied to Azure's well-being just as much as Mountain Hollow. Eliminating her would destroy us too. I have the Flock breaking up fights left and right."

Russet sighs. A hand rubs his temple. "I'll speak to them." He asks the doctor, "Is there anything I can tell them?"

Their eyes shift to me. The doctor smiles. "Ah, you're awake." He moves closer and introduces himself as Dr. Sage. He then performs a quick examination, checking blood pressure, my temperature, and the like. To Russet he says, "She's stable but has a good amount of recovery before her. We'll monitor her closely in case something changes."

"Thank you." Russet levels his gray eyes on Cerulean. "I'll be back in ten minutes."

Cerulean stiffens, his tone stern. "Nothing is going to happen to her."

Russet appraises Cerulean. Seeming satisfied, he strides out of the room. Emerald and the doctor follow.

"Overprotective much?" I say of Russet.

"He has every right to be," Cerulean mutters darkly. "I nearly got you killed."

I cup his cheek. "It's not your fault."

He covers my hand with his. "I shouldn't have stopped." His tone harshens again. "I should have just run Jex over."

I speak with conviction. "Cerulean, you're not responsible for somebody else's actions. I'm alive, and that's what counts."

"Thank feathers." Cerulean presses a light kiss to my lips. "So how do you feel about tackling the bathroom?"

I chuckle at the need I see in his eyes. "Let's try it."

I grab a fistful of his feathers while he climbs out of bed. He gently lifts me into his arms and carries me to the bathroom while I push the IV pole. He sets me on the toilet and turns around. When I finish, he places me on an adjacent white plastic chair and gives me a hand sanitizer bottle. I focus on rubbing my hands clean, giving him privacy. He carries me back to the bed and settles in beside me once we're both relieved and clean.

Cerulean grins. "Mission accomplished."

"Good job." I bend my head to lean against his, surprised at my complete lack of embarrassment.

Russet steps into the room, holding a paper bag and a drink carrier. "I brought food." He brings us cups of chicken noodle soup, sandwiches, and Sprite. "Best if you start with the soup, then see if you can handle more," he tells me.

"Thank you." I inflict my tone with gratitude. Despite our many arguments, I'm beginning to see he genuinely cares for me.

There's a knock on the door. Russet wears a secret smile. "My gifts have arrived." He lets in Bree, Jack, and Ben.

"Hey!" My back flies off the pillow as I lean forward.

Cerulean grabs onto me. "Easy there, you're still injured."

"Oh my goodness, Azure," Bree gushes. "You've had us worried sick."

"I'm all right guys. Er, at least, I will be." I refuse to entertain the idea that I might not be okay at all.

I'm given an hour to visit with them before Russet and the nurse deem I need my rest. During that time, I hear all about their epic tale of getting Cerulean and Jade to the gates of Soaring Heights.

"It took the three of us to load them into the back of the truck. Man, they're heavy. I thought we were going to drop Jade. Then we just kept going down the road, hoping we'd find the place," Jack says.

Then the showdown at the entrance. "Seriously, that gate guy thought we attacked them," Bree says. "He had guards surround us with guns at the ready. He was a total birdbrain."

Then about Cerulean running out of the hospital. "You should have seen him, Azure," Ben says. "He probably would've broken an Olympic record for sprinting out of here."

Next I hear how eerie it is that everyone here looks young. "Seriously, it's weird listening to Jade call Rose 'Mom' when they look the same age." Bree shudders.

"It sucks that you're not going to age with us," Jack says.

"Yeah, you get to keep your youth and beauty for hundreds of years, and we get only a couple of decades." Bree gives me a mock stink eye.

"Come on, Bree." I chuckle. "You know I'd rather you age with me. If I could give you my life span, I would."

I learn about the hundreds of Mountain Hollow residents camped out in the parking lot. "There are tents set up, food and drink stations. Some up-tempo music. Word is they're not leaving till you're released," Bree says. "Oh man, did they give us 'humans' a wide berth." She rolls her eyes. "I can't tell whether they hate us, are scared, or are simply disinterested." She shrugs.

"Probably all of the above," Jack says. "We're not anything special."

"No way. You guys are awesome," I encourage. "I couldn't ask for better friends."

"Same goes for you, so get better quick," Bree's tone borders on motherly.

"Yeah, we're supposed to be having the week of our lives 'camping.'" Jack makes air quotes. We laugh.

The nurse comes in then and ushers my friends out. I lean back onto Cerulean, resting my head on his chest, tired and grateful to be alive.

CHAPTER TWENTY-ONE

CERIL

Azure and I spend a good portion of the remaining day napping. Mom stops by with fresh clothes for me and a few card games to keep us occupied. Marigold also comes and brings stuff for Russet. I manage to change into something clean on one of our bathroom adventures.

Russet conducts business from his recliner. "Azure will stay under my watchful eye until we know why she was targeted." He proceeds to ask her for an account of her attack. "Any details you might be able to give us would help in figuring out this case."

With little feeling, Azure recounts what happened. Russet and I shift to high alert upon learning that Jex was working with someone else. Russet spreads this information to my father and among the Flock and Silver Guard. He also doubles the guard outside our hospital door.

Russet and I spend a maddening hour trying to come up with a list of suspects: friends or associates Jex might have. Jex still isn't speaking. The wolves haven't been able to get hold of Danyon. Best guess is he's off the grid in cat form. We may have to wait until the Summit for him.

We struggle to make sense of the attack. "It can't be a Wingai," I say. "Soaring Heights and Mountain Hollow are now connected. Killing Azure would condemn us both to be matchless. What Wingai would want to do that?"

We start discussing other shifters, but we "lovebirds" are considered the most peaceful among all the shifters. We've fought more with ourselves than we have with any other race. I sigh. "It just doesn't make sense."

"Does it have to make sense?" Azure asks. "Sometimes people go off the deep end and do something psychotic. Maybe Jex and whoever he was working with were angry about something else and took it out on us? Maybe someone offended them and they went crazy."

"Cat shifters do not just 'go off the deep end,'" Russet says, his fingers making a steeple. "Everything they do is expertly calculated. I don't believe this was a psychotic episode."

"Nor do I." I've always considered Jex to be pretty levelheaded.

"Then I guess we're going to have to chalk it up to a mystery until someone can get Jex to talk," Azure concludes.

"Mmm." Russet wears a sour expression. I can't help but feel the same.

Azure's soft whimpers wake me in the middle of the night. I press a button on the bed remote to turn on a night-light. Eyes closed, she pushes against me. "Let go, hurts." I start to move, worried I may have held her too tight while I slept. Has my power stopped? My heart starts to race. "Mama, please. Hurts." Feathers. She's having a nightmare. "Mama, no, don't. Hurts."

I cup her cheek. "Azure," I whisper.

Her eyes race behind her eyelids. She doesn't hear me. "Stop, Mama," she mumbles.

"Be a little more forceful, Ceril," Russet says from his recliner.

I certainly can't shake her awake with her injuries, so I speak up. "Azure."

Nothing.

Running out of options, I take her face in my hands and kiss her. Her response is instantaneous. She presses herself against me, her lips frantic. Her touch lights me up like nothing else. Feathers! With a muttered groan, I pull away. I can't have a make-out session when she's not in her right frame of mind and Russet's in the room. "Azure."

Her sleepy eyes finally open. "Cerulean." She blinks rapidly, confusion evident on her face.

"Hey there." I grin and brush her golden locks away from her face. "You were having a nightmare."

She frowns. Her brows pull low with awareness. Her anger and pain skid across my heart. She turns her head away from me. "I don't remember."

I softly call out her lie. "Azure."

"Go back to sleep, Cerulean." Her tone holds a note of finality to it.

She's got another thing coming if she thinks I'll do her bidding. I lean over her, locking her eyes with mine. "You don't want to talk about it, fine, but don't brush me off like I'm nothing. We're matches. I am irrevocably invested in you." I grab her hand and put it over my heart. "Your pain becomes my pain. Your laughs are my laughs. We're in this together, Azure. One day you're going to have to open up to me."

She stares at me in silence, weighing my words. Just when I think what I've said is for naught, she speaks. "One day, Cerulean, but my wounds are deep. You're not going to like what you see."

"I like you, wounds, scars, and all." I press a light kiss to her lips. A smile plays around her mouth. I settle back into bed and tug her close. I shut off the night-light. Wings touching hers, I open a mental connection between us. She stiffens, resistance filling her bones. *"Relax."* Exuding calm, I help her fall back asleep, wanting her to know how much she's treasured.

A fight breaks out the following morning when Dr. Sage comes in to check on Azure. "I need to be released by this evening, regardless of how I look," Azure says.

Russet's gray eyes flash at her. He places his hands on the bed rail beside her. "If there's even a hint of improper healing, you're staying right where you are."

Azure's expression hardens. "The shifter summit thing is tomorrow. My friends are here to be approved. I have to be there."

Dr. Sage cuts in before Russet can make his retort. "Why don't we take a look, okay?" He proceeds to pull back the bandages and examine. When he's finished checking her, he says, "Everything appears to be healing beautifully. I see no signs of infection around the stitches." His eyes dart between Azure and me. "You have a very strong match."

"What about her wing?" Russet asks.

"At the rate she's healing, I would like another X-ray this evening," Dr. Sage answers.

"So?" Azure asks.

Dr. Sage glances at Russet, then says, "To be on the safe side, I'd rather we release you tomorrow morning. We'll have to figure out accommodations for your leg. I don't want any pressure on it, and you'll need to be careful with your wrapped wing. No sudden movements or anything. I'll want you back for checkups as well."

"Fine," Azure readily agrees. "Russet?"

Russet sighs, his hand scrubbing across his stubbled face. "All right, we'll get your friends approved."

Azure beams at him. I think it's one of the first genuine smiles she's ever given him. "Thank you."

"You're welcome." Russet blinks, clearly put off guard by Azure's niceness.

Dr. Sage vacates the room. "Knock, knock," Magenta sings. She steps through the open door. Her pink heels clack against the glossy floor. A cloud of some cloying flowery perfume follows in her wake. She wears a formfitting hot-pink dress, her face is made up, and her wings are spritzed with glitter.

"Magenta, what are you doing here?" I ask coldly. Azure's intense dislike of Magenta smacks me in the chest. I take a breath to steady myself.

Magenta snorts. "Cool your feathers, Ceril. I'm on official business for Daddy." It's then I notice a pink canvas bag over her shoulder. She takes a black spiral book out of it and hands it to Russet. "Spring's recordings for you to review for the Summit tomorrow."

Cider pops his head in from his post outside the door. "Hey, Russet, any chance you could spare a moment? Parking lot's hollering for an update on Azure."

"I'll be there," Russet says. He turns to Magenta. "Is that all?"

Magenta pats her bag. "I have a few papers for Ceril to review, then I'll be on my way. Won't take more than a moment."

"All right. Back in ten minutes." Russet strides out.

Great. Now Azure and I are stuck with her. "You can set the papers on the table, then leave."

Magenta rummages through her bag, bringing out another spiral black book. She sets that on the table, then retrieves a five-by-seven picture frame. It's the two of us hugging each other wearing party hats. Magenta walks around to my side of the bed. "Your seventeenth birthday party. We were inseparable that night, remember?" When I say nothing, she adds, "You gave me my first kiss."

Azure stiffens. Feathers. "My lips never touched yours," I snarl.

Magenta scowls. "You want to deny it? Fine. But what about when you thought matches were stupid and overrated and you said you'd never be able to love a stranger? When you begged me to be your match when you couldn't find her?" She gestures to Azure. "When you wanted me above anyone else?" Her voice lowers. "When I completed you?"

"Magenta," I warn.

"Don't tell me you don't remember." She grabs a couple of pages from her bag. "I've printed some of our texts. Your match should know the type of man she's getting." She walks around the bed and hands them to Azure.

My eyes dart to the pages to see what vile Magenta has cooked up.

Magenta Pink for life: You want to be my match, Ceril?
Prince Ceril: You know I do.
Magenta Pink for life: What if I'm not?

Prince Ceril: Then let's make our own future. Who says you can find love only with your match? I don't want to marry a stranger. There's no telling if I could ever love her.

Magenta Pink for life: You think if we have enough love for each other, we could become our own match?

Prince Ceril: Why not?

Magenta Pink for life: I love you, baby.

Prince Ceril: I love you, princess.

Disgusted, I quit reading. "Come on, Magenta, you think I'd write that crap? You're overreaching." Azure sets the papers down on my lap.

"Not even close," Magenta says with surprising conviction. "I'm not naïve. I know the look in a man's eyes when he wants a woman. I can't count how many times I've seen it on you, every time we were together, sneaking around our parents to have time alone. You've always wanted me."

Azure's eyebrows raise. Her eyes are wide with uncertainty. Feathers! A small triumphant smile plays on Magenta's lips.

I ball my hands into fists, resisting the urge to leap out of the bed and shove Magenta out of the room. I won't dare leave Azure unprotected. My feathers are the only thing keeping her out of pain. "You go too far," I growl. "Get out before I get you banned from Soaring Heights forever."

Magenta laughs. "There's no way Daddy would let that happen. I'm his precious jewel."

I've had enough. "Out!" I yell, pointing to the door. Azure cringes at the strength of my voice.

Russet appears in the doorway, his expression stern, eyes darting about the room for a threat. "Is there a problem?"

"None at all. I was just leaving," Magenta says sweetly. Her green eyes lock on mine. "When you're done playing with the trash, you know where to find me."

Her wings knock over the IV pole as she walks out. Azure's IV rips out of her hand. Blood blossoms. My wings jolt with increased power to soothe the new injury. I snatch tissues to cover Azure's hand. Russet steps back out for help. Tulip comes in to bandage Azure's hand. Since Azure's doing so well, they decide not to put another IV in.

"I'm so sorry," I apologize. "The crazy chick doesn't know when to give up."

"You must have given her something for her to be so persistent," Azure deadpans.

"Friendship, that's all," I insist.

"Friends with benefits, perhaps?" Azure fishes. "Stolen moonlight flights?"

"Absolutely not!" I cry. "Look." I create a link between us, allowing her a front-row seat to my thoughts and memories. *"Yes, I did consider Magenta once upon a time. I may have even agreed on the possibility that we could be matches, but that was before I turned eighteen and knew for sure she wasn't. All thoughts of the conniving crow flew right out of my head after that."*

Glancing at the picture Magenta left of us, I think back through my seventeenth year. I didn't hug girls very often. She'd caught me off guard, and before I knew it, her mom snapped the picture, saying we'd make the perfect match. Magenta started coming around a whole lot more after that, trailing after her father at his meetings with Dad, sneaking up on me, wrapping her arms around me, giving me pouty lips. Her bottle-green eyes flashed with anger when I pushed her off or thwarted her plans to get us alone. I could have easily fallen into her machinations, but I didn't. My parents taught me respect for my future match—for Azure—and I worked exceptionally hard to become a man *she* would be proud to have by her side. And now Magenta . . . again.

Azure cups my cheek with her good hand. *"Hey. I trust you, all right? Magenta can't rip us apart."*

"You mean it?" I ask.

"I mean it." She kisses me.

Feathers, I think I'm in love.

AZURE

Unbelievable!" Russet slams his phone onto the table. I jump at the sound. My hand pauses from discarding the two of clubs. I look around Bree and Ben to see. Russet kicks at the recliner, his talons digging into his hair. I've never seen him so rattled. It makes me nervous.

"Russet, what's the matter?" I ask. Admittedly I've been immersed in card games with friends and haven't paid him much attention.

"Jex is unconscious. They think he's ingested some kind of poison," Russet says. "They don't know whether he's going to make it or not."

"Who made it past the wolves?" Cerulean asks, surprise in his voice. "Or was it self-inflicted?"

Russet scowls. "I don't know, but I believe it's Jex's counterpart trying to cover up their tracks."

Cerulean nods. "But to get past the wolves on their home turf? We're not dealing with an amateur—"

Russet cuts him off. "Anyone who can convince a cat shifter to do *anything* is definitely not an amateur. Cats don't take orders."

"What are we going to do?" I ask with some concern.

"Security will need to be vetted and tripled," Russet says. "Whoever it is will no doubt be looking for a second chance."

"If Jex was poisoned, you better be more careful with food preparation," Jack says, eyeing the half-empty containers of food we got from the parking lot grills. "Anybody could slip something in."

"Do you feel sick at all, Azure?" Bree asks.

"No, just numb." I shrug. "Anybody else?" Everyone else shrugs like they're fine as well. "All right then. We'll just be mindful from now on." I place the two of clubs into the discard pile.

Russet flies back into work mode. He stands by the door of my room, getting updates and interviewing Wingai from the Silver Guard. One of them let Jex's demise slip to the parking lot of people. I heard muffled shouting from my ground-level window.

Not long after, Emerald rushes into my room. "Russet you have to stop this. They're turning on Soaring Heights again!"

With a stream of muttered curses, Russet strides out with Emerald, but not before placing Onyx, Cider, and Crimson in my room along with Sky and several others outside.

"They're sure not taking any chances," Bree says, eyeing the men.

"Nope," I say.

Russet and Emerald appear decidedly disheveled when they return. They have tired lines on their faces, rumpled hair and clothes, and slumped wings, a few feathers sticking out at odd ends. How many brawls did they break up?

"This fighting between Soaring Heights and Mountain Hollow has to stop," I tell them. "We'll be on equal footing as soon as I finish recognizing everyone."

"Will that be your first order of business as Lead?" Russet asks. A corner of his mouth lifts into a half smile.

I nod. "It should be."

"Here's your slogan." Ben writes with a Sharpie in a spiral notebook. He tears the page out and hands it to me. "Azure, a Lead for peace."

Laughter circles the room.

The following morning, I tug Cerulean's wing down to hold onto a few of his feathers while he wheels me outside. Eyes shut, I turn my face upward to the scorching sun and inhale a lungful of fresh rose-scented air. Heaven.

Cerulean chuckles. "Nice, isn't it?"

Cheers and whoops reach my ears. A crowd of Wingai, some with children, stands together in the parking lot. All of their tents and grills have been packed away. A few hold "Get Well, Lead Azure" signs. A strange emotion hits my gut. Gratitude and nausea join together. I'm not sure how to handle all this attention.

Cerulean wheels me over, and I manage a shaky thank you. One by one the children come up to me with flowers and a rehearsed "Get better, Lead Azure." The queasiness and appreciation intensify as I gain a bouquet of roses, carnations, lilies, chrysanthemums, and more.

Mercifully, Sky pulls up with the SUV to take us to the Summit. Cerulean lifts me into the third row and slides in beside me. Russet and Marigold take the second row. I don't gain a proper breath until the doors are shut and we're driving away. Cerulean presses a kiss to my lips. "You did great."

"Mmm." I can't bring myself to say anything. Becoming Lead was the price I paid for my friends' acceptance.

Sky parks behind a black Chevy truck on a dirt-packed road. A forest filled with moss, ferns, and Oregon grapes surrounds us. Sunlight filters through the pine needles, dotting the ground. We wait for the Silver Guard to surround the vehicle, then Cerulean hops out and reaches for me. I wrap my arms around his neck, and my cheek rests on his shoulder as he carries me. I had petitioned for crutches, but Cerulean insisted on being my legs. "No pain meds either. My wings can do the work."

Bree, Ben, Jack, and Jade slip through the guard to join us. "You ready for this?" I smile as we walk down the path of parked cars. I suspect we may be the last ones to arrive.

"A meeting I might not come out of alive? Oh yeah, totally." Bree laughs nervously.

Ben and Jack laugh uncomfortably too.

"You guys will be fine, promise," I vow. "What I said still stands."

Cerulean's grip tightens on me. "It better not come to that."

"Come to what?" Russet asks, his eyes sharp on me.

I jerk my thumb in the direction of my friends. "They die, I die."

Russet's eyes widen. His skin flushes an angry red. "Don't you even dare suggest it." Marigold shakes her head at me too.

"I don't plan to, unless it becomes necessary," I answer, giving him a pointed look. I won't back down on this.

A dark cloud shrouds Russet for the rest of the walk.

"Here we are." Cerulean turns the corner, stepping onto a smaller dirt path that slopes downward.

The trees open up into a grove. An outdoor auditorium made of rough-hewn logs has been erected among the trees. Numerous benches face a small stage with a large stone firepit as the focal point. Firewood crackles and pops. Smoke curls upward, scenting the air.

Soft chatter from those who have arrived fills the grove. Multiple curious gazes turn on us. I resist the urge to bury my face in Cerulean. I may be injured, but that doesn't mean I can't appear strong in other ways.

Axel strides toward us. "Glad you could join us." His electric-blue eyes zero in on me. "How are you feeling?"

"Much better. Cerulean's wings are quite handy," I answer, giving Cerulean a quick smile. He kisses the top of my head. "Thank you for reaching me in time."

Axel smiles. "My pleasure, and my apologies for not keeping a better watch on Jex. Our lapse should not have happened." His eyes glow as a bit of his wolf emerges.

"How is Jex?" Russet asks.

"He's still hovering between life and death." Axel scratches his temple. "Samira of the fox shifter clan is looking in on him as we speak."

"Excellent," Russet says, seeming pleased. "I hope she can bring him back."

"If anyone can, it would be her," Axel says, but his face doesn't hold any hope, sending Russet back into his gloomy cloud.

Markers designating sections for each shifter group have been placed in the aisles. As we move to the sign marked Wingai, Cerulean halts, causing Jade to bump into us. "We are not sitting by Magenta."

Peering through people, I spy her, all glitzed out as usual. She sits beside her parents and I assume a younger brother with bronze tips. "It's assigned seating. Do we have a choice?" I ask.

"I don't care. We're not sitting within ten feet of her." He spins us around, presumably to find Axel.

Russet stops him. "I've sent Sky."

Axel leads all Wingai from Mountain Hollow away from the Soaring Heights Wingai. He places us on the other side beside the fox shifters. Rose flits over, her brow furrowed in confusion. "Why aren't you sitting with us?"

"They're avoiding Magenta," Jade answers.

Rose sighs, her eyes crinkling with disapproval. "Cut her some slack, Ceril. She really had her heart set on you two being matches. She's going through a hard time. Violet says she's been crying off and on for a week."

Cerulean doesn't show a bit of remorse. "Matches can't be chosen. She shouldn't have put so much thought into me."

"True," Rose concedes. "But Magenta—"

Cerulean interrupts. "Called Azure trash yesterday and purposely knocked over her IV pole, ripping out Azure's IV." He gestures to my bandaged hand. "For our health and sanity, I think it's best if we don't have contact with each other, at least until she claims her own match and gets over me."

Rose lets out a breath, her teeth sinking into her bottom lip. "All right. I'll relay this to your father." After Cerulean thanks her, she returns to her bench, her red wings bouncing with her steps.

Bree leans over me and muses at Cerulean. "If Magenta's so into you, could she be behind Azure's attack?"

Jade and Cerulean laugh like the idea is ludicrous.

"Magenta's too prim to get her wings dirty." Jade shakes his feathers.

"No, her bite isn't big enough to be killer," Cerulean says knowingly to Bree. "Plus she's not stealthy enough to get past the wolves. She's a flying neon sign." Jade and I laugh at Cerulean's description of her wings and clothing choices.

"So, she's one of those annoying yapping dogs that nip at your ankles," Ben says, causing Jade and Cerulean to chuckle more.

"Exactly. She'll be tamed once she gets her match," Cerulean says with confidence.

CHAPTER TWENTY-TWO

CERIL

A xel stands in front of the fire and holds his hands out for silence. "Thank you all for coming to our Summer Summit. It is a pleasure for us of the Cascade Mountain pack to host. I want to open this meeting with a wish of goodwill between all our people. May any issues brought before us be resolved, and let peace reign among us." The auditorium echoes with murmurs of agreement. Axel smiles. "As dictated from our last meeting, I believe the bears are up first."

Orson, chief of the bear shifters takes Axel's place. In human form, he's no less than a giant. His height tops out at six feet nine inches. He has a barrel chest, thick corded arm muscles, and hands that easily outsize mine. Once, I watched him fell an eighty-year-old fir tree with one punch.

He begins by going over the businesses they're involved in. Logging, masonry, carpentry, and high-end mountain construction. Bears enjoy working with their hands. Conversation flows freely from suggestions thrown out from other shifters to help them make use of their full potential.

Going into the second hour, he switches to more interesting accounts. "We said goodbye to three bears over the spring season: two to old age, and one to a mountain fall we suspect may have been a suicide." He grimaces. That must have been a hard one to swallow. "Five bears found their true mate. Nine cubs were born." He grins with pride. "Including one of my own."

"That makes five for you, doesn't it?" Trisha, Axel's mate, asks.

Orson bobs his head. "It does. Three boys and two girls." Congratulations ring out. Orson grins his proud-father smile again. He reports on their health. "Our bear blood continues to be strong, keeping our families safe." He takes a breath, his eyes focusing on the bear section of the benches. "Our last order of business is for the council to decide on a human. Luke, Jeska." He motions at two bears.

The two lead a red-faced middle-aged man with graying hair and an obvious beer gut.

Orson holds his hands out. "Would the council please step forward to confer?"

The leaders of each shifter group stand and make their way down. They include Dad, Russet, Danyon, Axel, Orson, and Imogen of the foxes.

Russet stops in front of Azure. "When it gets to our turn, you will be recognized, and our power will shift. For now I will retain the council position."

Azure smiles sweetly. "I'm in no hurry."

"Of course not," Russet drawls, his eyes rolling.

The council forms a circle around the human. They speak in low tones, allowing admissions and choices to be said privately. Marigold passes out chocolate bars while we wait. Soft chatter from the benches floats on the breeze.

The council steps away from the human and confers privately. The council members break rank. Orson calls out as he walks to the human. "The decision has been made." Orson rips the human's throat out with one slash of a shifted bear paw. Azure and her friends gasp with horror. Eyes popping, the man crumples to the ground, blood pooling out of his neck cavity. Luke and Jeska drag the body into the woods.

"I think I'm going to be sick." Bree covers her mouth.

"A warning would have been nice," Azure growls. Her anger hits me square in the chest. She scoots out of my grasp to focus on her pale-faced friends. I have to stretch my wing to its full extent to keep my touch on her.

I try to reassure her. "That's not going to happen to your friends. They saved mine and Jade's lives by getting us to Soaring Heights, and they've been nothing but supportive and helpful to you. They're going to be fine. That guy must've given off some real warning bells for the council to feel the need to eliminate him. We don't kill lightly."

"But it still should've been done out of the public eye," Azure grumbles.

"That would be ideal, but how do you propose we do that without giving the guy a heads-up that his life is at an end?" I ask. "His self-preservation instinct would kick into overdrive, and we'd have a fight on our hands. It's merciful to catch him off guard and make it quick so there's little suffering on both our parts. Most of the time, the humans brought to the summit aren't even told they face the possibility of death. They're kept away from the meeting until it's their time to be approved so they don't see anyone else executed and make a run for it." I take a breath. "Your friends are sitting here with us because there's basically no doubt they'll be accepted."

"You're probably right. Still, I can't believe how easily you reason a person's execution." Azure's disgust coils around my stomach. She shoves my wing off her. My mouth parts in surprise and hurt. She'd rather be in pain than be touched by me.

"Switch places with me please, Jack," she asks him. He stands. Azure slides into his spot. He takes hers. Her hands reach out to grab hold of Bree's and Jack's. Ben places his on top of Bree's and Azure's. "I've got you." They bend their heads to rest on each other, finding comfort in their friendship.

I retract my wings. My wounded heart burns with hurt and her simmering rage. I thought I could reassure her by explaining how we normally do things, thus allowing her to see that we've made exceptions for her friends. That approach failed.

Jade nudges me and says, "You should've been more sensitive. Azure's as human as a Wingai can get. She's not going to accept killing for our security."

I scowl. Jade's right, but I don't want to hear it. "You can't afford to be sensitive as a Lead."

Russet's eyes narrow on his return as he spots Azure's and my separation. "Whatever problem you two have created, fix it now," he hisses at us. "We can't afford our Lead's health to drop."

Azure straightens and glowers. "He's not the only one in trouble. You both should've thought to tell me we'd see someone get their throat ripped out."

"You knew humans coming to this meeting could face death," Russet counters.

She arches her brows. "Yes, but not that it would be viewed by everyone. Neither of you gave any regard to our sensibilities as first-time meeting goers."

Russet sighs. A frown peeks around the corners of his lips. "I should have considered that. I'm sorry. Now will you go back to your match?"

"I need some space to process and be here for my friends first," she says. "Give me that, and then I'll go back."

"A few minutes," Russet agrees, then sits next to his match on the bench above us.

Azure leans against Jack. I'm still a little hurt she pushed me off, although as I watch Jack give her a smile of gratitude, I acknowledge the selflessness she's exhibiting by being a support to her friends over her own well-being. Their love for each other is stronger than what I have with her. I'm terrified I'll never reach their level, that every time we have a disagreement or things get tough, she'll shove me away in favor of them.

AZURE

My body throbs, a consistent pound that seems to move to the beat of my heart. However, I'm not about to give in and go back to Cerulean—Mr. Casual-about-Human-Execution. I've felt worse pain. I can handle it for peace of mind.

Next to report are the wolves. Axel speaks for a good hour and a half in the same manner as Orson of the bears. My injuries make it hard for me to pay attention, and most of Axel's talk goes in and straight out of my head.

Cerulean scowls while he watches the proceedings. His expression softens the few times he glances my way but hardens again as he turns back. I'm not sure where his anger is directed. I assume he's mostly mad at me for rejecting him, but his "I'm fine with a no-warning public murder" attitude doesn't sit well with me.

Russet nudges me as Axel closes. "I think you've had more than enough time. Back now." He jerks his thumb in Cerulean's direction.

"Fine." I try not to sound curt. I'm surprised he waited this long to push me to return.

I switch places with Jack again. Cerulean releases his wings and extends one to mine. The aching ceases almost instantly. I shut my eyes, my shoulders dropping and breath exhaling in a moment of sweet mind-numbing bliss. A subtle unintentional connection opens between us, and I sense him sharing my relief, though emotionally rather than physically. I read his desire for a rock-solid relationship between us and a twinge of something else. Trying to understand, I delve deeper into our link. His gaze whips to mine. I run straight into a brick wall as he breaks the bond.

Quietly but firmly, he says, "I don't appreciate you riffling around to satisfy your curiosity. If you want to know what's going on with me, ask, like you'd want me to do for you."

I'm immediately contrite because he's totally right. "Sorry, I didn't mean to overstep."

He takes my hand in his and squeezes. "I'll try not to either."

Long tables are set up near the firepit. A line of mostly women brings a variety of dishes to the table. The scent of a sweet and smoky barbecue floats toward me. My mouth waters. I used up all my energy taking space from Cerulean.

"Come eat!" Axel gestures to the tables buckling with food.

Russet passes out sub sandwiches and bottles of pink lemonade from a wicker basket. "We're not trusting community food. Whoever poisoned Jex could have tainted what's there."

I sigh, wishing I could sink my teeth into the grilled fare. I hate having to watch my every move. Bree doesn't touch her meal, and Ben and Jack only pick at theirs. Guilt gnaws a hole through my stomach, and my appetite vanishes. I'm starting to wish I could go back in time and stop the miscommunication that revealed me to my friends.

"Who's up next?" I ask Russet.

"We are," he answers while screwing the cap back on his drink. "In light of your match to Ceril, Emerald and I have agreed to present together."

"All right." I hope the torture I've put my friends under will then cease. My gut clenches in resolve to use my threat just in case. They get out alive or I'm dead too.

"Hey, Ceril!" A girl greets him with a bright welcoming smile. Her vibrant red highlights stand out against her medium-brown hair. Her purple tank top that matches her eyes sports a fox with the words "I'm foxy" written across her chest. My lips quirk.

Cerulean turns on his charm. "Hey, Tinsley. How are you?"

"Good." Her purple eyes rest on me. "I wanted to meet your match." She extends her hand to me, and we shake. "Hi. I'm Tinsley, from the fox shifter pack."

I smile. "Azure."

"Who are your friends?" Her gaze drifts down to Jack, Bree, and Ben, then stops and lingers on Jack. Her pupils dilate, and her vivid purple eyes shine.

"These are Jack, Bree, and Ben," I say. "They are the most amazing friends you could ever want." My spirits lift when I get a grin out of them.

"That's awesome." I love how nonjudgmental she is of my human friends. Tinsley extends her hand to Jack. "It's nice to meet you."

"Same." Jack encloses her fingers in his. Tinsley's eyes glow. "Whoa." Jack lets out a surprised breath. He pulls his hand back quickly as if she'd shocked him with static electricity.

"Tinsley, come eat!" A guy I assume is her brother—based on similar features, red spikes in his medium-brown hair, and the fact that he's wearing the men's version of her foxy shirt—shouts at her.

"I'll be there," she calls over her shoulder. Her gaze sweeps across us again. "I hope we can chat again soon. Bye, Jack." She wiggles her fingers at him, a trace of heat in her expression, as she trots off.

"What was that?" Bree and I ask Jack at the same time.

Jack runs a hand through his hair, his expression bewildered. "I don't know. She touched my hand, and it was like sparks went off. Is that normal?" he asks Cerulean.

Cerulean shares a look with Jade. "Uh, yeah, it can be." He laughs almost apprehensively.

"Cerulean." I give him my best no-nonsense attitude.

He scratches his chin. "Tinsley was probably just messing with you," he tells Jack. "Foxes are super playful and like to tease."

"Oh." Jack frowns, then shrugs as if putting it out of his mind. "All right."

Other friends of Cerulean's stop by to say hello. I meet Hudson, Miles, and Sierra from the wolf pack and River and Lily from the bears.

The cat shifter girl who helped bring Cerulean to me to seal the match, hugs him. I learn her name is Kiana. She then apologizes to me about Jex. "Please don't think badly of us for the actions of one crazy cat shifter. I promise we're not all psychotic."

Except for the fox shifter Tinsley, everyone gives Bree, Ben, and Jack a wide berth. Their standoffishness irritates me and makes it hard for me to like them. Just because they're humans does not mean they are less or worse than shifters.

Once lunch is cleared away, Axel stands. "The Wingai are up next. Emerald and Russet will be presenting together due to the match of Ceril and Azure."

Russet and Emerald make their way to the stage, each carrying a black spiral notebook. Emerald nods at Russet for him to speak first.

"Shall we start with the good news?" Russet smiles at the crowd. "After nineteen years of hell, Mountain Hollow has gained a Silver-Tipped Lead. Azure, Ceril, would you come down here?"

I hold onto the ends of Cerulean's wing as he lifts me into his arms. Reaching Russet, Cerulean turns so we face the benches.

Russet speaks. "I would like to formally introduce you to Azure Hatch, daughter of Fire and Amethyst Tallon—"

"And match to Ceril," Emerald adds with a proud grin.

Russet smiles fondly at me. My chest twinges unexpectedly. I've never had a father figure before, but Russet might have some potential. "Last week, we started recognizing Silver Wingai. Soon we will no longer be matchless."

The auditorium erupts into claps, cheers, and whistles. I spot a few Wingai, Crimson and Marigold most notably, wiping their eyes. For a second time, the first being after I recognized some of the matchless, it sinks into me how much matching means to the Wingai. I see the joy and hope in their eyes and realize my wings are bringing so much good to the Wingai of Mountain Hollow.

The cheers die down, and Russet says, "I shall be spending—" His words are cut off by a loud screech from the audience.

Cerulean pivots toward the left side of the benches, where the Gold Wingai sit. Axel and Brexton have their hands around Magenta. Emerald, Russet, Cerulean, and I hurry over.

"What is the meaning of this?" Diamond demands. "Unhand my daughter!"

"We have reason to believe Magenta is behind the attempted murders of Azure and Jex," Axel says, his voice hard.

"What?" multiple Wingai ask, eyes wide.

"On what grounds?" Diamond asks.

"Jex woke up. He names Magenta as his counterpart," Axel says.

The color drains out of Magenta's face. She flaps her wings at Axel and Brexton. Talons out, she attempts to rotate her wrists out of their grasp. "Let me go!"

"Let me take her," Diamond pleads. Axel and Brexton hesitate. "She won't go anywhere, I promise." They release her into her father's arms. He twists her hands to make her nails retract, then holds her tight. "Magenta, what have you done?"

"Nothing!" she cries.

Axel's attention shifts, his eyes flicking up the sloping hill. "Here is Jex now."

I follow Axel's gaze. Jex walks slowly with a middle-aged lady with flaming red hair, probably the woman Axel mentioned, Samira. Two guards go before them, and two more make up the rear. Jex's golden eyes, tired and red rimmed, meet mine. Cold fear steals my breath and clenches my insides. My fight-or-flight instinct takes over. I shove against Cerulean's hold to get away.

"It's okay." Cerulean's fingers dig into me as he struggles not to drop me. I don't trust him.

Russet steps in to help. "Calm down, Azure. Nothing's going to happen to you."

He helps Cerulean sit on the edge of the stage with me. Ben, Bree, Jack, and Jade rush over and sit beside us. "We've got you." Bree takes my hand. The Silver Guard form a circle around us.

My terror eases now that I'm surrounded by protectors. My heart beats fast, but I settle against Cerulean. He presses a kiss to my temple. "You're safe. I promise."

I watch through the gap between Crimson and Sky. Jex sits on the first bench, flanked by guards. Danyon, Axel, Emerald, and Russet face him. Diamond holds Magenta off to the side. Orson and Imogen also stand nearby. The other Wingai have moved to benches closer to the stage. The air stills in anticipation.

"What have you to say for yourself, Jex?" Danyon asks.

"Magenta abused our friendship," he says, his voice scratchy. "She led me to believe the Silver-Tipped Wingai was a threat to shifters. Our world would end with her in it."

"In what way?" Emerald asks.

"Magenta said the Silver-Tipped was in love with humans," Jex continues. "She wanted many to live in our communities, and they would destroy what we have. Shifters would become lab rats at the mercy of human scientists. I was told if the Silver-Tipped were taken out, we would remain safe and anonymous. I saw three humans with the girl and believed Magenta."

"Feathers," Cerulean says.

Anger lights a fire in my chest. I would never.

"So you took Azure into the woods to dispose of the threat," Russet says.

Jex nods. "Magenta was supposed to meet me, but she didn't show. I called her, and she said she couldn't come."

"Why not?" Axel asks.

Jex rubs his forehead. "She said her father put her on lockdown due to the humans and that she couldn't get out of the house. She reiterated the threat the girl posed, saying she'd gotten her information directly from her father, who spoke with Lead Emerald. She said Lead Emerald and Acting Lead Russet were figuring out how to stop the girl from bringing in more humans but weren't sure it would be enough—because the girl was crafty." He takes a breath. "Magenta said it was up to me to save all shifters. No one but the cats would have the guts to do what needed to be done." He coughs hard, his body racking. Samira hands him a bottle of water. He downs half the bottle, then wipes his mouth with the back of his hand.

Scowls darken faces, and many eyes glow, everyone's animals close to the surface.

"Tell me about the poisoning," Russet orders.

Jex's face hardens, and his golden eyes gleam. "Magenta visited me in the wolves' holding cell. She smelled strongly of fear. I worried an invasion of humans had retaliated for my actions against the girl. I went up to the bars. Magenta stabbed me with a needle. Immediately I was overcome with weakness and slid to the floor. Magenta apologized and ran. I realized then that I had been betrayed and lied to."

Axel verifies Jex's words. "Magenta did visit with reports concerning the land we share."

"She also delivered a book of accounts to me in the hospital," Russet says. "Perhaps she picked up a needle and poison on her way out?"

All eyes turn accusingly to Magenta, held fast by her father. She's white as a ghost, her pink wings limp behind her back. Her lower lip trembles, an admission of guilt in her fear-ridden eyes.

"Oh, Magenta, what have you done?" Diamond cries.

Panicked, she wrestles with her father. Axel and Brexton step in again to restrain her. Diamond releases her into their care. He faces her, pain evident in his face. "Why, Magenta? How could you?"

Tears and mascara make tracks down her cheeks. "I needed her gone to make Ceril mine. He's supposed to be mine!"

Appalled gasps sound from the benches.

"Oh . . ." Cerulean exhales. His hold loosens on me. His face turns a shade of light green. He obviously underestimated Magenta's obsession with him.

"Called it," Bree whispers.

"You so did," I quietly acknowledge her.

"You were willing to condemn our entire race to extinction over this crazy infatuation?" Diamond shrieks.

Passion coats Magenta's voice. "We have the power to adapt. Bronze Wingai did it when they were at risk of dying out. We can do it again—gain the power to recognize ourselves and choose our own matches."

"Bronze adapting is a myth! Even if it were true, we have no way of knowing whether we could adapt again. If you succeeded and we couldn't evolve, you would have killed us all!" Diamond digs his claws into his hair.

Magenta shrugs. I'm repelled. Her selfishness knows no bounds.

CHAPTER
TWENTY-THREE

CERIL

I blink through the fog clouding my brain. Magenta? I know she's been rather overzealous, but to plot Azure's death? I never thought she had it in her. I shake my head, bewildered and sick to my stomach. I guess it goes to show people I've known all my life aren't always what they seem.

Russet walks over, his black journal tucked under his arm. "The council agrees that once Magenta and Jex have a chance to plead their case, the ones who were wronged will decide their fate. That means it's up to you two, Ceril and Azure."

"What about Jade?" Azure asks. "He was hurt too."

"That's true." Russet rubs his chin. "I guess I'll leave that up to you."

"We will consult with him," Azure says.

"Yeah." I scratch my head. How could a childhood friend turn into such a monster? My chest tightens. Had I been too harsh with Magenta? Had I driven her to do this? Azure startles me with a snap of her fingers in my face. "What?"

"There you are," she says. "They want to do the trial right now. We're supposed to move over there." She points to a bench placed near the firepit.

"Oh." I pick her up and walk over. Jade and a few members of the Silver Guard follow. Her friends have returned to their seats by Marigold.

Jade whispers to me. "I seriously did not expect Magenta to stoop so low. She's a mean crow when she doesn't get her way, but murder? That's a whole other ball game."

"I know," I say.

Jex sits on the bench placed ten feet before us. Azure stiffens, fear snaking around her heart. I take her into my arms and hold her against me. Jex grimaces at Azure's reaction, regret strong in his eyes.

Dad speaks to Jex, his voice solemn. "You have five minutes."

He clears his throat. "I do not ask for your forgiveness, but I do wish to offer an apology. My parents were shot and killed in their cat forms by a human hunter two winters back. My dislike of humans runs deep, and I try to keep myself apart." He coughs into his elbow. "Magenta preyed on this. When she contacted me in a panic about humans becoming involved with shifters, I believed her lies. I considered her a good friend and did not suspect she would toss me over the cliff to fulfill her own desires. I believed I was working for the good of shifters. I was willing to be hated if it meant I'd secured our safety for the whole."

My hands ball into fists, and ire heats my bones. Of course Magenta would remember Jex's hardships and use them to her advantage. Did she make a list of those wronged by humans and choose the deadliest one to pillage?

Jade asks, "Why did you take Magenta's word alone? Why didn't you check in with someone else?"

"Good question," I say.

Jex gestures to Azure. "She is a Silver-Tipped. I believed the Wingai's desire to save Mountain Hollow from being matchless would produce lies of peace."

"That's logical," Jade agrees.

Jex turns his attention on Azure. "Are you planning on getting more humans involved with us?"

I don't think he has the right to ask anything, but Azure answers him. "No!" she yells with such vehemence that I jump. "The humans I brought with me are my closest, dearest friends. They gave me protection when I needed it. I trust them with my life, and they trust me with theirs, hence they came to be approved as law requires."

Jex blinks, seeming taken aback by Azure's intensity. Murmurs pick up in the stands, and the shifters appear avidly interested in Azure.

"I am truly sorry." Jex shrugs. "That is all I can say."

The wolves take Jex away and put Magenta in his place. She wears a sullen expression, her eyes angry and red rimmed.

When it becomes clear she's not going to be the first to speak, I do. "I never thought twice of you after I learned you weren't going to be my match. Why didn't you do the same?"

"I couldn't," she says, her hands fisting at her sides. Her eyes fill with tears again. "I've been in love with you for years. I couldn't think of anyone else but you."

"You never should have allowed yourself to cultivate those kinds of feelings for me," I say sharply. "I certainly never did for you. You defied everything that makes us Wingai."

Magenta's lips flatten at my reprimand. Her bottle-green eyes glitter, and I see little remorse in them. My insides twist. "How could you think murdering Azure would bring me to you? Wingai get only one mate, and Azure and I have already claimed each other. If she died, I couldn't make a new match with you."

"Wingai who have lost partners have found comfort in another," she contests.

"Comfort because they don't enjoy being alone isn't the same as finding true love again. They will never be able to create what they had with their match." About ninety percent of matches made are when both Wingai are eighteen. Males always have to wait until that age for their mate-finder sense to activate. Females, however, can match as early as the end of their seventeenth year, and the latest I've heard is two days past their nineteenth birthday. Magenta won't turn eighteen till the first week of August. She still has a full year to be claimed. "What was your plan when your own match came knocking? Kill him too?"

Magenta's eyes dart to the side. I lean back, appalled. "I can't believe this! Have you lost all common sense? Do you have no conscience anymore?" I'm ready to weep at the loss of Magenta's sensibilities.

"All I've ever wanted was you," Magenta says with conviction. "When you first couldn't find your match, I thought there must be a glitch. You just needed a few days to work it out, and then you'd find me. When that didn't happen, I was heartbroken. I decided it didn't matter whether we were matches in the true sense. I could love you enough to make up for it, and we would adapt."

Not likely.

"I was secretly overjoyed as the months ticked by and you still hadn't found her." Magenta wrinkles her nose in disgust at Azure. "It gave me more time to convince you to be mine. And then you started going on those stupid little match quests until finally you brought this piece of trash home and called her yours."

"Don't talk to my match that way!" I snarl.

Magenta rolls her eyes. "I realized quickly that *Lead Azure* didn't deserve you. I heard all about your fight to claim her, and I knew she could never love you like I could. You have your hands full trying to make her fall in love with you when she's never wanted you in the first place."

My breath catches as Magenta's barb hits its target.

Her lips curve, satisfaction glowing in her eyes. "From what I've heard, her mother was coldhearted and malicious. Azure might be incapable of love. She certainly can't see it on you. I thought you would be relieved that I saved you from a fruitless cause."

"I've heard enough," Azure snaps. "If you truly loved Cerulean, you would have respected his wish for a true match. Instead you put your own selfish desires above his, and you got nothing." Azure snuggles into my side. "Cerulean's wings chose me. He will never be yours."

"Then he won't be yours either!" Magenta pulls a syringe from her pocket. She lunges at me, her arm raised high.

Azure launches herself, tackling Magenta with talons out. Magenta flails, screaming as Azure's momentum sends them toppling. Magenta swings her arm with the needle toward Azure as they fall. Azure twists to the side to avoid it. They hit the dirt. Both gasp in pain, and then there's silence. Azure pushes herself off Magenta and sits up, wincing heavily. Magenta lies motionless, her eyes open and glassed. The needle sticks out the left side of her chest.

Body tight with concern, I fly out of my seat to get to Azure. I wrap my wings around her. She tips her head back and sighs. Her aching expression clears.

"Magenta!" Diamond lurches forward and drops on his knees before her. He yanks the syringe out and picks her up. He cradles her still form as tears rapidly fall down his cheeks. "Oh, my darling girl."

"Let me see." Samira sits beside Diamond and places her hands on Magenta. Her amber eyes flare. A moment later, she shakes her head. "Her soul has moved on. I grieve your loss with you."

Magenta just tried to kill me. Azure saved my life, and now Magenta's dead. Blood rushes in my ears, drowning out sound. My heart pounds. Body trembles. Breath quickens. Stomach churns. Feathers.

Azure rubs circles on my lower back. "Breathe, Cerulean," she whispers.

Her gentle presence is the only thing giving me strength.

AZURE

Russet has Samira check me over to make sure I haven't injured myself further. Once I'm deemed fine, Cerulean picks me up, and we return to the bench. They take Magenta's body away. Her family returns to Soaring Heights to grieve. The auditorium is grave, and yet all I can feel is relief. She will never get between Cerulean and me again. I can focus on healing without needing to look over my shoulder for a killer. I'm grateful.

"You tackled Magenta and saved my life." Cerulean smiles, but I still sense a bit of shock. "You're amazing. Thank you." He presses a quick kiss to my lips.

"I couldn't afford not to," I say. For more reasons than I can count. Losing him when he's really starting to grow on me could very well turn me into my mother.

Russet turns to us. "You haven't decided on a punishment for Jex."

"I don't think his punishment should be too harsh," Jade says. "Magenta duped him, and he's shown remorse."

"I suggest thirty days isolation to let him think over his actions, and therapy to help him with his issues against

314

humans," I say. "I would like to see him become a better man out of this, not just be thankful he got out of the noose."

"Sounds good to me," Jade says.

Cerulean nods. "All right. We'll go with that." He delivers the judgment to Jex.

Jex nods, accepting his punishment without a fight. Tension eases out of his shoulders, giving me the impression he expected death. The wolves return him to his holding cell, and Cerulean, Jade, and I return to our seats in the crowd.

Russet stands to address the shifters once more. "What an interesting turn of events this Summit has brought us. I wish to express my gratitude for all those who have helped Mountain Hollow protect our Lead." He grins. "Our future is bright once again." He garners a round of appreciative clapping.

He proceeds to read Mountain Hollow's accounts, and the Summit moves on like nothing murderous ever happened. I'm appalled and intrigued at their ability to easily switch tracks.

It's a different story on my bench. Cerulean watches Russet, but his eyes are glazed, distracted. He wears a pinched frown, brows pulled low, shoulders hunched as he rests his elbows on his knees. Guilt comes off him in waves, and I assume he thinks it's his fault Magenta went off the deep end. Bree's knees bounce. Her hands run up and down her thighs. Ben fiddles with Marvel's Avenger charms on a hemp bracelet Bree made him for Valentine's Day. Their guilt, fear, and dread feed into me until I'm rigid as stone.

Jack nudges me. "Azure."

"Yeah?" I focus on him. Concern slams into me when I see the worry in his eyes. "What is it?"

He holds up his arm. Black lines trail down the back of his hand to the middle of his forearm in the shape of a swirly tree. I watch as more black ink appears, creating roots, filling in the trunk, adding leaves, until the shape reminds me of a mandala tree from an adult coloring book. "I don't know what's going on, but I'm a little freaked out right now."

"Oh my goodness, Jack," I say, alarmed. I grab his arm and rub at the marks. It's as if he just walked out of a tattoo parlor. I lightly tap Cerulean to get his attention. Then I show him Jack's forearm.

Cerulean jumps, startled. "Feathers!"

"What is it?" Jack and I ask.

"It's a fox declaration," he says, eyes on Jack. "You must have had some dormant fox blood in you from a relative who mated with one. Tinsley probably sensed it and activated that part of you when she shook your hand. Your markings mean your fox side is waking up."

"What?" Jack, Bree, and I whisper-shriek.

"I'm a fox shifter?" Jack exclaims. He holds his arm out as though it's diseased. I grab his hand and enfold his fingers in mine.

"I'm not an expert on foxes—they're secretive—but I think so." Cerulean leans around me and sniffs him. "Yeah, sorry. You smell like a fox now."

I smell him too and notice a scent that definitely wasn't there a few hours ago, like cinnamon and nutmeg thrown on a wood fire. "Your aroma *is* different."

Cerulean smiles. "At least you don't have to worry about getting approved."

"Like that matters!" Jack complains. "I'm so dead the second my parents see this."

"Maybe not," I disagree. "If you have fox blood, then one of them has to as well. Maybe it's dormant in them like it was in you, so they've ignored it and went about life as normal humans. It's possible they didn't want to burden you with something they probably didn't think would be an issue."

Jack sighs. "If they know something and didn't tell me, I'm disowning them as my parents." He rubs his forehead, his eyes on the new tattoo. "I can't believe this!"

"It'll be okay," I encourage. "We'll figure it out together."

Russet shuts his black book and tucks it under his arm. "Our last agenda item is the approval of Lead Azure's friends. Would those involved and the council please step forward?"

This is it. I turn to face my friends. "I've got you."

"We trust you, Azure," Bree says.

Jack, Bree, and Ben sit on the bench Magenta and Jex sat on. The council stands in front of them. With a small smile at me, cradled in Cerulean's arms, Russet gestures to his spot in the line. "Would you like to take your place as Lead?"

I don't hesitate. "Absolutely." Cerulean moves us into his place. On impulse I reach out and touch Russet's arm before

317

he's out of reach. "I'd like it if we could vote together. Your influence still carries—if that's all right."

Russet nods. "That's acceptable." Cerulean makes room for him.

Danyon flashes me a grin. "Tell us about your friends, Azure."

"These are Bree, Ben, and Jack. I love them as family," I say with pride. "They came into my life when I was extremely vulnerable. I had just survived the car accident that killed my mother, and I was more skittish than a wild animal. I lacked just about everything in terms of sociability. I was envious of people who seemed well put together. So I decided to do something about it and went to school. These three beautiful souls took me in and taught me everything there is to know about living—how to have fun and be social, how to take charge and be fearless, how to offer support and empathy even when I couldn't relate."

I take a breath. "Before them, I was a broken shell. I had nothing inside of me and no reason to keep living except that I felt obligated to. Their friendship changed that. I literally would not be the person I am today without them."

"Nor would we," Bree chimes in, bringing a smile to my lips.

"I didn't mean to reveal my wings to them. I was terrified of their rejection," I say. "Since finding out, they have been nothing but loyal and protective. Our friendship has only gotten stronger."

"Thank you, Azure," Danyon says. "Does anyone on the council have any questions?"

Orson addresses my friends. "Are you prepared to keep your knowledge of shifters to yourselves? That means not telling family, not writing about it in your diaries or on social media."

"Yes," Bree, Ben, and Jack say in firm tones.

"Should a war break out between humans and shifters, are you willing to defend us?" Orson asks.

"Are you planning a war?" Ben asks.

"We have no plans to start one, but we have policies in place should the humans engage us," Orson says.

Ben scratches his chin. "If people are harming you through no fault of your own, then yes. I'd see that as a problem and want to help. I prefer to stay on the side of good regardless of people."

"Me too," Bree and Jack agree.

"I'll accept that," Orson says.

After a beat of silence, Emerald says, "Shall we put it to a vote?"

Imogen speaks. "I see no reason to vote on Jack." She points to the mark on his arm. "Tinsley discovered fox blood in him and woke it up. He's entirely shifter now."

The other council members bob their heads, conceding.

Jack pales, and his body sways. Bree grabs hold of him before he can faint. The council members chuckle.

Imogen's lips curl into a sly grin. "You've got a lot to learn about us foxes, my dear Jack. Let me be the first to say welcome to the family. We're pleased to have you."

Danyon speaks. "All those in favor of approving Bree and Ben into the fold, raise your hand." All hands go up. "Congratulations, you two. You're approved."

"Yes!" I squeal, pumping my fist into a cheer.

Bree places a hand over her chest. "Oh, thank goodness!"

"My sentiments exactly," Ben laughs.

The rest of the summit goes by in a flash. Emerald announces the business dealings of Soaring Heights, mostly stock market changes and investments, then Danyon speaks for the cats. "Trail cameras are becoming more popular among humans. I have asked all cats to be on the lookout for them in the woods before they shift."

Last, Imogen speaks for the fox shifters. Her most notable moment happens when she comments on Tinsley's tinkering on Jack.

"I'm pleased to announce Tinsley's awakening powers have finally developed as she managed to find the fox in Jack and bring him out," she says.

The fox shifters in attendance cheer and whoop. Tinsley blushes, her lips stretching into a beaming smile. Jack wears a devastated expression like someone just ripped up his prized collection of baseball cards. Maybe they did. How is he supposed to go on to play major league ball?

Imogen's purple eyes find Jack's, her lips curving into that sly smile again. "Don't run from us yet. You may not know it, but you're going to love your new self."

"Fox shifters are great," Cerulean says to him.

Jack manages a small smile. "I hope so."

A party ensues that evening. More wood is added to the fire, creating larger flames and additional heat. The wolves lay out a huge feast of meats, potatoes, beans, salads, pies, cakes, and cookies. The bears bring speakers and blast up-tempo music. Conversation, dancing, and laughter light up the night. With the threat on my life over and my friends approved, I join in the fun as best I can with my injuries.

I wrap my legs around Cerulean's hips, my arms around his neck, and we dance to a slow pop song. His wings enfold us in a cocoon, giving us a semblance of privacy. His cheeks are flushed, and his sea-green eyes look dazzling in the firelight. His wide, pleased smile sends butterflies into my stomach and warms my heart.

Cerulean creates a mental link between us. *"I'm sorry about earlier,"* he says, referencing our fight about human approval. *"I've been going to these Summits for years. What happens here doesn't faze me anymore. But this is your first time, and you had stakes in the game. I should have been more sensitive in my attempt to be supportive."*

"Yes, you should have." My heart warms with how genuine he is with his apology, and even though we had a disagreement, I appreciate that he's trying.

"Will you forgive me?" he asks.

I scrunch my face. *"Hmm, let me think."*

Cerulean laughs in mock offense. *"Oh, come on!"*

"Of course I forgive you." I press my lips against his.

"Yes!" Cerulean deepens the kiss, and his hands roam to anchor me closer—if that's even possible.

The butterflies in my stomach transform into molten lava, sending delicious warmth to the coldest recesses of my body and soul, a place I vowed I'd never let someone in. Cerulean smashes through the defenses around my heart, claims love I didn't know I could feel, and declares victory.

CHAPTER TWENTY-FOUR

CERIL

Azure and I sit together on an exam table in the hospital three days after the summit. Russet hovers nearby.

Dr. Sage removes the wrappings around Azure's leg.

He prods the stitched area. "Looks good," he says. "You can start putting weight down."

Azure grins. "About time."

I sigh. "Guess you won't need me. You can hobble off on your own."

Azure laughs. "That's right."

"There'll be none of that," Russet says to Azure. "Ceril's touch stays until you're one-hundred-percent healed."

"Let's see that wing of yours." Dr. Sage removes the bandages. The X-ray Dr. Sage took this morning shows the bone has fused back together, compliments of my constant contact. He has me hop off the table, taking my touch off her. "Can you stretch it out?" he asks her.

Azure grimaces as she slowly extends her wing. "It's sore."

Dr. Sage nods. "Expected. See if you can give it a few flaps." Azure winces as she does. "Excellent. Let's take this outside and see what you can do." He helps Azure to her feet.

I take her hand in mine and wrap my feathers around her. Azure walks out of the patient room under her own power, an exultant smile on her lips. We step out into a light summer drizzle.

Dr. Sage holds out his hands. "I want you to take this slow. No cross-country flights." He chuckles. "Pump your wings, and let's see if you can hover."

"You've got this." I press a quick kiss to her lips and step back.

Azure unfurls her wings and stretches them taut. She scrunches her face as she gets her wings moving. With a little jump, she pushes herself into the air. "Ouch!" She drops to the ground. I catch her as she stumbles.

Dr. Sage examines her, his fingers feeling around her feathers. "They might not be strong enough to support you yet." His light-green eyes find mine. "Ceril, keep your touch on her for another couple of days, and then we'll try this again." He turns back to Azure. "I want you to stretch for now. Give your wings a few flaps here and there. Let the damaged one get used to working again."

"Fine." Azure's disappointment snakes through me.

I pull her close and press a kiss to her forehead. "It'll be okay. We'll make a flier out of you again."

"Yeah." She sighs.

We say goodbye to Dr. Sage with the promise to see him again in a few days, then amble to Russet's car. Azure and I slide in the back.

Russet turns in the driver's seat. "Don't be discouraged. You're healing quicker than any common Wingai. You've made significant progress for a week's time."

A brief smile touches Azure's lips. She snuggles into my side for the ride to our nest. I bend my head to rest on hers. We've gotten closer since the shifter summit. She doesn't shy away from my touch as often as before. I'm eager to take our relationship to the next level. Though neither of us has said it yet, I'm pretty sure I've won her heart over. She's definitely got mine.

Russet parks. I look out and see my parents' house. Dad sits in a rocking chair on the front porch reading the Soaring Heights paper. Russet gets out, prompting Azure and me to do the same. We walk around the car and up the path. Dad tucks the paper under his arm and approaches.

"Why are we here?" I ask.

"Yeah, my friends are leaving in the next hour," Azure says. "I need to be home to say goodbye."

"Emerald and I just want to talk to you both for a minute," Russet says, his face the picture of innocence. I don't buy it.

Neither does Azure. She arches an eyebrow. "About what?"

"A timeline of sorts," Russet answers evasively.

Dad ushers us into the living room. Seventies rock music blasts above our heads. Mom's in her creative space.

"What's this about?" I ask the second we've all sat.

"Have you seen today's paper?" Dad tosses his copy at me.

"No." I unroll the paper to read the headline.

In bold capital letters, it reads, "The Most Anticipated Baby for Our Rising Generation." Underneath the headline is a zoomed-in picture of me pressing a kiss to Azure's cheek while she laughs, ice-cream cones in our hands. I snort. Soaring Heights paparazzi at its finest.

Azure snatches the paper from me, her mouth parting. I read the article over her shoulder.

In an unprecedented move, our very own Gold-Tipped Cerulean Hatch of Soaring Heights is matched to Silver-Tipped Lead Azure Tallon of Mountain Hollow. Sources say our drama-besieged couple is finally settling down. We hear the two are becoming quite cozy and, dare I say it, in love. The question now arises: is there a baby in the works?

"Unbelievable!" Azure crumples the paper into a ball. Her anger plows into my chest, burning my heart.

I put my hand on hers. "It's just a silly article to generate sales and keep people entertained. There's no need to get worked up."

Azure's dark-blue eyes flash. "It's rude and invasive to speculate on our personal lives."

I shrug. I'd rather take this news report over the ones they wrote a few months ago questioning my lack of a match, thus dooming Soaring Heights to be matchless. "We're Tipped. It comes with the territory."

Azure scowls. Dad swoops in to speak before she can retort. "Write-ups and inquiries like this will pop up until something is announced. Wingai need to see their future secured."

Azure's wings flick with irritation. Dad holds up his hands. "We're not telling you to make it a priority right this minute. We're simply asking for the promise of children to assure everyone."

I thread my hand through Azure's. "Give us a few minutes alone to talk about it." I wait until Dad and Russet leave the room before I speak. "Before we even have this conversation, I think there's something else we need to address."

Azure tenses. "What's that?"

I take a breath of courage. "I love you."

She stills. Her brows furrow and lips pinch. My heart plunges into my stomach. She casts her eyes to our clasped hands. Feathers, I've said it too quickly. I brace myself for another rejection. She says, "I think . . . I love you too."

My jaw slackens. What? I put a hand on my forehead and dig my fingers into my hair. "Did you . . . I mean, really?" Feathers, she loves me.

Azure laughs at my dumbfounded expression. "Yes." She cups my face in her hands and touches her lips to mine. I kiss her back, funneling my excitement into it.

Aware that I'm in my parents' house with Russet and Dad probably listening around the corner, I force myself to break it off. "So about—"

"I'm not ready," Azure says firmly.

"Tell me honestly. With a plan in place and support, could you be ready sometime down the road?" I pray she says yes, because the thought of her carrying my child fills me with happiness and warmth. I honestly think she'd be an awesome mother. She is fiercely protective of those she loves. Our children would not lack in support and love. Plus, I don't want to doom our entire race.

Azure sinks her top teeth into her bottom lip. "It's possible, yeah," she admits.

Hallelujah. No Wingai destruction for us. I grin. "That's all I ask."

AZURE

Russet's mouth splits into the widest grin I've ever seen on him when Cerulean announces I've agreed to the request of children sometime in the future. A good ten years away, I hope. I'm sensible enough to know I'm not all put together yet. While my body is on the fast track to being fully healed, I still have some scars from my mother that need mending. I foresee some hard talks with Cerulean concerning my childhood. With his encouragement and love, I trust that all my fears with commitment and the trauma my mom inflicted will be taken care of. I look forward to the day that I become the best version of myself that I can be.

Russet drops Cerulean and me off at our nest with plans to see me the following day for official Lead training. Oh joy. We'll resume recognizing when my health is one hundred percent.

The front doors open as we walk up the drive. Ben heads to the open trunk of Jack's car, bags in hand. "Azure's here!" he yells over his shoulder.

Jack sprints out of the house and skids to a halt a few inches away from me. Panic laces his face. He grasps my upper arms. "You've got to do something, Azure. I can't be a fox shifter!"

Alarm bells ring. "What's happened?"

"Look at this." He lifts his forearm, showing the fox declaration. The leaves on the tree have filled in with vivid green. Upon closer inspection, I notice the color fading and deepening as though in tandem with his breaths.

I grab his arm and press a finger to the leaves. Nothing changes. "Oh my goodness, Jack. This is—"

"I know!" he interrupts. "Tinsley is supposed to be here in a few minutes. She apologized for waking me up. She said she felt compelled to meet me at the summit, and when she shook my hand, her fox acted out before she could stop herself. Now she insists on taking me under her 'paw' to train me since it's her fault." He throws a hand up as he talks, barely taking a breath between words. "I have to go home today. My parents will throw a fit if I don't. So now she's coming along. She'll get to witness the big confrontation that's gonna go down. Dad is going to throw me into the meat grinder when he realizes I can't be a baseball player anymore."

"Really?" Cerulean asks with genuine curiosity.

Bree steps out, twisting the cap on a water bottle. "Oh yeah. Jack's dad wanted to be a major league baseball player in high school, and he had some real talent, but then he got Jack's mom pregnant. Her family kicked her out, so he had to quit playing and take on two jobs to support her. Jack is now their golden ticket. His parents are determined that nothing stands in his way."

Cerulean frowns. "Oh." He pats Jack on the shoulder. "Tough luck, man. Fox shifters are pretty awesome, though."

"That's not going to matter if I'm dead!" Jack cries.

I cup Jack's face with my hands, meeting his eyes with mine. "Take a breath. It will be okay. You're not alone. You've got friends in your corner." I drop my hands.

He closes his eyes, inhales deeply, and exhales slowly. Bree makes him do it again until his shoulders relax. I fish in my pocket for my keys and pull off the set to my place in McMinnville. I hand them to Jack. "My house is open to you anytime. Use it."

Jack gives me a heartfelt smile. "Thanks, Azure. I don't know what I'd do without you."

"You'd be in a lot less trouble probably," I tease.

Ben finishes loading up Jack's Honda and gets the key. Tinsley arrives in a cute yellow Beetle, sending my approval rating of her higher. With hugs, I say my goodbyes to Bree, Ben, and Jack. We'll plan a date to meet up soon.

I read the nerves on Jack as he gets in Tinsley's bug. "You think he's going to be okay?" I ask Cerulean as we wave them off.

"Oh yeah," Cerulean says confidently. "He's in for a roller-coaster ride, but he'll be all right. Just like you."

"It's been a ride, all right." I laugh.

Cerulean turns on a megawatt smile. My heart melts and sizzles. "Let's go on a new one." With lightning speed, he sweeps me off my feet.

Cerulean carries me through the threshold and up the stairs, placing expert kisses on my forehead, lips, and chin, in the hollow of my neck, and behind my ear. Butterflies and rising heat erupt in my lower belly. I'm ready for a new adventure.

EPILOGUE: THREE YEARS LATER

AZURE

I step out of Dr. Sage's office, my hand enfolded in Cerulean's. Late-afternoon snow falls lightly, tickling my face. It's the first snowfall of December. I tilt my face up to marvel at it. Cerulean chuckles softly at me. A silver SUV pulls up in front of us. We get in.

Russet turns in the driver's seat to face us, his eyebrow raised. "Well?"

Cerulean rubs my swollen belly, a beaming smile on his lips. My heart melts a little at the pure joy emanating from him. He's been nothing short of ecstatic since finding out we're expecting. While tendrils of fear on motherhood still hold me in their grip, his support and love have been greatly alleviating. "Doc says any day now."

Russet grins, his enthusiasm matching Cerulean's. "Excellent."

As we roll out of the parking lot, I pounce on Russet. "So now are you going to tell us why you insisted on driving us to the appointment?"

His gray eyes flick to the rearview mirror. I read a gleam in them. "You'll see soon enough."

I huff in mild annoyance, though in truth I'm not really worried. During the past three years, Russet has shown enough care and consideration to become like a father to me. And, as I've embraced my role as Lead with a campaign of personal growth and healing, peace has been achieved among all in Soaring Heights and Mountain Hollow. "Why don't I like the sound of this?"

Cerulean laughs. "There's definitely been some scheming going on behind our feathers."

Ten minutes later Russet parks in front of the Mountain Hollow Community Center in the "Reserved for Lead" parking space. Casting my eyes around as I get out, I note almost every spot in the whole parking lot plus the adjacent street is taken. It's usually only this full when we're hosting our monthly town hall meeting. I wonder what big event Russet has planned.

Chatter and music emanate from the community center's doors. A party? Russet ushers us inside and down the brightly lit hallway. We stop in front of the open doors of our largest event room. Cerulean and I peek inside. My eyes are hit with an explosion of decorations—streamers, balloons, and confetti in varying shades of blue and pink. Tables run the length of the room with alternating pink and blue tablecloths. A pile of presents rests in one corner. In another, several Wingai run a DJ station. Against the back wall, a potluck-style dinner has been set up, smells of roast beef, ham, peppermint, and ginger wafting in the air. A host of Wingai from Soaring Heights and Mountain Hollow mingle all over the place. A large banner hangs from the ceiling reading, "Baby Hatch! Congratulations!"

I turn on Russet, my voice slightly incredulous. "A baby shower?"

"We never had a party for you and Ceril when you sealed your match. We're not letting this achievement slide too." He gestures to my baby bump, his tone firm. "Wingai enjoy celebrating their Leads' accomplishments. They need to feel connected to you."

I hold my hands up in a show of backing down. "All right." I don't think a baby shower is necessary. We have everything we need for the baby, and while I like parties, I'm not particularly fond of ones focused on me. It's probably because Mom and I never celebrated anything growing up. Even after all these years, partying still gives me a weird feeling.

Pushing those thoughts aside, I touch Russet's arm, inflecting sincerity in my voice. "Thank you."

His gray eyes brighten, making me glad I chose not to resist. "You're welcome."

Cerulean tucks me into his side, an excited grin on his face. My lips quirk. He's always up for a party. "Shall we go in?"

Cheers erupt as we enter. The bright atmosphere draws me in, making it easy to express surprised delight. I make a show of looking around the room with appreciation. As the noise dies down, I say, "Wow, you have really outdone yourselves!"

"Yeah, this is amazing," Cerulean adds. "We can't thank you enough for putting this together and for your excitement for Baby Hatch." He puts his hand on my stomach, then chuckles as the baby pushes against his hand. The little chick always seems to have a kick for him.

"What's the news from the doc?" Rose asks us. Soft chatter ceases as everyone quiets to listen.

"No concerns. Everything's looking great. It's anytime now," Cerulean says with enthusiasm.

This earns a round of whooping and clapping.

Marigold shouts, "Don't forget to cast your votes for gender and wing color!" She points to a big poster board with four columns: boy, girl, wing color, and a place to write your name.

Despite living in the modern age of ultrasounds, it's common practice for Wingai to wait until birth to find out the gender. I haven't minded. Admittedly, my anxiety about becoming a mother has been my main focus. Besides, there are plenty of gender-neutral clothes and accessories, and there's no use coming up with a name beforehand. We name our kids after their wing color. Dr. Sage says chicks are born with them tucked in. They'll release once the baby feels comfortable enough outside of the womb, usually a few hours after birth, barring any complications. Their talons usually come in sometime after six months, sort of like teeth.

Rose bids everyone to eat, and the party jumps into full swing. We fill ourselves up with good food, music, conversation, and laughter. Having worked tirelessly to bring Soaring Heights and Mountain Hollow together by fixing the matchless problem, I'm overjoyed to see Gold, Silver, and Bronze Wingai sitting among each other with open friendliness and ease.

People flit to and from our table to offer their congratulations on Baby Hatch. Some innocuous questions are raised, such as "Are you hoping for a boy or girl?"

"Doesn't matter," we say.

Some crack jokes. "Too bad you're not having twins. We could get one Gold and one Silver-Tipped in one fell swoop."

"Wouldn't that be nice." Cerulean chuckles lightly as if we haven't heard this the entire pregnancy.

One lady from Soaring Heights tells us her experience of having her second child without her match. "Clover always goes on a morning flight to start his day. I was feeling a little off, but I wasn't too concerned, so I told him to go. Ten minutes after he took off, our little Ivory decided to come. Worst. Pain. Ever."

At this Cerulean says to me, "You've got nothing to worry about. With how close we are, I'm not leaving your side for anything longer than a shower." He brushes a kiss on my temple.

I lean into him, meshing my feathers with his. "Fine with me."

The unspoken hope that Baby Hatch will be Tipped shines bright in everyone's eyes.

The baby shower ends. Russet and Marigold drop us off at our nest with plans to deliver the many shower gifts the following day. We offer them many thanks, then slowly walk up the drive to the front door, our boots crunching in the snow. I turn to Cerulean. "How much disappointment are we going to face if our chick doesn't come out Tipped?"

He shrugs. "Some, but it doesn't matter. Wingai will just look forward to the next one." Stopping at the threshold, he wraps me in a hug, his wings cocooning me. "Don't let yourself get caught up in what our baby should or shouldn't be. Our chick will be loved whether he or she is Tipped or not. I'm going to be happy with whatever we have—even if our baby's wings have rainbow polka dots and stripes."

A laugh escapes my lips as I instantly relax. "Me too."

I wake in the early hours of the morning feeling constricted. Sleepily, I push at Cerulean, who holds me against him, his wings acting like a blanket. "Loosen up," I ask.

"Sorry." He rolls away from me, taking his touch away.

I jerk and gasp sharply as I'm hit with intense pain. In a flash, Cerulean flips around, covering me with his feathers again. The fire abates and the tightness eases up. I inhale a loose shaky breath.

He hovers over me, worry etched in his brows. "What's wrong?"

Heart pounding, I stare at him with wide eyes. "Call Dr. Sage. I think it's time."

"Feathers." He reaches for his cell on the nightstand.

Fifteen minutes later, Dr. Sage arrives and checks me over. "You're almost there."

Cerulean's jaw slackens in surprise. "Already? You must've been laboring all night and not noticed with my touch on you."

With my stomach increasingly tightening and loosening, I say, "I notice now."

Cerulean phones his parents and Russet and Marigold to tell them it's go time. They hurry over. Emerald and Russet remain downstairs while Marigold and Rose come to help Dr. Sage guide our chick into the world. Cerulean's touch and gentle words of encouragement keep my anxiety at bay. I feel relief at the baby's first cry.

"It's a boy!" Dr. Sage exclaims as he gently lays the baby on my chest. "Congratulations!"

A boy. I'm a mother. I stare at the wailing little bundle in my arms with wonder. Warmth fills every crevice in my soul. I'm in love already.

CERIL

I hold Azure, her back to my chest, my wings wrapped around her. Jolts of energy shoot out of my wings as I soothe her. I peek around her shoulder to see our child. A son. I can't believe it.

Marigold gently cleans the top of his head with a warm washcloth, revealing locks of Azure's blonde hair. I reach out to stroke his cheek with a finger. He's the softest thing I've ever felt. His blue-green eyes open and close. "He's perfect," I murmur with pride to Azure.

"Mm-hmm," Azure agrees.

Her love for our son swells inside of me, mixing with my own. Tears of joy spring into my eyes. I'm so happy I can barely think.

Once assured Azure is well, Dr. Sage takes our son to give him a full once-over. We watch with our hearts in our throats as he's poked and prodded. Grinning, Dr. Sage hands our chick back to Azure. "You've got a strong, healthy boy. Now we just wait for his wings to release."

I'm dimly aware that Mom left, and now she steps back in with Dad and Russet. My eyes remain glued on our son as he adjusts to life on the outside. Snuggled up with Azure, I softly stroke his back near the two perfectly formed ridges. Abruptly he squirms, his back arching. Two dark wings emerge. Unfurling, they reveal tiny feathers as black as the darkest recesses of a cave. Next to his spine where his wings begin, I see one strip of silver and one strip of gold. My eyes fly to his feather tips. Everyone gasps. The ends are patterned gold, silver, gold, silver. He's double Tipped.

"Would you look at that?" Dr. Sage whispers.

I look to Russet and Dad. "Did any of you think . . . ?"

They shake their heads in obvious bewilderment. "No."

"They're beautiful," Marigold gushes. "I don't think there's a shade darker than his. What are you going to name him?"

"How about Obsidian?" Mom suggests.

"No," Azure and I say together. Slightly surprised at our unplanned mutual objection, I lean around to meet her gaze. A name seems to reach our minds and cross our lips at the same time. "Coal." We give each other warm shaky smiles of love and approval.

Marigold beams. "Coal Hatch it is."

Azure leans into me, holding our baby close. "Our little fire starter."

NOTE TO THE READER

Thank you so much for taking the time to read *Matching Feathers*. I am thrilled you chose to add it to your home library. If you enjoyed reading this book, it would mean the world to me if you could leave a review wherever fine books are sold online—and, of course, spread the word! For more information you can visit www.TaraLytle.com

ABOUT THE AUTHOR

Tara Lytle prefers to start every day with a steaming cup of hot chocolate, her Spotify playlist, and an open Word document. She is an avid YA-fiction reader with a particular love for fantasy and paranormal. She writes what she wants to read. While wrangling four kids and a husband, she crams in as much writing and reading time as a day can hold.

Made in the USA
Middletown, DE
04 September 2022

72214021R00208